KIM BOCK

ERENOR'S DAWN

BOOK 2

The Chronicles of Erenor

The Series: The Chronicles of Erenor

AN OVERVIEW

In *The Chronicles of Erenor*, readers are pulled into a captivating world of magic, adventure, and destiny. From the first introduction of Lysandra in *The Last Mage* to the cosmic rift that distorts reality in *Erenor's Dawn* and the climactic battle against the evil sorcerer Malachor in *Erenor's Destiny*, this epic fantasy series weaves a compelling tale of intricate characters, rich world-building, and thrilling action.

Every page is filled with tension and wonder, inviting readers to embark on a journey where ancient prophecies, untamed magic, and the power of courage and friendship hold the keys to survival and victory. *The Chronicles of Erenor* is a must-read series that guarantees an unforgettable adventure, seamlessly blending romance, profound themes, and the eternal struggle between light and darkness.

Contents

Chapter 1

FRIENDS

Lysandra's muscles coiled and were released with the grace of a striking serpent, her runic sword tracing arcs of silver fire in the dappled sunlight. Each blade sweep sliced through the air, a whispering promise of lethal precision.

She danced across the training field, her footwork as meticulous as the runes etched along her weapon—a language of power that hummed against her skin and resonated with her every move.

"Swift as the wind, Lysandra," she murmured to herself, the words a mantra to sharpen her focus.

A rustle from the underbrush snagged her attention, and she pivoted on the ball of her foot, sword poised.

Shadow appeared his coat a meld of night and smoke, his eyes glittering with intelligence that belied his feral form. He padded to the edge of the clearing, a silent sentinel watching her practice.

She offered him a slight nod, a gesture imperceptible to most but as clear as if he'd spoken out loud. His ears twitched in response, the subtlest of affirmations.

They were a team, connected by more than the shared trials that had forged their bond. They were two halves of a whole, each the other's shadow in this dance of light and darkness.

"Stay sharp," Lysandra said, not breaking her rhythm as she transitioned into a series of complex thrusts and parries. "The enemy is cunning, but we are even more cunning."

Shadow's tail flicked once, in amusement or agreement. It didn't matter. He was like a steadfast presence at her back.

Her movements grew bolder, the edges of her sword catching the sun in flares that made the air appear as if it was on fire.

Aerin's voice reverberated in her mind, an echo of all the lessons he'd given her in the past. "Let the blade be an extension of your will, Lysandra. Your resolve made manifest."

And as much as she fought it, a thrill coursed through her veins at the thought of him—their battles, their unity, their combustible connection.

But this was her moment, her fight to face alone.

Without warning, she lunged forward, driving the point of her sword into the heart of an imaginary enemy.

She breathed hard, the only sound of her panting and the rustling leaves beneath Shadow's paws as he approached.

"Enough for now," she said, lowering her weapon with a slow exhale. She allowed herself to gauge its weight in her hand and its balance—much like the balance she sought within herself.

"Good work today," she whispered to Shadow, who nuzzled her palm with his wet nose. His loyalty was a given, unwavering, but it never ceased to warm the hidden corners of her soul.

"Let's rest," she suggested, though they both knew there was little time for true rest. There were shadows to chase, evils to vanquish, and a world to save. But for now, for this fleeting moment, they could pretend that peace was theirs to keep.

The sun was cresting the horizon when the unmistakable sound of footfalls approached Lysandra. She pivoted on her heels, and muscles tensed for a new confrontation—a sparring match with her closest allies.

Aerin emerged first, his dark hair catching the light as if waging its battle against the encroaching shadows. The daggers at his side glinted ominously, a silent promise of the swift dance to come.

"Ready for another round?" he called out, a grin playing on his lips that did not quite reach his stormy eyes, reflecting an inner turmoil mirroring her own.

"Of course," Lysandra replied, her grip tightening around the hilt of her runic sword.

Feyla arrived next, her crossbow slung across her back and a satchel of inventions bouncing against her thigh.

Her pixie cut framed her determined face, a stark contrast to the others with their magical prowess—her human vulnerability was her strength, her will unyielding.

"Let's see if you've improved since yesterday," Feyla teased, loading her crossbow with practiced ease.

Master Elarion, the old wizard with wisdom etched into every line of his face, completed the quartet. His staff hummed with latent power, a beacon of the ancient magic they fought to restore.

"Mind your defenses, child," he reminded Lysandra, a twinkle in his eye betraying his affection for his protégé.

Together, they moved through the motions of battle, no blow too harsh, no spell uncast, the air crackling with the energy of their unity.

Beyond the city walls, the golden scales of Harrow shimmered as the dragon lay recumbent, his lonesome figure a reminder of the fractures marring their world.

As steel clashed against steel, Lysandra's mind wandered to the darkness lurking within her veins, the heritage that linked her to both the First Mage and the demon that she'd banished.

With each swing of her blade, doubt crept in, whispering seductively of power untamed, of a lineage cursed.

"Concentrate, Lysandra!" Aerin barked, snapping her from her reverie as his dagger came dangerously close to her skin.

"Sorry," she muttered, parrying away and regaining her footing. The struggle within her raged—a tempest of light and shadow vying for dominance.

The joy of the fight, the camaraderie of her friends. It was all tinged with the fear that she might one day succumb to the darkness that beckoned.

"Your thoughts are elsewhere," Master Elarion said his voice carrying the weight of centuries. "The balance you seek is not found in the blade alone but in accepting all facets of yourself."

Lysandra met his gaze, finding only solemn understanding. "I know. It's just...harder some days than others."

"Strength comes from struggle," Aerin added, nodding solemnly. "We all have our demons to face."

"Even without magic, I know that much," Feyla chimed in, offering a supportive smile.

"Indeed," Master Elarion agreed. "And we face them together."

"Thank you," Lysandra said, heartened by their unwavering support. Together, they paused, panting from exertion, yet bound by an unspoken oath to stand against whatever darkness threatened their land.

"Let's rest," Lysandra finally suggested, sheathing her sword. A collective sigh of relief spread through the group as they relaxed their stances.

"Rest, but be ready," Master Elarion warned. "The shadows never get tired."

They shared a look of mutual understanding, each carrying their scars, their hopes. As the training session wound down, Lysandra could feel the weight of her destiny settle upon her shoulders—not as a burden, but as a mantle she was learning to wear with pride.

Lysandra's muscles tensed as she resumed her stance, the runic sword reflecting the harsh light of the midday sun.

Taking a breath, Lysandra prepared herself for another series of strikes against the training dummy, which could dodge and weave like a true enemy.

"Focus on your strength, not your fears," Aerin said, stepping close enough that his voice reached her over the clash of metal.

His presence was like a grounding force, pulling her back from the brink of her internal abyss.

She glanced at him, noting the earnest concern in his blue eyes, framed by dark locks that had escaped the leather tie at the nape of his neck.

He stood with his daggers sheathed, the warrior's poise never quite leaving his body. "Strength isn't always enough," she murmured, her grip tightening on the hilt of her blade.

"Sometimes it is," he replied, a faint smile touching his lips. "You've proven that time and again, Lysandra."

Their gazes locked, a silent exchange passing between them. They were warriors, both marked by pasts they wished they could rewrite, but finding solace in the battles they now faced together.

It was a bond forged in fire and magic, one that was deepening with every shared glance and unspoken thought.

"Let's show this dummy what we're made of," Aerin suggested with a nod toward the wooden figure that had moved again.

"Agreed," Lysandra replied, emboldened by his faith in her.

The dummy lunged forward unexpectedly; its movements more erratic than before. A malfunction, or perhaps another layer of their training exercise?

Feyla raised an eyebrow from where she stood, her crossbow loaded but lowered. "Looks like it's picking up the pace," she called out.

"Stay sharp," Master Elarion warned, leaning on his staff with deceptive casualness.

Lysandra parried a strike from the dummy, the feeling shot up her arm.

Aerin moved in sync beside her, his daggers flashing as he intercepted another attack meant for her flank.

They danced around each other, a deadly ballet of blades and precision.

"Use the shadow within," Aerin breathed, as if sensing her hesitation.

"Like you use your earth?" she retorted, a smirk tugging at her lips despite the situation.

"Exactly," he said, his own smirk mirroring hers.

Feyla stepped in, firing a bolt from her crossbow that struck the dummy squarely in the chest. It paused, giving Lysandra the opening she needed.

With a shout, she summoned the magic coursing through her veins—a blend of light and darkness—and channeled it into her strike.

The sword's runes glowed as she delivered the final blow, cleaving through the enchanted wood.

The dummy shuddered and came apart, harmless splinters scattering across the ground.

"Teamwork," Feyla stated with a grin, reloading her crossbow with practiced ease.

"Definitely," Lysandra agreed, panting slightly as she wiped the sweat from her brow. She met Aerin's eyes again, warmth spreading through her at his obvious pride.

Together, they had faced the challenge head-on, their trust in each other unwavering.

"Well done," Master Elarion praised. "But remember, real enemies won't fall apart so easily."

"Then we'll be ready for them," Lysandra declared, her resolve hardening. The path ahead would be fraught with darkness, but with Aerin and her friends by her side, an ember of hope flickered within her.

"Ready for anything," Aerin echoed, resting his hand on her shoulder—the warmth of his hand and the gesture promised support and she felt the thrill of a shared destiny.

As they regrouped, the sense of anticipation was palpable.

The world outside the walls of Tyrannis awaited, full of unknown magic and the lurking threat of Aviara. But for now, they had each other, and the knowledge that together, they were unstoppable.

Lysandra's shoulders heaved with the effort of battle as she dropped her runic sword to the ground, its blade now silent.

She leaned on her knees, catching her breath, and glanced up and saw Shadow padding toward her. His massive wolf's form was a comfort after the hard training in the yard. His tongue lolled out in what Lysandra swore was an amused pant.

"Conceding at last?" Aerin teased, his dark hair sticking to his forehead with sweat, eyes alight with the thrill of their mock combat.

"Never," Lysandra shot back, straightening up. "Merely... strategizing."

"Is that what you call it?" Feyla chimed in, her pixie cut framing her face in disarray. She twirled a bolt between her fingers, her brown eyes dancing with mirth.

"Careful, or she'll strategize you right into the mud next round," Master Elarion warned with a sage nod, his voice carrying the weight of years and wisdom.

Their laughter mingled with the rustling leaves as they made their way out of the city, seeking solace in the open fields where Harrow, the golden-scaled dragon, lay basking in the sun's embrace.

As they approached, the dragon lifted his head, eyes gleaming with ancient knowledge. He rumbled a greeting, a sound like distant thunder rolling over the hills.

"Ah, Harrow, old friend," Lysandra greeted, her voice softening. "How fares your solitude?"

"Lonely skies," he replied in the deep, resonant tones of his own language, which they had all learned to understand. "But brighter with your presence."

"Let's hope we can keep those skies safe," Aerin remarked, his gaze sweeping over the expanse of Erenor. "We've come far in healing the land, but there's much left to mend."

"Indeed," Feyla agreed, slinging her satchel over her shoulder. "And with each piece we restore, the stronger Erenor becomes."

As they settled into the grass, a figure approached from the direction of Tyrannis—a messenger bearing the King's insignia.

Even before they exchanged words, the urgency in their stride showed that they brought dire news.

"Champions," the messenger began, bowing deeply. "I bring a plea from the throne. An encounter with the shadow deity Aviara has left one of our own gravely wounded. Her darkness spreads once more."

"Aviara..." Master Elarion murmured, stroking his beard thoughtfully. "A being of malice, forgotten by time, yet not vanquished."

"Her touch corrupts the very essence of life," Lysandra added, recalling the tales of Aviara's cruel reign. "She's a blight upon the land."

"His Majesty seeks your aid," the messenger implored. "Will you stand against this threat?"

"Stand and fight," Aerin confirmed, his hand instinctively finding the hilt of his sword. "For Erenor, for magic, for all that is good."

"Tell the King," Lysandra said, rising to her feet with a determined glint in her eyes, "we will meet this danger head-on. For we are the light that will banish Aviara's shadows."

"Your bravery honors us," the messenger said, relief flooding their features. "I shall relay your message with haste."

As the messenger departed, the companions shared a solemn look. The path ahead was fraught with peril, but their resolve was unshakeable. Together, they would face the darkness.

"Then it's settled," Lysandra stated, her voice ringing with command. "We prepare at dawn. Tonight, we rest; tomorrow, we fight—for the heart of Erenor."

"Until the end," they vowed in unison, a pact sealed beneath the watchful eye of Harrow, whose fiery breath whispered promises of protection and warmth.

With the sun dipping on the horizon, casting long shadows across the land, they returned to Tyrannis.

They were buoyed by their bond, forged in fire and tempered in battle. As night fell, they readied themselves for the journey beyond—the realms of magic awaiting their courage.

Lysandra's breath fogged in the cooling air, her mind tumbling back through time as the twilight murmur of Tyrannis wrapped around her.

The clink of sword against sword faded, replaced by a distant memory—a whisper of a moment that had bound her fate to both shadow and light.

She was but a child, hiding behind an ancient oak within the Enchanted Forest, watching the First Mage, her ancestor, confront a being made purely of darkness. The First Mage's voice was firm yet filled with sorrow as he sealed away the dark entity.

His last words before vanishing into legend echoed in Lysandra's ears: "Balance is the hardest battle one will ever fight."

The memory flickered and died as reality set in, the weight of her heritage heavy upon her shoulders.

She knew that within her flowed the same potent mix of light and dark magic that had once challenged the greatest mage of Erenor. It was this balance she sought to master, the balance that would define her destiny.

"Thoughtful tonight, aren't we?" Aerin's voice cut through her reverie; his silhouette edged by the fading light. His presence, a constant reminder of strength and resilience, grounded her.

"Memories," she replied, her voice tinged with resolve. "They shape us, drive us forward."

"Then let them fuel your fire, not dampen it," he said, his dark eyes reflecting the last embers of daylight. "We have a plan to forge."

Gathered in a circle, their determination and purpose intertwined with the approaching night, they stood.

Harrow's deep rumble echoed like distant thunder, as he rested just beyond the city walls. Feyla, her eyes gleaming with inspiration, meticulously tinkered with her collection of inventions in her satchel.

"Aviara's resurgence is no coincidence," Master Elarion stated, stroking his silver beard thoughtfully. "Her power grows from the fractures left in magic's weave. We must seal these rifts before confronting her directly."

"Agreed," Lysandra nodded. "Our first step is to seek out the Forgotten Altars. They hold the key to mending what has been torn asunder."

"Forgotten Altars?" Feyla interjected, curiosity piqued. "I've heard legends, but I assumed they were just that—legends."

"Legends rooted in truth," Lysandra confirmed. "These are ancient power sites, harmonized with the ley lines of the land.

By reactivating them, we can amplify the magic of Erenor and diminish Aviara's sway."

"Seems like we'll have to explore every corner of the kingdom," Aerin pondered, absentmindedly tracing the runic engravings on his daggers. "It's a dangerous mission, but it's necessary."

"Indeed, it's full of peril," Master Elarion agreed. "But with Lysandra's incredible magical abilities and your growing earth powers, Aerin, we have a fighting chance."

"Then it's settled," Lysandra declared, looking into each of their eyes. "We'll set off at dawn to reclaim the altars and restore balance, not just within me, but throughout all of Erenor."

"Balance," Aerin echoed, his voice a whispered promise. "And redemption—for all of us." Feyla chimed in, a mischievous grin on her face as she brandished her crossbow.

"Let's not forget cunning and invention. Magic isn't our only weapon." Harrow growled, his deep voice resonating through their bond. "Indeed, Feyla. Together, we are a force that even the gods will fear."

Their plans took shape in the gathering darkness as stars pierced the velvet sky. Words of strategy and support intertwined, strengthening their determination.

They were not just warriors, but guardians of a world on the brink of chaos. "Tomorrow, we embark on our journey towards hope," Lysandra proclaimed, her runic sword gleaming under the starlight.

At the edge of Tyrannis, where cobblestones met untamed

grasses whispering tales of uncharted lands, Lysandra stood alone with her faithful wolf companion, Shadow, who focused on the symphony of the night.

Her friends' laughter faded into the background, their warmth uplifting her spirit but unable to quiet the storm brewing within her.

Closing her eyes, she took a deep breath, filling her lungs with the cool air. Her thoughts turned inward, to the spaces between light and shadow, to the essence of her lineage.

The demon's snarl still echoed in her dreams, a grim reminder of the darkness she wielded as skillfully as her sword.

However, with each passing day, the radiance of her heritage grew stronger, casting long shadows and illuminating the path ahead.

"Balance," she whispered, a vow to the stars above. "I will not be consumed." The words were a lifeline, a beacon amidst the storm of her soul.

She had danced on the knife-edge between destruction and salvation, and there she found her strength, tempered like steel in the fires of adversity.

A quiet rustle alerted her to Aerin's approach, his silhouette a dark contrast against the city's glow. His magic hummed beneath his skin, an earthy echo to her fantastical surge.

"Ready?" he asked, his voice steady despite the uncertainty ahead.

"More than ever," Lysandra replied, opening her eyes to meet his gaze. In them, she saw the reflection of her resolve, the shared knowledge of what they had been through and what was to come.

They turned together, beckoning to Feyla, Master Elarion, and Harrow, who emerged from the shadows, their figures etched with purpose.

They gathered their belongings, the familiar weight of armor and weaponry grounding them as they prepared to step into the unknown world outside Tyrannis.

"Beyond these walls lies the genuine test," Master Elarion said, his voice a rumble of wisdom earned through years.

With her crossbow slung across her back and her satchel of inventions bumping against her hip, Feyla added, "Let Aviara tremble," wearing a confident smirk.

Harrow's voice reverberated, his glistening golden scales capturing the moonlight, a reminder of the ability to change and find redemption.

Each carried their battles and scars, but Lysandra understood that their collective strength created a tapestry of resilience.

With a glance at Shadow, his loyalty to her was a silent promise to follow her wherever she led.

"Then we move at dawn," Lysandra declared, her clear and unwavering voice cutting through the night.

"For Erenor, for the magic that binds us, and for the future we will carve from the darkness."

As they faced the gate, the first beams of morning sun cast a glow on the path in front of them.

It was a treacherous journey, a path leading into the depths of the unknown, yet their eyes remained filled with hope.

Guided by Lysandra and accompanied by Shadow, they seamlessly merged with the morning mist as they entered the day.

The magical realms they came from were now in the past. The unknown lay ahead, waiting for them.

Chapter 2

TWO HALVES OF A WHOLE

The clash of steel echoed as Lysandra defended against Aerin's strike, the force sending vibrations up her arm. As she steadied herself on the uneven ground, her eyes locked with his fierce, dark gaze.

"Predictable," she taunted, feinting left before spinning right, her blade aimed at his side.

With a grunt, Aerin only just dodged her attack, and their swords collided, producing a burst of silver sparks. "Maybe," he retorted with a surprising amount of power, given his lean physique.

They engaged in a sparring session filled with a dance of shining blades and moving shadows, accompanied by the sound of boots hitting the ground and occasional grunts of effort. The forest echoed with the rustling of leaves as if the surroundings were witnessing a fierce fight.

As Aerin advanced, Lysandra leaped back, a mischievous grin

on her lips. "Not bad for a former witch hunter."

"Be on your guard, Lys," he warned, his voice hushed and teasing. "Complacency is a killer."

She laughed; the sound sharp as a knife's edge. "Worry about your own—"

As the air crackled with energy, she stopped talking and the space between them shimmered with the raw power of her fantastical magic. Like ethereal serpents, ribbons of light twisted around her arms, seeking liberation.

"Dammit, Lysandra! Control it!" Aerin barked, his earthy magic instinctively rising to meet hers—a grounding force emanating from his palms, green tendrils snaking through the dirt and stone beneath their feet.

"I am in control," she snapped, though the pulsing light betrayed her struggle.

"Like hell you are," he shot back, the green glow intensifying around him. It clashed with her radiance, causing a sizzling sound to fill the clearing as the two magics fought for dominance.

"Stop it!" Lysandra commanded; her voice laced with frustration. She closed her eyes, taking a deep breath as she attempted to rein in the chaotic energy within her.

"Easy for you to say," Aerin grumbled. "Your magic is all whims and wonder. Mine's stubborn, tied to the earth. It doesn't yield easily."

"Neither do I," she replied, opening her eyes to find his gaze steady on her. The moment held a silent understanding—they were both creatures of power, yet completely different in their essence.

"Again," she said simply, lowering her sword.

"Again," Aerin agreed, nodding curtly as they reset their positions.

Their residual power permeated the air, a constant reminder of the potent blend of their abilities. Their task was to uncover a means of blending their strengths, not only to strengthen their bond but also to benefit Erenor.

"Let's focus on the harmony, not on the conflict," she murmured, to both herself and to Aerin.

"Harmony," he echoed, a hint of a smile touching the corner of his mouth. "We'll see about that."

They exchanged a shared nod and charged ahead, their swords colliding in a dazzling spectacle of light, symbolizing their commitment to working together.

As the last echoes of their swords meeting faded, Feyla made her way over, her arrival a stark contrast to the lingering magical atmosphere between Lysandra and Aerin. The young woman's eyes sparkled with a mix of determination and excitement, drawing both warriors' attention despite their smoldering argument.

"Enough with swords and spells for a moment," Feyla announced, holding up a curious contraption made of gears and polished wood. "I've created something that doesn't need magic to be powerful."

Intrigued, Lysandra took a step forward and examined the

device. It was compact, fitting neatly in the palm of Feyla's hand, yet its intricate craftsmanship spoke volumes of its potential.

"Is that—" Lysandra started, but Feyla cut her off with a proud nod.

"A repeater crossbow," Feyla declared, revealing a cartridge filled with bolts. "It holds six shots. Less reloading, more fighting." She aimed at a nearby tree and fired. Bolts whistled through the air, each finding its mark in quick succession.

"Remarkable," Lysandra admitted, her gaze shifting from the pierced bark back to Feyla. "Your mind is truly your greatest weapon."

Despite their earlier conflict, Aerin couldn't resist smirking at the spectacle. "It appears that we all have our special brand of magic," he commented, acknowledging Feyla with an approving nod.

"Indeed," Lysandra agreed, the corners of her mouth lifting slightly. "We're lucky to have you by our side."

While the group marveled at Feyla's ingenuity, Aerin caught Lysandra's eye, gesturing for her to join him away from the others. At the edge of the clearing, the shadows grew denser, creating an atmosphere of intrigue as the canopy above murmured secrets to anyone willing to pay attention.

"About what happened earlier," Aerin began, his voice a rough whisper, "we can't keep letting our powers clash. There must be a way to—"

"Blend them?" Lysandra finished for him, her eyes searching his face. "Our magic are reflection of ourselves, Aerin. Yours is grounded, and resilient. Mine... it's untamed, unpredictable."

Acknowledging the opposites in nature, Aerin took a step closer. The magnetic pull of their contrasting energies was hard to ignore. "Yet here we are, drawn together, seeking the same end."

"Balance," she whispered, the word hanging between them like a fragile promise.

"Exactly," he replied, reaching out to brush a lock of hair from her face. "I worry that I may lose myself to this earthy power—that I'll become the very thing I once hunted."

"And I fear the darkness within me will one day win," she confessed, her voice barely above the rustling leaves. "That I'll succumb to the demon's blood and destroy everything we fight for."

"Then we'll find our balance together," Aerin vowed, his hand lingering near her cheek. "I won't let the past define me—not when our future depends on us."

"Nor will I be defined by my heritage," Lysandra declared, her hand firmly resting on top of his. "Uniting forces, we become more powerful."

Lysandra and Aerin stood together in the peaceful forest, surrounded by ancient trees that had experienced countless seasons. Their deepest fears were exposed. Their souls were linked by an unspoken bond, finding solace in their shared challenges.

"Let's return to the others," Lysandra suggested after a moment, her resolve strengthened by their connection.

"Right behind you," Aerin agreed, his spirits lifted by the

depth of their alliance.

Hand in hand, they made their way back to Feyla, who proudly showed the reloading mechanism of her invention. The atmosphere brimmed with a fresh understanding, a shared understanding that their unity was the crucial element in safeguarding Erenor and each other.

Energy filled the atmosphere, as the earthy scent of the forest blended with the distinct smell of ozone. Lysandra tightened her grip on her staff, squinting against the approaching darkness. It was as if the shadows were alive, writhing and twisting in both grotesque and oddly familiar figures.

"Stay on high alert," she hissed, feeling the power within her surge as a response to the surrounding darkness. With a swift motion, Aerin brandished his sword, its sharp sound breaking through the quiet, as his other hand deftly readied a dagger.

"Here they come," he grunted, and the woods erupted into chaos.

Emerging from the twilight thicket, the Shadow Hounds, twisted beings born from the tainted essence of the Celestial Fracture, unleashed snarls that shattered what little peace remained. Their forms were fluid, a nightmarish blend of smoke and sinew, teeth bared in eternal hunger for magic and flesh.

"Bind them!" Aerin commanded, stepping forward as his earthy magic rose in response—roots, and vines breaking through the soil to ensnare the shadow beasts.

With a vibrant thrum, Lysandra's staff channeled her otherworldly power, illuminating everything around her with a brilliance that was almost painful to look at. She unleashed a barrage of glowing projectiles, each one hitting its target with deadly accuracy, aiming for the core of darkness.

"Charge together!" she shouted, realizing that the clash of their magic had become a weapon in itself. As Aerin's roots held the creatures fast, she unleashed a burst of pure light that turned the binds into ethereal chains.

"Left side, be careful!" Feyla's voice broke through the chaos, the snap of her crossbow underscoring her caution. A bolt narrowly missed Lysandra and struck a Hound in the mouth, causing it to erupt in flames from Feyla's alchemical fire. Retreating, the creature emitted haunting howls as it dissolved into the shadows.

"Impressive shot!" Aerin commended, blocking an attack from another creature with his dagger before swiftly dispatching it with a deadly strike from his sword.

"Cover me! I've got this one!" Feyla shouted, loading another bolt into her crossbow—a new design developed from her recent invention. She dove and rolled, coming up to kneel at a vantage point that offered her a clear shot at the heart of the skirmish.

"Take care, Feyla!" Lysandra warned, her staff cutting an arc in the air as she summoned a shield of shimmering force around them. It flickered with the potency of her heritage, a reminder of the balance she sought between light and darkness.

"Always," Feyla replied sharply, unleashing a storm of bolts that hit their targets with deadly precision, each one tipped with her own powerful concoctions capable of eroding darkness like acid through paper.

"Push them back!" Lysandra cried out, her voice rising above the roars and clashing steel. Together, she and Aerin advanced, his earthly might and her radiant spells weaving together in a dance of destruction.

"Give me three more!" Feyla declared, swiftly reloading with precision. By being there, she proved that cleverness triumphed over natural strength, showcasing deadly mental acuity and manual skills that were as deadly as any form of sorcery.

"Let's end this," Aerin growled, and the trio pressed forward, a united front against the encroaching tide.

In a chaotic clash, magic, metal, and expertise collided with darkness. Lysandra's light flared, Aerin's determination grounded them, and Feyla's ingenuity provided the edge they needed. Finally, with a resounding cry from all three, the last of the Shadow Hounds dissipated into nothingness, leaving behind a forest scarred but safe—for now.

"Thank you, Feyla. Without your support..." Lysandra let the sentence trail off, knowing words were unnecessary.

"Teamwork," Feyla replied simply, a small smile playing on her lips as she checked her crossbow for damage. "That's how we'll win this war."

"Certainly," Aerin affirmed, sharing a knowing look with Lysandra that said it all. Through the trials of battle, they fought together as a unit, their determination unwavering and their bond growing stronger.

With a graceful stride, Lysandra proclaimed, "Let us proceed," aware of the weight of destiny that she carried on her shoulders. "Erenor depends on us, and we will not fail."

Moving further into unexplored territory, the companions left behind the fading echoes of their past victory, their memories serving as a reminder of their capabilities as they prepared themselves both in mind and in spirit for the coming trials. Even though they still had a long way to go, their unwavering unity made them invincible.

In the last moments of the battle, echoes reverberated through the forest, and the air carried the lingering scent of charred shadow, creating an atmosphere that reminded one of a bitter perfume.

With her chest rising and falling rapidly, Lysandra released her hands, causing the magnificent light that had been pouring from them to diminish into a soft glow before ultimately extinguishing altogether. When she locked eyes with Aerin, she instantly recognized the clarity in his gaze, undeterred by the traces of their disagreement on his face, acting as a steadfast anchor for her emotions.

"Are you hurt?" he asked, his eyes scanning her body for any signs of injury.

"Only tired," she replied, leaning into his touch more than necessary. "The same cannot be said for the woods."

"Regrowth takes time," Aerin murmured, pulling her close. His breath was warm against her ear, his voice steady despite the tremor of adrenaline still coursing through them both. "Just like healing."

Resting her forehead against Aerin's broad shoulder, Lysandra allowed herself to show a rare moment of vulnerability. Surrounded by the aftermath of their joint destruction, she couldn't ignore the contradiction of her heritage—the radiance of her ancestors locked in combat with the darkness she carried. Aerin, in a true paradoxical fashion, had transitioned from being a predator to becoming the ultimate protector of her kind. Their embrace was a wordless agreement, a pledge to repair the shattered pieces inside and out.

"Look at us," she whispered, a half-laugh escaping her lips. "Two halves of a whole, each fighting our own shadows."

"Yet stronger together," he returned, his grip tightening. "Whatever darkness lies ahead, we face it as one."

The word "Always" slipped from Lysandra's lips, cementing their unspoken oath.

Feyla, standing nearby, saw their interaction, her crossbow hanging idly at her side. The unique blend of contrast and unity in Lysandra and Aerin's bond struck a deep emotional chord with her.

Her existence resided in a realm that lacked both darkness and brightness, instead existing in the physical realm of mechanical components like gears and spring-loaded bolts. However, right here, following their spellbinding storm, she could feel an overwhelming sense of unity.

With a gentle stroke, she caressed her satchel, tracing the contours of her latest invention beneath the aged leather. Her strength did not waver, despite the absence of magical or inherited abilities flowing through her veins. It motivated her to become more determined. Resilient.

"It's not just magic that has the power to change the world," she whispered to herself, a newfound determination strengthening her resolve.

"True," Lysandra agreed, having caught the tail end of Feyla's self-assurance. "Your mind is as sharp as any spell, Feyla."

"Sharper," Aerin added, releasing Lysandra to clap a reassuring hand on Feyla's shoulder. "We'd be lost without your cunning."

Feyla looked into their eyes, a surge of pride in her chest. "Then let's ensure we're never without it. I have plans, ideas that might turn the tide when we next face our enemies."

Lysandra stepped back to stand next to Aerin, urging Feyla to take the lead. "Lead the way, Feyla," she said with a smile. "Show us the path your ingenuity has forged."

With a nod, Feyla shouldered her crossbow and stepped forward, her silhouette cast long by the setting sun. They were a trio bound by fate and choice, each carrying their own scars and strengths, ready to face whatever twisted creatures lay in wait.

"Stay alert," she called over her shoulder. "The shadows may have retreated, but they're never truly gone."

"Neither are we," Aerin declared, his hand finding Lysandra's once more. United, they followed Feyla deeper into the heart of Erenor, their spirits intertwined in the dance of darkness and light, innovation and ancient power.

Lysandra's breath misted in the cool air of twilight as she paced the perimeter of their makeshift camp, the last vestiges of sunlight glinting off her sword. The weight of Aerin's gaze upon her was tangible, a silent sentinel from where he leaned against an ancient oak. Their eyes met, and without having to say a word, they both were aware that it was time to unburden their hearts.

"Ever since the Demon," Lysandra began, her voice barely above a whisper. "I've experienced this...rift within me. As if my soul is a battleground for light and darkness."

Aerin pushed off from the tree, his boots crunching on fallen leaves as he closed the distance between them. "And I've been fighting my own shadows," he confessed, the steel in his voice softened by vulnerability. "The magic I once hunted now thrums through my veins, a constant reminder of what I can't undo."

With a gentle touch, their hands found each other's, their fingers weaving together in a familiar dance of solace. "We are two halves of a broken whole," Lysandra said, her gaze lifting to the crescent moon peeking through the branches. "But together, we can mend not just ourselves but Erenor as well."

"Redemption and balance," Aerin nodded, his thumb caressing her knuckles. Despite our checkered pasts, we have an unlimited potential for our future. "It's ours to mold, Lysandra," he declared, his eyes filled with resolve.

Hidden in the shadows, Feyla strained to hear their exchange, her heart pounding with the resonance of their words. She clutched her crossbow tighter, its familiar contours grounding her resolve. They were warriors, battling inner demons and external foes alike, and she, too, had a role to play.

"Then let's vow," Lysandra's voice rose with conviction. "To unite against any adversity."

"Let's make a vow," Aerin echoed, placing his free hand over his heart. "To serve as a beacon of hope for one another when everything else is engulfed in darkness."

Stepping backward, Feyla's leather attire made a gentle rustling sound, harmonizing with the night's symphony. She cast her eyes upward, witnessing the gradual appearance of stars in the velvety night sky. 'I may not wield magic,' she thought resolutely, 'but I wield will and wit. And that alone is sufficient power.

"Take me into account" and that is potent enough.'

"Count me in on that vow," she murmured to herself, a steely edge to her tone. 'With or without magic, I am Feyla, unyielding and undeterred.'

Like a river that breaks free from its confines, determination flowed through her. She would skillfully construct traps to ensnare their adversaries, fashion shields using her collection of ingenious inventions, and serve as the sharp-minded strategist alongside their formidable magical abilities. Their unity made them a formidable force, impervious to the influence of shadow hounds and corrupted beings.

"Come," Lysandra whispered, aware of Feyla's presence before she appeared. You are as much a part of this oath as we are, so please join us.

"Without exception," Feyla answered, stepping into the muted glow of their encampment's fading fire. With an intense determination, she joined hands with her companions and her eyes sparkled. "When we join forces, there are no limits to what we can achieve."

Beneath a deep blue sky, three individuals united by a common goal stood in silence, prepared to face the challenges of Erenor. Each person brought their own strengths into play.

With each step they took on the rolling terrain of Erenor, the earth trembled beneath their boots, a testament to the untamed beauty that surrounded them and the hidden dangers that lay in wait. Lysandra, her gaze sharp and her staff held tightly, took the lead as they ventured through the thick foliage, acutely aware of the subtle murmurs of magic that teased their senses.

"Stay near," Aerin directed, his voice a deep growl, blending with the sounds of the forest, like the whispering leaves. His eyes swept across the terrain, ready to strike with his daggers, while his earthy magic hummed beneath his skin.

With a loaded crossbow and a satchel of inventions against her side, Feyla followed closely. She quickly scanned the shadows, her eyes alert for any signs of movement, her human senses unaffected by the absence of magic.

The three of them synchronized their movements, silently promising to protect one another with every step.

"Something is amiss," Lysandra murmured, halting in her tracks. The atmosphere crackled with a palpable, unsettling energy that sent shivers down her spine.

"An ambush?" Aerin questioned, shifting into a defensive stance, his instincts honed from years of hunting.

"Possibly," Feyla added, skillfully inspecting her crossbow with her nimble fingers. "Or, to make matters worse."

As soon as she finished speaking, the ground erupted in front of them. Dark, distorted figures emerged from the earth, their snarls creating a chorus of wickedness.

With a hiss, Lysandra addressed the corrupted individuals and channeled her magic into a glowing shield that encased the entire group.

Aerin yelled, "Stay back, Feyla!" as he lunged forward with a battle cry, swiftly cutting through the dark shapes with his blades.

However, Feyla was not just a spectator. Maneuvering between the creatures, she unleashed bolts with lethal accuracy, demonstrating her ingenuity and skill.

"Keep an eye on your flank!" she exclaimed to Aerin, who reacted to defend against a brutal strike from one of the corrupted.

"Thanks," he grumbled, recognizing her life-saving help.

As Lysandra chanted, her hands moved skillfully, creating intricate patterns that conjured radiant torrents of light, driving away the encroaching shadows.

"Focus, Lysandra!" Aerin yelled above the clamor, reminding her of the balance she sought between light and darkness.

Side by side, they engaged in combat with a savage passion

that arose from their interconnected fates, their enchantments and determination combining with an indomitable energy. As each enemy fell, their trust in each other grew stronger, solidifying their bond against the spreading corruption.

With the disappearance of the last being, Lysandra was both drained and triumphant, slumping in exhaustion. Aerin hurried over to her, extending her arm for support, which was as sturdy as the surrounding ancient trees.

"Are you hurt?" he asked, concern etching his rugged features.

"Nothing I can't handle," Lysandra replied, a wry smile touching her lips despite the exhaustion that crept into her bones.

"Your inventions saved us again, Feyla," Lysandra said gratefully, turning to their companion, who was already collecting spent bolts.

"Magic isn't the only power in Erenor," Feyla responded, her brown eyes gleaming with pride.

"Indeed," Aerin agreed, sheathing his daggers. "It's our combined strength that will help us along this journey."

Despite the destruction of the battle, they stood together, their bond strong and unbroken. The sun descended below the horizon, casting the sky in vibrant shades of red and orange, and they experienced a sense of being one and ready to confront whatever awaited them.

Under a starry sky, Lysandra and Aerin perched on a weathered outcrop, their gaze reflecting the celestial conflict going on above them. The only company they had was the murmurs of the night and the far-off cry of a nocturnal predator.

"Just look at them," Aerin murmured, nodding toward the sky. Each star battles to shine the brightest of all the stars, despite the shadows' attempt to overshadow their radiance.

As she followed his gaze, Lysandra absentmindedly ran her fingers over the hilt of her sword—a habitual response that signaled her deep contemplation. "It's quite similar to us, don't you think?

"Exactly," Aerin's voice resonated like a deep rumble, carrying the same earthy power that flowed within him. "But I dream of a day when the balance is restored—when our battles are distant memories recounted around campfires."

"Where magic isn't feared or hunted but embraced as the lifeblood of Erenor." She leaned into him, her head resting against his shoulder as if drawn by gravity itself. "And where our love flourishes, untouched by the cacophony of battle."

"Love," Aerin murmured as if the word held a secret power, barely audible yet full of meaning. As he turned to face her, she saw depths of her soul reflected in his dark eyes. "Yes, I want that too. For us to not just survive but thrive. To build something new from the ashes of the old."

Their hands intertwined, fingers lacing with an intimacy born from shared scars and whispered dreams. The moment hung between them, delicate and potent.

"Yet here we are," she sighed, half in resignation, half in resolve, "bearing the weight of the world when we should be free to love without restraint."

"Freedom often comes at the end of a long struggle," Aerin said, his thumb caressing her knuckles. "But I believe it will be worth it. We are worth it, Lysandra."

From the shadow of an olivine thicket, Feyla observed the pair, unseen yet feeling the resonance of their words. Her heart swelled with a mixture of admiration and yearning. They spoke of magic and balance, of a future bright with promise—a future she dared to share in her own way.

She brushed her hand over the leather satchel at her hip, following the contours of her latest invention. It was more than gears and springs; it was hope forged into steel. With every bolt she crafted and every mechanism she perfected; she carved out her place in this magical world.

"Let their dreams be my beacon," she whispered to herself, drawing strength from their conviction. "For as long as shadows cast, I'll be the light they don't expect."

Feyla stepped away from the cover of leaves, her silhouette outlined by the moon's silver embrace. She approached Lysandra and Aerin with purpose in her stride.

"Whatever tomorrow brings," she declared with a voice filled with determination, clear and unwavering, "I'm ready to stand shoulder to shoulder with you, to fight for that world of balance and love."

Lysandra and Aerin turned toward her, their eyes filled with warmth, reflecting the sincerity in Feyla's words. With an unspoken vow passing between them, the trio made an oath to chase the dawn together, their determination growing stronger with each step.

Not long after, Lysandra's blade sliced through the air, its sharp sound harmonizing with the narrow beam of moonlight reflecting off its gleaming edge, clashing against Aerin's with a powerful clang. Each move in their sparring was executed with precision and grace, their bodies moving in perfect harmony.

"Your form has improved," Aerin grunted, a rush of adrenaline coursing through him as he countered her attack with a sweeping low strike.

With a playful smirk on her lips, she leaped back. "Your footwork, hunter, has certainly come a long way."

The air crackled with tension as their eyes locked in a fierce battle of wills, each one ready to strike at any moment. No longer a simple clash of steel, their training had metamorphosed into a nuanced dialogue conveyed through the ebb and flow of combat.

Feyla, hidden in the shadows, kept a watchful eye, her crossbow nestled in her arms, poised for the perfect moment to join their magic-filled skirmish. Despite her lack of arcane power, her presence commanded respect and awe.

"Ready?" Aerin called out, his voice clear and unwavering.

"Always," Lysandra replied, her voice filled with unwavering determination, before launching herself at him with renewed vigor.

Their exchange escalated, the clash of swords echoing through the air with a ferocity that could reshape the course of fate. The symphony of clanging metal and the intensity of strength filled the air as they refined their edges with each step.

Amidst the clamor, Lysandra's sharp command, "Strike now!" resonated, accompanied by a subtle hand gesture directed at Feyla.

With perfect timing, Feyla stepped into the light, her fingers preparing her invention—a bolt infused with a shimmering concoction that radiated with boundless possibilities. Letting loose the projectile, she looked as it sailed through the air, finding its mark between the dueling pair.

The bolt erupted into a burst of blinding radiance, causing Aerin and Lysandra to freeze in their tracks and shield their eyes from the intense light. With the fading light, a breathtaking sight emerged—a barrier of interwoven light and shadow, an otherworldly creation born from Feyla's ingenuity and the convergence of their magical energies.

"Trust in unity," Feyla said, stepping forward. "Together, we are more than our strengths."

"Indeed," Lysandra breathed, her heart swelling with pride at the sight of their collaborative creation.

With a nod, Aerin lowered his sword, his body language reflecting his acknowledgment of the truth in Feyla's words. Our bond, a weapon forged in trust and loyalty, is our greatest strength.

Drawn by the captivating luminous barrier, they gathered, their hands meeting its glowing surface, perceiving the pulsating power emanating from it. It stood tall, a symbol of their unity and a reminder of their collective potential.

"Through darkness and doubt, we've forged a path forward," Lysandra said, her voice filled with resolute determination.

"Side by side," Aerin added, her voice filled with determination, "we'll reclaim this fractured world."

"And I'll be right with you," Feyla asserted, her voice filled with unwavering support.

As their gazes met, an unspoken vow lingered in the air, binding them together. A melding of fantastical magic, earthy resolve, and human ingenuity defined their triad. It was their unbreakable love, fierce enough to challenge the fabric of destiny, that tied them together.

Lysandra declared, "Let's walk this path together," as she reached for Aerin's hand, her eyes extending an invitation for Feyla to join them.

"United," Aerin affirmed, clasping Feyla's shoulder with his free hand.

"Unwavering," Feyla concluded, completing the circle.

With the barrier bearing witness, they shifted their focus to the uncharted horizons, every footstep away from the clearing serving as a resounding testament to their unwavering commitment—a pact sealed by their shared conviction and the unwavering spirit of togetherness.

Chapter 3

A WARNING VISION

Lysandra sat cross-legged on the cold earth outside the fortress of Tyrannis, her breath coming slow and deliberate, a steady rhythm in contrast to the chaos of her thoughts.

As her fingers danced along the intricate runic tattoos that adorned her arms, she could feel the ancient power coursing through her veins, a constant reminder of the darkness she battled against. Dew-laden grass tickled her bare ankles, and the pre-dawn air was sharp with the scent of pine and impending rain.

Her constant companion, Shadow, lay sprawled at her side, his dark coat blending seamlessly with the velvety blackness of the night. The gentle rise and fall of his flank provided a calming presence amidst the storm of her emotions. Like a soothing balm, his loyalty eased the turbulence that plagued her soul.

A whisper escaped her lips as she uttered the name "Aviara," causing a surge of emotions to course through her. The King's messenger had spoken without hesitation or sugarcoating. As Lysandra's determination grew stronger, her skin reacted with a prickling sensation, disregarding the chill in the air.

She couldn't afford to waver or let the internal conflict overpower her, especially with so much at stake. "I have to be ready," she murmured, her voice resolute and piercing the silence. "The shadows within me pale in comparison to the abyss she would unleash upon us all". Nobody was there except for Shadow and he just pressed his warm body closer against her legs.

Like a storm, the vision crashed into her mind's eye, bringing with it a torrent of sights and feelings that left her breathless. Aviara stood tall and imposing, a ghostly presence shrouded in the shadows of ancient times, her eyes empty yet burning with malevolence. Under her shadow, the once vibrant and teeming land of Erenor withered, its magic unraveling like a delicate tapestry.

With each beat, Lysandra's heart echoed like a war drum, urging her to take action. The urgency of their mission weighed on her, a burden more crushing than any armor she had donned. The twisted forests loomed before her, their gnarled branches reaching out like skeletal fingers. The pained cries of corrupted creatures echoed through the air, filling her ears with a haunting melody. She couldn't help but experience the essence of the world groaning in agony, a heavy weight pressing down on her soul.

"By the First Mage," she swore, her fists clenching in the dirt, "I will not let this dark prophecy come to pass." Shadow lifted his head, nudging her comfortingly with his nose.

Lysandra stood up and realized that her meditation session had ended. The battle for Erenor's soul began with her, along with others, and she was determined to see it through to the end, even if she had to confront death with her magic blazing brightly, defying the darkness.

Lysandra's breath fogged in the chill air as she walked towards her companions, who huddled together by a dim campfire. The shadows cast by the flames danced across their faces, illuminating the concern etched into each line and crease. Aerin, with his dark hair falling over his forehead, looked up from the whetstone and blade in his hands.

"Your face tells a story of its own, Lys," Aerin said, his voice low, eyes searching hers.

"Aviara," she whispered, her voice carrying the weight of impending doom. "She's a storm on the horizon, threatening to break upon Erenor with fury we've not yet seen."

Feyla, petite but fierce, bristled at the mention of the deity's name. Her crossbow lay beside her, as if ready for immediate use. Harrow shifted nearby, a rustle of golden scales and the soft clink of his talons against stone betraying his agitation.

"Is it as dire as you say?" Master Elarion asked, his aged eyes sharp with intelligence, his wizard's staff planted by his side.

"Worse," Lysandra replied, her gaze flitting between them. "Our land was... dying. Aviara's darkness, like a blight, consuming everything."

"Then we fight," Aerin declared, setting aside his blade, resolve hardening his features. "We always knew it would come to this."

"Without question," Feyla added, a determined glint in her brown eyes. "Magic or no magic, I stand with Erenor."

"We cannot allow her evil to go unchallenged," Master Elarion declared, his voice carrying the weight of centuries of wisdom.

"We won't allow it to worsen," Harrow growled with a deep, dragon-like voice, the resonance carrying a certain promise.

Drawing on the unity of her friends, Lysandra nodded, gaining strength. "As a team, we take on the challenge of facing her."

"Let's confront Aviara," Aerin declared, standing up and positioning himself next to her. "Root out this evil."

"Defend the innocent," Feyla added, her fingers wrapping around the handle of her crossbow.

"Preserve our world," Harrow rumbled, his eyes gleaming like molten gold.

"Restore balance," Master Elarion concluded, his voice echoing the gravity of their shared oath.

Lysandra echoed the word "balance," preparing for the fight that lay ahead. "For Erenor, for the magic that binds us all, I swear it."

"Well then, let's get ready," Aerin stated, locking eyes with Lysandra, his dark gaze matching her intensity. Since our enemy won't wait, we have to leave at dawn.

"Nor shall we give her a quarter," Lysandra affirmed. Together, they turned their thoughts to the journey ahead, the trials they would face, and the hope that their courage could turn the tide of darkness threatening to engulf their world.

With a graceful touch, Lysandra's fingers danced across the hilt of her runic sword, gently tracing the intricate glyphs that had been meticulously carved into the steel—a powerful language that pulsed with energy beneath her hand. She made sure there were no scratches on it and sharpened the edge to perfection before securely placing it in its sheath, the satisfying click foreshadowing their upcoming adventure.

"Is this all?" Aerin's question cut through the heavy silence as he inspected his twin daggers, their blades gleaming in the pre-dawn light filtering through the armory's narrow windows. His hands moved with lethal grace, every swipe against the whetstone a whisper of death for their enemies.

"Every potion, every herb," Lysandra replied, her gaze lingering on the leather packs brimming with supplies. "And enough food to sustain us until we reach Aviara's borders."

With one last strap secured on her satchel, Feyla carried a collection of her ingenious creations—gizmos and snares that could act as a backup plan in case their magic fell short. Lysandra and she exchanged a meaningful glance, silently conveying their preparedness.

"In that case, we should devise a plan," Harrow uttered, his voice resonating with a harshness akin to the sound of grinding stones, while his golden eyes remained fixed on a map that was unfolded on a table made of wood. The depiction showed the dangerous landscape they were about to traverse, an unfamiliar stretch marked with symbols of danger.

"Beware," warned Master Elarion, pointing to a darkened domain adorned with foreboding symbols. "Our risks extend beyond the battlefield."

Lysandra took a firm stance, stepping forward, and clarified that succumbing to fear or doubt is not an option. She leaned over the map, her shadow merging with the dark ink. To avoid any complications, we navigate around the Iron Mountain, bypassing the territories of the dwarves who do not align with our cause.

"Let's go through the Whispermire," Aerin proposed, his forehead creasing in concern. However, the fog is dense.

Feyla whispered about the treacherous illusions ahead, but her eyes gleamed with the inquisitiveness of an inventor, intrigued by the challenge.

Lysandra remained steadfast in her conviction as she spoke. "However, if we stay on the familiar path, we can harness the power of the mists to benefit us."

"Risky," Aerin conceded, his glance holding a storm of emotions—fear, determination, and something fiercer that sent a shiver down Lysandra's spine. "But bold. It may just work."

"We shouldn't disregard the hidden creatures," Harrow warned, his scales twitching. "I sense their restlessness, like whispers in the wind."

"We shall silence them," Lysandra stated firmly, adjusting her posture. "With blade, bolt, and fire. We will not falter."

"Nor will we fail," Aerin added, stepping up beside her. The way he stood spoke volumes, silently pledging his loyalty by her side.

"With each step we take, we edge closer to triumph," Feyla proclaimed, casually draping her satchel over her shoulder.

"Or a deadly dance," Master Elarion cautioned, though his eyes sparkled with the excitement of the adventure. "Stay alert, my students."

"We shall overcome the darkness," Lysandra pledged, her hand intertwining with Aerin's as if compelled by an unseen energy. Their combined strength, her light, and his emerging earthy magic formed a bond that felt unbreakable.

"Then we shall courageously enter the unknown," declared Aerin, his hold strong. "Together."

"Into the mists, into the fray," Feyla agreed, hoisting her crossbow with resolve.

"Towards destiny," Harrow affirmed, his wings unfurling with a sound like thunder.

"Strike true, strike fast," Master Elarion finished, his tone solemn yet laced with pride.

"We must act as a unified force," Lysandra concluded, sensing the immense responsibility of determining Erenor's future. Together, they began the methodical task of strapping on their armor, the clinks and clanks of metal a prelude to the symphony of war that awaited them beyond the safety of Tyrannis' walls.

The steady rhythm of Lysandra's breath misted in the morning air as she peacefully sat cross-legged on the rugged terrain outside Tyrannis. Despite her closed eyes, she remained acutely aware of the world's whispers and the power pulsating within her. A silent sentinel, her runic sword lay beside her, its familiar silver glimmer catching the eye. Silent and watchful, Shadow laid his head on his paws, his gaze unwavering and fixed upon her.

She murmured "inner peace" to herself, delving into the depths of her being, where a perpetual battle between darkness and light raged on. Dragging in her breath, Lysandra embraced a sense of calmness. She was aware of Aerin's presence in the distance, his magic connected to the earth, his roots intertwining with his essence, a sharp contrast to her otherworldly powers.

"Balance," Aerin groaned, his hands planted on the ground as green energy tendrils spiraled up, wrapping around his arms like ivy. With his dark hair cascading over his forehead, it created a stark shadow against his resolute expression. With intense concentration, he tapped into the unbridled strength of the earth beneath him, yearning for mastery and a chance to atone for his irreparable past.

"Your magic has grown stronger," Lysandra said without opening her eyes, the current of his power brushing against her consciousness.

"Your guidance," he replied, his voice gravelly with concentration. "I learn from the best."

A smile tugged at the corner of her mouth, but it was fleeting, overshadowed by the gravity of their mission.

Outside Tyrannis' protective walls, the kingdom stretched into untamed lands—the enchanted woods of murmuring willows, where rustling leaves safeguarded hidden secrets. Awaiting them was Aviara's domain, obscured by darkness, where the magic they were familiar with turned into grotesque parodies because of her vile influence.

"The Shadow Hounds are nothing compared to what's coming," murmured Feyla, loading her crossbow. With a resolute posture, her brown eyes shone with a hint of steel. As she lightly tapped her satchel, brimming with her most recent innovations, her ingenuity thrived in a realm where enchantment reigned.

"Shadowy and wicked creatures," Master Elarion reflected, running his fingers through his gray facial hair. Beings born from dark dreams and malice.

"Still, we have to confront them," Harrow rumbled, his radiant golden scales capturing the first rays of dawn. The ancient language he spoke, though unfamiliar, conveyed a truth that everyone understood.

"I agree," Lysandra affirmed, standing up, her calm state of meditation replaced by a firm resolve. Our challenge lies not only in confronting Aviara, but in confronting the essence of our fears.

With determination, Aerin declared, "We will carry the torch of courage," his hands still stained with the remnants of his magic—soil and the energy of life.

"Courage and cunning," Feyla remarked, a mischievous smile gracing her face.

"Strength and sagacity," Harrow intoned, his wings flexing in anticipation.

"Unity and determination," Master Elarion concluded, acknowledging with a single solemn nod.

As they ventured into the unknown, the air buzzed with anticipation and the promise of a fierce battle. The barrier between dimensions weakened, beckoning them into a realm where even the trees could be enemies and every shadow posed a danger. Yet, they had prepared themselves, equipping not only weapons but also carrying an undying hope and a resolute determination to restore Erenor, regardless of the consequences.

As the first rays of sunlight touched the rugged terrain, Lysandra prepared herself for the journey ahead, adjusting her backpack, which held essential supplies. Mist veiled the path before them, and every step they took solemnly revealed the path that awaited them. Aerin's figure appeared beside her, providing a constant source of comfort as they moved together towards the unfamiliar.

"Don't forget," he whispered, his voice blending with the rustling leaves, "every breath we inhale brings us closer to Aviara."

"Every breath," Lysandra echoed her tight grasp on the mystical sword at her hip showing her preparedness.

In the dim light of twilight, they moved stealthily, their figures breaking through the mist that hung low on the ground. The sound of distant roars and cries filled the air, yet Lysandra stayed resolute. Her heart raced, not with fear, but with excitement—a warrior's intuition expecting the forthcoming battles.

"It's like entering a dream," Feyla remarked from behind,

her crossbow hanging on her back, her gaze sweeping the dense forest.

"Or perhaps it's a horrifying nightmare we are bound to awaken from," Harrow interjected, his voice emanating as a deep rumble that sent tremors through the ground beneath them.

"Whether we like it or not, our dreams shape us as much as our swords," Aerin stated, giving a quick look to Lysandra, who concurred with a nod.

"Together, we will mold this dream into our ultimate success," she proclaimed, her tone reflecting the relentless spirit that had propelled them forward.

"Into our destiny," Master Elarion corrected his aged eyes reflecting the spark of youthful fervor.

With each step they took into the forest, the canopy above them grew denser, creating a captivating display of shadows and illumination. The atmosphere in this location was vibrant with tangible and potent magic, encasing them like a protective shroud. Lysandra could feel it pulsating through her veins, a melody of ancient energy that resonated with who she was.

"Stay focused," she commanded, her senses attuned to the intricate melody of the forest. "Aviara's influence could manifest in any form."

"Then we shall cut through her lies with precision," Aerin declared, unsheathing his daggers that concealed their deadly intent.

Feyla interjected, "Clear paths lead to clear minds," as she placed her hand on a pouch filled with her latest inventions, poised to challenge any hidden obstacles.

"Mind and blade, both honed to perfection," Harrow affirmed, his scales shimmering with an inner light that cut through the gloom.

With each passing mile, the sense of anticipation grew stronger and more noticeable. A current passed between them, igniting sparks of excitement as they moved closer to Aviara's realm.

With unwavering determination, Lysandra proclaimed, "Today, we tread where others dare not," her eyes locked on the horizon where the sun vanished into the land. "But we do not falter. For Erenor, we brave the heart of darkness."

"United," they all voiced as one, an oath bound by the shared heartbeat of their mission.

Their journey had begun—not with fanfare, but with the steadfast beat of determined footsteps marching towards a future only they had the power to forge.

As the group navigated through the tangled underbrush, the shadows grew longer, enveloping the once lively place now tainted by an unexplainable gloom that undoubtedly emanated from Aviara. The sound of laughter reverberated through the trees, a rebellious tune in the face of looming fear. With a snort, Harrow expelled a cloud of smoke, his brilliant golden scales reflecting the last rays of daylight, while he regaled them with a thrilling tale from the Iron Mountain that had everyone in fits of laughter.

Lysandra laughed and said, "Harrow, you think we'll believe that you outsmarted a goblin king with a riddle about fishbones?"

The dragon's deep growl, in its ancient language, resonated within them, implying that the reality was even more extraordinary than the legend.

"Fishbones," Aerin pondered, a mischievous glint in his eyes as he gazed at Lysandra. Without uttering a word, they exchanged meaningful looks, creating an invisible bond.

"Truth can be stranger than fiction," he whispered, his voice filled with an undertone that went beyond the current discussion.

"Especially in Erenor," Lysandra replied, her heart fluttering like the wings of a caged bird.

"Let's hope our truth won't be written in pain," Feyla interjected, her crossbow slung over her shoulder, a symbol of readiness and resolve.

As darkness fell, the conversation dwindled, weighed down by the foreboding presence of Aviara. Amended: Twisted into unnatural shapes, the leaves of the trees give the appearance of being scorched by an unseen blaze. The atmosphere, suffocating any remnants of the day's lightheartedness, grew heavy with negativity.

Lysandra's voice was commanding as she urged, "Stay vigilant," her hand gripping the sword's hilt, its inscriptions glowing with anticipation.

"Definitely," Aerin responded, equally attentive.

The sound of rustling caught their attention, and they saw distorted creatures emerging from the twisted underbrush—a group of shadow hounds, their bodies flickering like smoke.

Lysandra hissed, pouncing forward with graceful agility, ready to confront Aviara's minions.

With every elegant movement, her blade sang a lethal tune, separating darkness from reality as she maneuvered through the pack of hounds.

Aerin was beside her, his daggers a blur of steel. His earthy magic pulsed from him in waves, knitting wounds closed with a glow that fought back the dark.

"Watch your flank!" he called out to Lysandra, who spun, slicing through a hound that had crept too close.

"Thanks," she breathed out, her pulse thrumming in her ears.

"Anytime," he shot back, a lopsided grin flashing despite the danger. The connection between them ignited brighter with each enemy felled.

"Need a hand?" Feyla shouted, notching a bolt to her crossbow with practiced ease, her lack of magic no hindrance to her deadly aim.

"Cover Harrow!" Lysandra replied, noting the dragon's focus on a larger beast emerging from the darkness, his flames ready to scorch it from existence.

"Got it!"

The conflict was intense, a harmonious clash of determination and steel. Lysandra's arm throbbed with pain, yet she brandished her sword with unwavering passion, her indomitable spirit matching the unyielding dawn they fought to defend. One by one, the shadow hounds vanished, leaving the forest to be reclaimed by silence, with only the exhausted victors' ragged breaths breaking the stillness.

"Are we all—" Lysandra began, scanning her companions for injuries.

"Alive? Yes," Aerin finished for her, wiping his brow with the back of his hand. "But let's keep moving. Aviara has shown her hand, and it's as twisted as we feared."

"Let's continue," Lysandra declared with determination, her voice resolute. "For the sake of Erenor, we mustn't waver."

"And we won't," Aerin affirmed, falling back into step beside her. The path ahead may be uncertain, but their determination has never been stronger. A looming shadow cast its vast, shapeless form against the twilight sky.

Feyla released a bolt from her crossbow, its sharp note resonating through the air. With unwavering concentration, she tracked the missile's trajectory. The shadow convulsed as the projectile struck its mark, dissipating into the ether with a shriek that echoed through the forest.

"Another one down," Feyla called out, reloading with deft fingers. She reached into her satchel, following the familiar shapes of her handmade gadgets—coiled springs, vials of incendiary concoctions, and serrated bolts designed for maximum carnage. With her thoughts racing, she contemplated how to best employ her arsenal against their unearthly adversaries.

"Watch your left flank!" Aerin's voice cut through the din of battle, his daggers a blur as he parried an attack from a twisted creature borne from Aviara's corruptive influence.

Feyla spun on her heel, her crossbow finding its target before she completed her turn. A satisfying thunk resonated as the bolt embedded itself in the creature's eye, halting its charge. "Thanks!" she shouted back, sparing a quick grin for Aerin before scanning for their next adversary.

The forest was alive with malice, shadows skittering between trees and over roots. But Feyla moved with purpose, her lack of magic no detriment to her effectiveness in combat. Each invention she deployed turned the tide in their favor—a net of woven steel fibers ensnaring a beast, a flash bomb blinding another, and her explosive bolts wreaking havoc in their ranks.

"Your toys might just save us all," Harrow rumbled appreciatively, his words a guttural symphony that transcended language.

"Let's hope so," Feyla replied, adjusting the straps of her satchel and squaring her shoulders. She had grown up believing that magic was the pinnacle of power, but here, amidst the chaos, she wielded her own brand of might.

Lysandra cleaved through another assailant, her sword leaving trails of light in the darkening air. "We're pushing them back! Feyla, what do you have for that cluster there?"

"Got just the thing." Feyla pulled out a spherical device and twisted it before hurling it toward the gathering darkness. It erupted mid-air, sending shards of cold iron scattering among the creatures, their unholy screams testament to its efficacy.

"Brilliant, Feyla!" Lysandra cheered, her voice carrying over the clamor of their relentless advance.

As the last shadow dissolved under their onslaught, the group paused, catching their breaths amid the now-quiet woods. Lysandra's gaze swept over her companions; each face mirrored the same fierce determination that burned within her.

Lysandra commented, "We've made some serious progress," sounding tired but keeping it together. Aviara is waiting, and Erenor's fate hangs in the balance.

"Then let's end this," Aerin declared, clasping Lysandra's shoulder with a supportive grip. Their eyes met, a silent exchange of resolve passing between them.

"We're all in this together," Feyla said, taking a step forward. The mundane human among a group of mages. Yet her spirit was indomitable. "For our home, for our future."

"United," they echoed, a chorus of shared conviction.

With renewed vigor, they set off once more, their path illuminated by the stars that pierced the night's canopy. Each step carried them closer to destiny, to the confrontation that would decide the fabric of their world.

The dangerous encounter finished with their silhouettes marching resolutely into the unknown, the promise of dawn just a whisper on the horizon. Their journey was far from over, but together, they carried the hope of Erenor on their shoulders.

Chapter 4

EOLANDE & AN ENCOUNTER WITH DARKNESS

Lysandra's boots sank into the soft earth, the scent of decay hanging heavy in the air. Shadow growled at her side, his fur bristling, eyes reflecting the faint glimmers of light that pierced through the dense canopy.

The woods used to be full of life, but now they are quiet, and something is seriously wrong.

"Stay alert," she whispered, her eyes scanning the shadows.

Their path led them further into the heart of this messed-up wilderness, where even the bravest of Erenor's people wouldn't dare to go. Without Master Elarion around, Lysandra couldn't ignore the weight of responsibility on her shoulders. Tyrannis was defenseless without its guardian mage, and she couldn't—wouldn't—let them down. Master Elarion had to stay.

"Something's happening," Feyla said, gripping her crossbow

and scanning the trees. Her hair was stuck to her forehead, all sweaty.

A horrifying creature emerged without warning from the bushes and charged at them, its teeth dripping with evil. Lysandra reacted instantly, swinging her sword smoothly. Sparks flew from the intricate runes on the blade, creating creepy shadows on her determined face.

"Go back!" she ordered, confronting the creature head-on.

The forest resounded with the clash of steel against hide as she skillfully deflected every fierce assault, her motions a graceful and deadly dance.

Aerin entered the chaos of the fight, his daggers moving so fast they became a blur, fighting alongside Lysandra in perfect harmony. The bond between them was palpable in their coordinated strikes.

"Watch the flanks!" he called out, his voice filled with urgency.

With a nod, Feyla let loose a bolt that hit its mark finding its way into the wide-open mouth of another enemy. The being tripped, its scream abruptly silenced, but others were quick to replace it, emerging like ghosts from the darkness.

"Aviara's minions are relentless," Lysandra said through gritted teeth, her brow covered in sweat and dirt. She experienced the impact of her dual heritage, experienced the surge of power flowing through her, a constant clash between light and darkness, each struggling for supremacy.

Aerin responded confidently, stating, "Let them come," his

determination mirroring the unyielding nature of the iron breastplate he donned. In perfect harmony, they joined forces, their combined strength and sorcery pushing back the unyielding wave of adversaries.

"Stay focused, Lysandra," Harrow's timeless voice echoed in her thoughts, his radiant scales shining amid the disorder. The key to your strength is maintaining balance.

Taking comfort in the dragon's wisdom, she nodded in agreement. With each swing of her sword, she harnessed the strength of her ancestry, using the legacy of her forebears to fuel her unwavering determination. The creatures stumbled as her enchanted blade relentlessly attacked; the air filled with the crackling of released energy.

"Stay resilient," she shouted to her fellow warriors, her voice cutting through the chaos of the fight. "We're together in this battle!"

They advanced together, presenting a united front against the encroaching darkness that aimed to conquer their world. They had to fight hard for every victory, and rather than being discouraged, their resolve only grew stronger with every adversary they vanquished.

"Until the end," they vowed, their voices merging into a single, defiant cry.

Aerin's breath came in ragged gasps as he wove through the melee, his twin daggers a silver blur in the gloom. Each strike was precise, aimed at the twisted creatures that hungered for their flesh and magic. The healers' light within him flared with every heartbeat, an emerald glow seeping from his palms, knitting closed the gashes on his arms even as he fought.

"Behind you!" Feyla's voice cut through the din, sharp as the bolt from her crossbow.

Without looking, Aerin pivoted, his dagger finding the throat of a shadow hound that had leapt silent as death itself. The beast dissolved into black mist, and the healing magic surged through him, eager to escape its confines and mend more than just cuts and bruises. But he couldn't let it—not yet. Control was everything; without it, he might save a body but lose a soul.

"Careful, Aerin! Don't overextend," Lysandra called out, parrying a blow from a creature twice her size. Her sword sang a bright counterpoint to the daggers' lethal dance.

"Trying not to," he gritted back, catching her eye for a moment—long enough to exchange a nod of understanding. They were both walking a razor's edge between their powers, striving for balance in the face of chaos.

The battle's fever pitch crescendoed when a new figure burst from the shadows. Tall and lithely muscled, an elf with hair like spun moonlight and eyes reflecting the starless night joined the fray. Eolande moved with an otherworldly grace, his bow singing as arrows flew, each finding its mark in the hearts of darkness.

"Who—" Feyla began, pausing only long enough to notch another bolt.

"Doesn't matter!" Harrow's voice thundered, his wings stirring the air. "He fights!"

Eolande offered no introduction, his focus absolute as he stepped seamlessly into their rhythm. His presence was a solace, a reinforcement they had not looked for but needed. There was no time for questions, only the grateful acknowledgment of aid as they fought back-to-back.

"Stay vigilant," Aerin warned, casting a glance toward the newcomer.

"Without fail," Eolande replied, loosing yet another arrow. As it soared through the air, it emitted a melodious hum before finding its mark - the eye of a furious creature.

"We definitely owe you," Aerin said between breaths, acknowledging the elf's prowess.

Eolande responded, his tone light and almost musical. "You owe me nothing. I choose to walk this path, just like all of you."

"We need to confirm that we have a viable way forward," Aerin remarked, and in unison, they fought against the encroaching darkness, united by the singular aim of staying alive.

Emerging from the depths of the corrupted forest, the Shadow Hounds launched themselves forward, their rapid movements and malevolent energy creating a blur of darkness, while the cacophony of battle echoed through the trees.

Lysandra moved past her enemies, her sword acting as an extension of her arm, shattering the delicate barrier that divides the realms of brightness and darkness. A sense of pure magic filled the buzzing air.

"Watch out on the left!" she yelled; her voice unwavering despite the approaching swarm.

Feyla spun around, crossbow in hand, to confront the unexpected danger, her heart pounding. While she fired bolt after bolt into the chaos, Eolande's presence became an intriguing distraction.

Standing mere steps away, the elf's bowstring hummed with deadly precision. During a momentary pause in their breathing, their gaze locked—a bond formed amidst the intensity of combat.

"You have a precise aim," he murmured, his voice soft and barely audible, yet piercing through the loud background noise.

"Thanks," Feyla replied, cheeks flushed from more than exertion. "You're not too bad yourself for someone who appeared out of thin air."

"Perhaps there is magic in serendipity," Eolande mused, rewarding her with a half-smile before releasing another arrow.

"Keep your head in the game, Eolande," she shot back, but the elf had already turned, his silhouette melding with the shadows as he moved to intercept a fresh wave of enemies.

Lysandra unexpectedly encountered one of Aviara's lieutenants—a menacing individual whose dark energy appeared to have a tangible weight. It let out a deafening roar, causing the leaves to tremble and fall from the trees, before charging towards her.

She braced herself, feet planted on the ground, the conflicting forces of her ancestry coursing through her veins. "Come then," she whispered, as the gigantic beast swung its clawed arm towards her. With the agility that necessity had given her,

Lysandra ducked beneath the blow, her sword shimmering with blinding light as it arced upward. The creature stumbled backward, clearly unaccustomed to facing such resistance. It snarled, its jaws gathering dark energy, preparing to unleash chaos.

"Enough!" Lysandra's voice rang out like a clarion call, her words infused with an indomitable will. Her blade grew brighter, the runes on its metal glowing with power. With a determined thrust, she pierced the creature's chest, aiming for its heart, if it even had one. A bloodcurdling scream escaped the lieutenant's lips, tearing through the night, as its body dissolved into fragments of darkness that faded away like nightmares at the break of dawn.

Lysandra stood victorious, though her breath came in ragged gasps.

"By the Ancients, Lysandra," Feyla exhaled, having witnessed the intense battle. "That was... incredible."

"Let's hope they all prove to be as easily vanquished," Lysandra replied, although her eyes revealed the toll the victory had taken on her. She surveyed the battlefield, prepared to face the next wave of enemies, her spirit unyielding.

Eolande returned to Feyla's side, nodding in acknowledgment of Lysandra's leadership. "Your leader is truly formidable."

"Of course, she is," Feyla grinned, reloading her crossbow. "She's got us backing her up."

"Indeed," Eolande agreed, a newfound respect kindling in his gaze. "Together, you are a storm Aviara can't weather."

"Well, then let's unleash our power," Feyla declared, and they both rejoined the chaotic symphony of the battle.

Through the ashen fog and the contorted shadows of the battlefield, Aerin's gaze never strayed from Lysandra. Her form was a dance of deadly grace, her runic sword an extension of her will.

He could see the strain on her face, the sweat beading her brow beneath raven locks, yet she moved with a ferocity that both inspired and unsettled him.

"Watch out!" he called, his voice cutting through the cacophony of clashing steel and dark incantations.

Aerin ran towards her, sensing the ground beneath his boots react to his every step. With a simple gesture, he summoned vines from the earth, ensnaring a menacing shadow hound that had leaped towards Lysandra. The pounding in his chest wasn't just from the effort he put in, but also from the intense fear of losing her.

"Thanks," Lysandra panted, not looking back as she trusted him to cover her. She didn't have to; their bond had grown beyond the need for words.

"Of course," he replied, maintaining a steady tone while a storm raged within him.

Feyla skillfully cranked her crossbow with swift precision, just a few paces to her left. She scanned the field, searching for targets and evaluating potential dangers. Despite lacking magical powers, she seamlessly blended into the background, her existence often disregarded by their adversaries until it was too late.

She yelled "East flank!" as she released a bolt that pierced the eye of yet another twisted creature. The sound of its howl filled the air as it tumbled to the ground, momentarily diverting the attention of its comrades.

"Well done!" Aerin acknowledged with approval.

"Keep them coming," Feyla responded, already loading another bolt. She glanced at the terrain, her mind weaving through possibilities like a spider spinning a web. She pulled a small contraption from her satchel—a Tanglefoot trap—and tossed it into the midst of an advancing group of minions. The device sprung open, ensnaring limbs and buying precious moments."

"Let's close this gap," she said, moving to stand back-to-back with Aerin. "They're trying to encircle us."

"We're on the same page," Aerin nodded, tapping into his connection with the earth below, commanding roots and vines to rise and form a protective barrier against the encroaching darkness.

"Your tricks are impressive," he admitted, watching Feyla work with a mixture of admiration and gratitude. "We'd be overrun without you."

"Magic isn't everything," she quipped with a smirk, shooting down another shadow hound that threatened to break through their defenses.

"Indeed," he conceded, slashing down a minion with his dagger before it could reach Feyla. "It's strength and cunning that keep us alive."

The fight continued relentlessly, with every moment passing like an eternity and each breath cherished. Their battle was not only for their own survival but also for Erenor, striving to restore the lost balance. As each enemy fell, the flicker of hope grew stronger, pushing back against the overwhelming gloom.

"Stay resilient," Aerin urged, standing alongside Feyla as they braced themselves for the next wave. "We unite and fight together."

"Always," Feyla repeated, her determination as strong as the steel in her backbone. Side by side, they defended their ground, their boldness serving as a guiding light amidst the confusion.

The arrows whizzed through the air, their feathers a blur of green and silver. It was as if the forest had summoned Eolande into existence, his silent but lethal presence commanding attention. He jumped from one twisted tree root to another, unleashing arrow after arrow, hitting the dark bodies of Aviara's followers.

He whispered amidst the chaos, "May the winds direct my aim," as if reciting a spell.

"Who is he?" Lysandra panted, ducking a wild swing from a creature whose claws dripped with malice.

"Doesn't matter!" Feyla shouted back, reloading her crossbow with deft hands. "He's on our side!"

Aerin grunted in agreement, driving his dagger into the heart of another twisted being. The earth responded to his call, vines wrapping around monstrous ankles, pulling them down as his companions exploited the new openings it provided.

"Come together!" Harrow's voice echoed; the archaic language interpreted through their deep connection. As he unleashed a blazing inferno upon the encroaching horde, the shimmering golden scales on his body caught the eye.

"Form a defensive line!" Aerin ordered. They advanced together, their defenses locking seamlessly, Lysandra's sword cutting through the darkness, while Feyla's bolts found their mark with lethal precision.

"You have perfect timing, stranger," Lysandra exclaimed to Eolande, her voice full of gratitude as his arrows kept reducing the number of their attackers.

"Fortune favors the bold," Eolande replied with a cryptic smile, notching another arrow. For a moment, his gaze locked with that of Feyla, acknowledging their shared understanding before they refocused on the ongoing battle.

"Watch out on the left side!" Feyla cautioned, noticing a group trying to sneak up. Eolande turned and unleashed a rapid succession of arrows that pierced through the shadows, resembling the first light of day.

Lysandra instructed, "Shield Harrow!" as she sensed the dragon's battle against a savage monster. Both she and Aerin surged forward, their collective power overwhelming the creature's resolve.

"Keep your eyes on the heavens!" Harrow's shout served as a well-timed caution as menacing winged creatures swooped down.

The bow in Eolande's hands emitted a melodious sound,

his aim deadly and precise, as Aerin's mastery of earth magic formed a protective covering of thorns over their heads.

"Keep moving!" Lysandra urged, pushing them forward through the mire of conflict. "Can't let them surround us."

"Agreed," Aerin said, his gaze meeting hers with a fierce determination. "We push through!"

"Behind you!" Feyla cried out, launching a bolt that took down a minion inches away from sinking its teeth into Aerin's flesh.

"Thank you," he exhaled, nodding before resuming the relentless assault.

"Stay focused," Eolande advised, his calm demeanor a stark contrast to the surrounding chaos. "These creatures are relentless."

"In that case, we are as well," Lysandra announced, her voice cutting through the noise of the battle. "It is crucial for Erenor!"

They moved together seamlessly, each strike carefully planned for their survival, every step a graceful dance with danger. Arrows, blades, and spells relentlessly rained down upon the minions as the heroes defeated them.

The companions took a moment to catch their breath, their gaze fixed on the path ahead as the final wave disintegrated into dust. The forest stood ominously, murmuring of greater challenges and more formidable adversaries. Bound by their shared purpose and a newfound sense of camaraderie, they formed a diverse and determined team, prepared to confront the twisted darkness that awaited them as they worked to bring balance back to Erenor.

Lysandra's sword sliced through the shadows, a gleaming silver streak amidst the shifting darkness. Her muscles resonated with effort, every motion graceful and exact, an expression of her determined resolve to reach Aviara and put an end to this suffering.

She yelled, "Retreat!" but it wasn't a directive to back off—it was a calculated move, a trick. With a swift spin, she released a beam of light from her enchanted sword, obliterating the shadow hounds that chased them. A vibrant energy emanated from her, filling the air with a crackling power that seamlessly intertwined the realms of light and shadow.

Aerin flanked her, his daggers a blur, as they found a home in the hide of a beast larger than the rest. "Impressive," he grunted, admiration lacing his voice despite the grim set of his jaw.

"Make sure to keep them away!" Lysandra responded, her voice conveying a blend of authority and motivation. They were warriors intertwined in battle, their bond deepening with every enemy felled.

Bolts flew from Feyla's crossbow, finding their mark with deadly precision. "We make quite the team," she said, a flash of pride in her brown eyes. Her presence, though lacking the shimmer of magic, was no less vital. She was the heartbeat of their group, her ingenuity their saving grace.

"Indeed," Eolande chimed in, as his arrow found its mark in the heart of an advancing minion. His calm in the storm, his graceful shots weaving through chaos, added a layer of lethal elegance to their defense.

The Harrow roared above, golden scales gleaming—a beacon of ancient might. He swooped, talons extended, snatching creatures from the air that dared to descend upon them. His language of roars and bellows became their anthem of war, understood by all.

"Your heritage shines through, Lysandra," Aerin said, watching her dispatch another minion with a blend of swordplay and sorcery. "You're the light guiding us."

"Only because you all stand with me," Lysandra answered, her gaze meeting his for a moment of shared understanding. They were two sides of the same coin—his earthy strength complementing her ethereal light.

They maintained an unwavering rhythm. Lysandra's sword sliced through the dark magic, Feyla's traps captured unsuspecting victims, Aerin's thorns protected them from danger, Eolande's arrows ensured quick and decisive victories, and the Harrow's fiery breath cleared the battlefield.

"Aviara will fall," Lysandra vowed, her declaration more than mere words—it was an oath, a promise woven into the fabric of their unity.

"I agree," Aerin asserted, his voice determined.

"By our will," Feyla added, reloading with a steady hand.

"By our honor," Eolande affirmed, notching another arrow.

"By our bond," Harrow's rumble appeared to say, a sentiment clear in the depth of his ancient gaze.

Together, they were a force forged in adversity, assessed by darkness, and unbroken in resolve. Each victory, each moment of trust, fortified their alliance—five souls against the tide, unwavering in their quest to restore balance to Erenor.

The twilight of Erenor crept across the land, casting long shadows that slithered and merged with the darkness. Lysandra's breath came out in sharp puffs, her sword still humming with residual magic from the battle. Shadow paced restlessly at her side, his fur bristling, sensing the weight of their task ahead.

"Keep moving," she urged, her voice a whisper that carried through the still air. The surrounding forest was a twisted labyrinth, the trees gnarled with corruption, their branches clawing at the sky.

Aerin advanced beside her, his eyes scanning the underbrush, daggers at the ready. He had been silent since their last skirmish, the burden of his past etched into the lines of his face. But there was a fire in him too—a fierce determination to right the wrongs he'd once served.

"Aviara's not going to make this easy," he said, breaking the silence.

"Since when do we back down from a challenge?" Feyla retorted, her crossbow slung over her shoulder. The stains of oil and dirt on her hands from setting up the last of her traps showcased her resourcefulness.

Harrow's golden scales shimmered in the dying light as he let out a growl, a sound that resonated with strength and loyalty. The dragon had become more than just a companion; he was a symbol of hope, a beacon of what they fought for—Erenor itself.

"Nor will I," came Eolande's smooth voice, as he stepped lithely over a fallen log, his bow in hand. His presence, other-worldly and calm, brought an odd sense of comfort despite the looming threat.

They pushed ahead on the unfamiliar landscape, requiring them to stay alert. The weight of her heritage pressed upon Lysandra, a tapestry crafted with elements of brightness and darkness, the threads becoming taut as her encounter with Aviara drew closer.

As darkness fell, they set up camp in a clearing, cautious yet desperate for some rest. The fire crackled to life, its flames licking the air as if to defy the encroaching darkness. They huddled close to the comforting heat, the dancing glow of the light casting shadows on their tired faces, exposing their exhaustion.

"Tell us, Eolande, where do you come from?" Feyla asked.

"From the Elven city of Aeloria," he began, his gaze distant. Aviara's darkness consumed it. I was the only one who escaped, and I made a promise to help those who would stand up against her.

"Your skills are unmatched," Aerin acknowledged, nodding toward the elf.

"Your cause is just. It is my honor to fight alongside you," Eolande replied, accepting the waterskin with a nod.

As Lysandra observed the exchange, her mind buzzed with a flurry of strategies and spells. She turned her attention to the map they had spread out before them, tracing the path to

Aviara's stronghold. "We have one chance at this," she said. "One chance to end her reign and heal our world."

"Then we'll make it count," Aerin promised, reaching out to squeeze her hand. His touch sparked something within her, a reminder of why they fought—not just for Erenor, but for each other.

"Tomorrow, we face our destiny," she declared, her voice steady. "For Erenor, for the lives lost, and for a future free of Aviara's tyranny."

"Until then, we rest," Harrow rumbled, settling his massive form nearby, a living bulwark against the night.

As they settled down, the cozy glow of the fire protected them from the cold. Surrounded by the calmness of the forest, they sought solace in the companionship of their allies, united by a common goal. Although their journey was still ongoing, they were determined to confront any obstacles that came their way.

Chapter 5

NIGHTMARES AND VISIONS

Lysandra's heart pounded against her chest, its frenzied beat mirroring the fear that gripped her during her deep sleep. She opened her eyes suddenly and was greeted by the dim light of dawn seeping into their improvised camp while the lingering remnants of her terrifying dream clung to her like spiderwebs.

Aerin was lying next to her, his arm draped over her waist, his calm breaths contrasting with the anxiety consuming her.

"Aviara!" she exclaimed, the bitterness of her archenemy's name still on her tongue. Within the world of dreams, she had stood beside Aviara, her hands engulfed in dark flames that reflected the sinister gleam in the sorceress' gaze. The image was incredibly intense, filled with horrifying potential...

Aerin woke up, his well-honed instincts immediately sensing her distress. His eyes, as dark and tumultuous as stormy seas, locked onto hers. "Lysandra? What's worrying you?" He reached for her, his calloused fingers brushing away the damp tendrils of hair from her forehead.

"Darkness...it's trying to claim me," she whispered, her voice trembling as much as her body. She could still feel the phantom warmth of the shadow fire, a stark reminder of the bloodline that both cursed and empowered her.

"Never," Aerin vowed, pulling her closer and enveloping her in the protective circle of his arms. "I won't let it."

But how could he understand? This was not mere darkness; it was a part of her, a heritage that threatened to consume her will, her soul. Shadow, ever-present and keenly aware of the turmoil within her, nuzzled against her cheek with a soft whine, offering solace in its way.

Aerin's touch, meant to soothe, was now like shackles, reminding her of the potential threat she posed to him, to all of them.

"What if I can't control it?" Lysandra's voice cracked, the words spilling from her lips like shards of ice. "What if, in facing Aviara, I became what we want to destroy?"

"Then we face that together," he said, his resolve as unyielding as the iron breastplate he wore. "You are not alone in this fight, Lysandra. Your battle is ours."

But could she allow it? Aerin, with his earthy magic still untamed, Feyla with her inventions and unwavering spirit, even Harrow with his ancient wisdom—they had all chosen to stand with her. They deserved a leader who wouldn't lead them into the darkness they sought to vanquish.

"Promise me," she started, her eyes searching his, "that if I fall—if the darkness takes hold—you'll do what must be done."

"Stop," Aerin cut in, his jaw set. "Don't ask that of me. You're stronger than any curse, Lysandra. You've proven that time and again."

The conviction in his voice was a lifeline, but the doubts continued to churn within her, a tempest that threatened to sweep away her resolve. Her gaze drifted to the flickering shadows cast by the dying embers of their campfire, each one a spectral reminder of her internal struggle.

"Then help me believe it," she implored, her eyes locking onto his once more.

"I promise," he said, sealing his vow with a kiss that conveyed both past and future battles—a blend of courage and resolve, shadows and hope. In that instant, Lysandra clung to the possibility that love could serve as the guiding beacon to navigate her through the encroaching shadows.

Lysandra's breath came in ragged gasps, each exhaling a fog in the chill air of dawn. Another dream!

Pushing herself up from the bedroll, her fingertips grazed Aerin's arm as he rested beside her, his chest rising and falling with each breath of peaceful slumber. The remnants of her terrifying dream persisted, casting a shadow over her mind.

"Another one?" Feyla murmured, appearing like a wraith, her crossbow slung over her shoulder, her eyes alert despite the early hour.

Lysandra nodded, her gaze fixed on the distant tree line where shadows danced with malevolent grace. "It's getting worse," she confessed, her voice a whisper. "The darkness... it's not just around us—it's within me."

"Aviara's doing?" Feyla asked, her brown eyes narrowing.

Lysandra replied, her hand tracing the lineage mark beneath her leather cuff, a constant reminder of her mixed ancestry.

"Your fear has never been as strong as your strength," Feyla said with conviction. "Don't forget that."

"Strength can be a double-edged sword," Lysandra countered, her heart heavy with the weight of her mixed blood. Her magic had the power to both heal and harm, to create and destroy.

"Perhaps it would be safer for everyone if I..."

"If you what?" Aerin's voice cut through the morning haze, tinged with concern as he joined them, his dark hair tousled from sleep.

Lysandra hesitated, but the truth clawed at her throat, desperate to be spoken. "If I left," she finally admitted. I am a potential threat to everyone here.

"Stop." Aerin's command was soft but firm, and the angles of his face were sharpened by the early light. "Lysandra, we've all experienced darkness. You're not alone in this fight."

"Your battle with your nature is no different than mine with my past deeds," he continued, his calloused hand encompassing hers, his touch grounding. The crackling of the nearby fire filled the air, casting flickering shadows on their faces.

"We've both walked through fire and come out stronger. You

won't face Aviara alone, and you won't become her either." The scent of burning wood mingled with the crisp night air, creating an atmosphere of determination.

"Easy for you to say," Lysandra muttered, pulling her hand away to wrap her arms around herself. The chill of the night crept through her clothes, sending shivers down her spine. "You haven't seen what I've seen in those dreams. The things I'm capable of—"

"Are these the same things that will defeat Aviara," Aerin insisted, stepping closer. His voice carried a sense of conviction, cutting through the darkness.

"Your power doesn't define you. Your choices do."

"Choices that could cost lives," Lysandra argued, her eyes haunted by the specters of the night. The moonlight illuminated the anguish etched on her face.

"Or save them," Feyla interjected, her practical tone slicing through the tension. The sound of her voice brought a sense of reassurance.

"We didn't come this far to back down now. And we sure as hell didn't follow you because we thought it'd be easy."

"Besides," Feyla added, offering a rare, encouraging smile, "who else would keep Harrow from accidentally setting fire to the forest?"

A faint chuckle escaped Lysandra's lips, dissipating some of the gloom that clung to her spirit. They were right; abandonment was not the answer. Not when so much depended on the strength they found in unity and in the bonds that tied them together.

"Thank you," she whispered, the first rays of sunlight piercing the canopy and warming her skin, a silent promise of the day ahead. "For everything."

"We're in this together, Lysandra," Aerin said, his voice resonant with conviction. "To the end."

To the end, she echoed her resolve, hardening like steel tempered in the forge. Aviara would be met with a confrontation, where she must confront the darkness within and face the fate of Erenor. How could she even consider walking away with friends like these by her side?

"It's time to go," Lysandra directed, her voice steady again. "We have an adventure to wrap up."

They packed up their camp, extinguishing the fire and setting off on the trail ahead.

The forest pulsed with the vitality of unseen creatures, a melodic hush that stirred the leaves and moved through the thickets.

At the forefront of their small band, Lysandra walked as the morning light created patterns of shadows. The heavy air carried the fragrance of moss and damp earth, a reminder of Erenor's enduring strength despite the fractures jeopardizing its magic.

"Aviara is a curse," she declared, shattering the silence as they traversed the rugged landscape. Nods of agreement followed her words, showing a shared understanding of the upcoming task. "She festers at the core of our lands, poisoning the magic that binds us."

Aerin matched her stride, his piercing gaze reminiscent of the steel in his sword. "If we refuse to confront her," he warned, his face bearing the burden of his past struggles, "Erenor will be swallowed by darkness."

The truth echoed within Lysandra's bones. The corruptive force of the Celestial Fracture was just a taste of the destruction Aviara's storm would bring. She was determined to continue her journey, even as the shadow inside her fought for control and tried to seduce her with its power.

With her hands clenched into tight fists, her nails dug into her palms. The pain provided a welcome diversion from the inner turmoil she was experiencing, a battle that was just as intense as those fought with weapons. The luminous legacy of the First Mage, representing her ancestral line, waged war against the encroaching darkness, remnants of a demon's lineage.

"Lysandra, we're practically doomed without you," Feyla interjected, her voice unwavering despite the uncertainty in her brown eyes.

The young woman's faith comforted Lysandra's weakening determination, but it also had drawbacks. To safeguard them, to safeguard Aerin, she had considered withdrawing and sparing them from her internal turmoil. Nevertheless, how could she safeguard them from a menace that demanded her being to vanquish?

"Moving further from Aviara means embracing darkness for all of Erenor," she whispered, speaking more to herself than to her companions. Though almost inaudible, her voice emanated a firm resolve that had propelled her to this point. I refuse to let fear control my decisions, and I won't let my actions bring harm to those I love.

"Onward we go," Harrow boomed, his time-honored words reverberating like the roll of faraway thunder. His golden scales gleamed in the stray sunbeams, a testament to the power that lay with them, not against them.

As they advanced, the crunch of their boots on the gravel path reverberated, each footfall resonating with determination and defiance. The air was thick with the scent of anticipation, a heady mixture of adrenaline, and the earthy aroma of the surrounding forest.

Their shadows danced and flickered in the dim light, casting elongated silhouettes that stretched toward the unknown.

Lysandra, the epicenter of this swirling vortex of bravery and trepidation, could feel her heart pounding in her chest, a rhythmic reminder of the immense stakes at hand.

"We must hurry," she ordered, her voice filled with a new-found determination that contrasted with her inner fear. The words hung suspended in the air, intermingling with the distant rustle of leaves and the faint howl of the wind.

Despite the growing magnitude of their shared objective, Lysandra remained resolute in her determination. "Our destiny awaits, and together, we shall confront it," she declared, her voice carrying a steadiness that surpassed."

Their relentless march persisted, defying the encroaching fate, as they embarked on a journey fueled by necessity and an unwavering determination to experience the dawn following the longest night.

Lysandra's heart was pounding against her ribcage, matching the quick rhythm of their march through the thick under-brush of Erenor's untamed wilderness. The early morning mist twirled around her like ethereal dancers, and every rustle in the foliage appeared to carry a whisper of what could have been—or what might still happen.

"Are we certain this is the right path?" Aerin's voice cut through the silence, his steely gaze searching the woods as if he could discern fate itself hidden among the trees.

"Every step forward is a choice," Lysandra replied, her fingers trailing over the hilt of her sword, the cool metal a fleeting comfort. Her magic pulsed beneath her skin, a reminder of the power she wielded—and the danger it posed.

"Decisions that affect us all," Feyla said, fixing her satchel strap where her inventions, their lifelines in endless battles, were resting.

"Especially for those without magic," Lysandra murmured. The thought of Feyla, valiant but vulnerable in a world where shadows had fangs, and darkness clawed at the light, tightened an invisible vice around Lysandra's heart.

"Your magic has saved us more times than I can count," Aerin said, stepping closer, his presence a grounding force amid

the roiling uncertainty within her. "But your heart, Lysandra…
that's what truly guides us."

She wanted to believe him, to let his confidence seep into her
bones and brace her resolve. Yet the vision of Aviara shrouded in
malice, loomed large in her mind, casting doubt upon her every
decision.

"Pressing on means risking you all—sacrificing you to my
whims, my lineage." Lysandra halted, the forest seeming to hold
its breath with her. "If I am the vessel of our doom…"

"Then we sail together," Aerin interrupted, fierce determination etched onto his face. "We knew the stakes when we joined
you. Your fight is ours."

"Besides, what use is my crossbow if not to protect our
cause?" Feyla chimed in, the corner of her mouth lifting in a wry
smile that failed to mask the gravity of her words.

"Your cause," Lysandra corrected, her gaze flickering between
her friends. "I cannot—"

"Will not," Harrow's rumble interjected, his voice resonating
through the crisp air. The dragon's massive form emerged from
the shadows, golden scales contrasting with the dark foliage
around them. "You will not face the darkness alone."

"Then we must proceed with caution," Lysandra admitted,
the weight of her responsibility keeping her grounded in the
present moment. She carefully watched the expressions on her
companions' faces, finding comfort in their unwavering loyalty.
"Our bond, our unity, is what Aviara fears. We will need every
advantage, every ounce of cleverness, to outsmart her."

"Agreed," Aerin responded, drawing his daggers and allowing the first rays of dawn to gleam off their blades. "Let us begin then. There's darkness to conquer and a world to rescue."

"Right behind you," Feyla chimed in, loading her crossbow. The click of the bolt sliding into place punctuated their determination. They continued their journey, their movements orchestrated with stealth and vigilance, creating a muted symphony.

Although the path ahead was dangerous, Lysandra's companions provided unwavering support, bringing her solace. Their shared resolve strengthened her spirit for the challenges that lay ahead.

As the edge of the Ironwood Forest loomed before them, Lysandra's breath caught in her throat. The gnarled trees cast long shadows that whispered hidden dangers. A chilly breeze swept across her skin, causing goosebumps to rise. She tightened her grip on her sword, attempting to ignore the trembling in her hands.

"Stay close," Aerin murmured, his voice a thrum that resonated with an authority born from battles past. "The forest is alive with more than just our prey."

Though her focus wavered, she nodded, drifting to the heart of their journey—the confrontation with Aviara.

The question of facing the Deity who had nearly torn Erenor apart seeded doubt in Lysandra's mind.

Could she, the last descendant of the First Mage, truly harness the darkness within her to defeat such evil? Or would it consume her, turning her into the thing she sought to destroy?

"Something troubles you," Aerin said, halting to study her with his dark eyes that seemed to see right through to her soul.

"It's nothing," Lysandra lied, averting her gaze. How could she confess her fears—that her power might be insufficient against Aviara or worse, that it might betray her at the crucial moment?

"Your eyes betray you, Lysandra. They hold a storm," Aerin said. "Share your burden."

"Every step we take, every spell I cast... I feel her—Aviara. It's like she's already here, inside my head." Lysandra's confession tumbled out, whispered. "What if I can't control it? What if I fail all of you?"

"Then I will be there with you," Aerin vowed, his hand finding hers, his touch grounding. "To catch you, to fight with you. You won't face this alone."

"Nor will you," Feyla added, stepping beside them. Her crossbow was at the ready, her brown eyes resolute. "We've come too far to let fear dictate our fates."

A rustling sound from the underbrush snapped them to attention, and they moved into formation—Aerin at the lead, Lysandra by his side, and Feyla covering their backs.

"Whatever comes," Lysandra breathed, willing her magic to rise to her call, "we face it together."

"Always," Aerin affirmed, drawing his sword as a shadowy form slinked between the trees.

Lysandra's heart started racing; Yet, even as she prepared for combat, a flicker of hesitation remained. Was she the true savior of Erenor, or did she bring destruction upon them all?

Lysandra was torn between uncertainty and confidence as she pushed forward. Each rustle and snap of a twig made her more anxious.

Right before they reached the center of the forest, where it was pitch black and hope was nowhere to be found, a scout from Aviara's legion popped up. Lysandra held her breath, her mind going all over the place. It's about to go down, war was imminent.

"Prepare yourselves," she whispered, her staff and sword glowing with an ethereal light that cut through the gloom.

"Wait!" The shout came not from her comrades but from within her mind—a voice laced with malice and honey. Aviara.

Lysandra's vision blurred, the edges of reality fraying. She stood between light and shadow at the threshold, her fate—and that of Erenor—poised on the edge of her blade. Would she step forward into battle or retreat into the darkness that beckoned her with whispers of power and glory?

Lysandra lifted her sword high, her magic shining and determination written all over her face, yet her eyes hinted at an ongoing battle.

The path ahead lay shrouded in mist, her choice obscured by the fog of her doubts. As the scout charged, weapon drawn, Lysandra's decision hung suspended in the silence before the clash of steel.

Chapter 6

A PASSIONATE ENCOUNTER

The scout's body was all crumpled up on the forest floor, its eyes staring into nothing. Dark magic stank in the air like a nasty mist, reminding them of Aviara, their relentless enemy.

Lysandra stood over the dead body, her hand shaking a little as she closed its eyes, like the soft breeze in the trees.

"Rather die than betray her, it appears," Aerin whispered, his voice serious as he came over. His shadow blended with hers in the moonlight, and his dark hair fell across his forehead, a stark contrast to the paleness of his warrior's skin, honed from battles past.

Lysandra nodded, a tight line forming on her lips. "We've won this skirmish, but the war rages on."

They returned to their camp, where the fire crackled and popped, making everything cozy and keeping the darkness away.

Their friends were crashed out around the fire, dead asleep.

Feyla, with her hair spread like a dark halo on her cloak, held onto her crossbow even in her sleep while The Harrow's golden scales shimmered, proof of his watchful rest.

Aerin settled beside Lysandra, stretching his long legs toward the fire, its heat seeping into their weary bones. "Do you remember when we first met?" he asked, breaking the silence. "When all I saw in magic was the pain it caused?"

Lysandra's gaze met the dancing flames, her mind casting back to those days of suspicion and fear. "I do. You've come a long way since then, Aerin. We both have."

"Indeed." He ran a hand through his hair, dislodging a leaf caught in the tangles. "You showed me that magic isn't inherently evil; it's simply a tool. And like any tool, it reflects the intent of the one who wields it."

"Sometimes I worry," Lysandra confessed, her eyes not leaving the fire. "About the darkness within me. The balance I strive for always feels just out of reach."

Aerin's expression softened, and he leaned closer, his body's warmth and tangy scent mingling with hers. "But you keep reaching, Lysandra. That's what matters. Your determination gives us all strength, especially on nights like these."

"Strength..." She echoed the word as if tasting it, seeking its essence. "It's something we find in unexpected places, isn't it? In friends, in battles, even in our enemies."

"Especially in each other," Aerin added quietly. They sat in companionable silence, the crackle of the fire accompanying their shared reflections.

"Perhaps our magic clashes for a reason," mused Lysandra after a moment. Yours is earthy and grounded. Mine is...less so. But together, they create something new, something stronger."

"Like us," he said, smiling faintly. "Our internal and external battles forge us together in ways we never imagined."

"True," she agreed, a small smile on her lips. "And there's comfort in knowing that whatever lies ahead, we face it as one."

The fire's glow painted their faces with light and shadow, an artist capturing the complexity of their journey. They sat close, two souls united by fate and choice, the bonds of their growing love woven through their words and the silent language of their bodies.

Aerin's fingers brushed against Lysandra's, a silent promise in the simple touch. She turned her palm upward, allowing his hand to envelop hers, the warmth from his skin seeping into the cold she didn't realize had settled deep within her bones.

His thumb traced the lines of her hand, a gentle exploration that spoke volumes, banishing the chill of isolation that crept up on her whenever darkness threatened to overwhelm her.

"None of us are alone," he said, his voice a rumble against the crackling backdrop of the fire. "We stand together, bound by more than just our cause."

Lysandra caught the flicker of flame in his eyes as he looked at her, an earnest intensity burning the dark depths. In that gaze, she saw not just Aerin, the warrior, but Aerin, the man who had once walked a path darkened by loss and vengeance—the same man who had learned to see the light within magic, within her, and within himself.

"Strength isn't always about wielding a sword or casting a spell," he continued, squeezing her hand ever so slightly as if to emphasize his point. "It's in the way we rise after falling, in the way we push back against fear and doubt."

She nodded, the weight of his words settling around her heart. It was true. Yet they sat side by side, finding solace in shared silences and unspoken understandings.

"Your battles," he whispered, leaning closer, the scent of earth and smoke clinging to him, "they've never been yours to fight."

"Nor yours," she answered, her voice barely above a whisper, as she mirrored his pose, leaning into him, their foreheads nearly touching. "We are entwined, you and I—our magic, struggles, and spirits."

"Entwined," he repeated, a soft smile curving his lips. The word was a vow that held all the certainty of dawn following the darkest of nights.

The fire popped, sending a shower of sparks skyward, a fleeting constellation that mirrored the determination kindling within them. They were warriors, mages, protectors—two halves of a strength forged through adversity, a strength that would help them through the looming battle and beyond.

"Whatever comes," he said, his breath warm and moist against her cheek, "we face it tomorrow together."

"Together," Lysandra affirmed, and at that moment, as embers glowed and hearts beat in synchrony, the darkness was just a little less daunting.

The heat from the fire did little to ward off the chill that crept into Lysandra's bones, a coldness born not from the night air but from the shadows that lurked within her soul.

She gazed into the flames, watching the dance of red and gold twist and turn like the battle that raged in her heart.

"Sometimes," she began, her voice a mere thread of sound, "I feel as if the darkness is a tide lapping at my spirit, threatening to pull me under." Her eyes, bright with unshed tears, flicked to Aerin's face, seeking the solace only he could provide.

Aerin's hand tightened around hers, an anchor in the tempest. "Lysandra, you've faced that darkness head-on and emerged victorious every time. Yes, it's a part of you, but it does not define you."

Her breath hitched, the honesty of his words piercing the veil of her fears. "But what if one day I'm not strong enough? What if—"

"Stop," he interrupted, tender but firm. "Do not dwell on 'what ifs.' Remember who you are—the last descendant of Erenor's First Mage. Your light outshines any shadow within you."

She drew a shaky breath, absorbing the conviction radiating from him. His belief in her was a lifeline thrown across the chasm of her doubts.

"Every day, we stand against Aviara and her minions; we do so together," Aerin continued, his voice a deep thrum that resonated in the hollows of her weariness. "Our unity, our connection—more than just a source of strength. It's a beacon that cuts through the darkest night, a signal to all of Erenor that hope persists."

Lysandra let his words wash over her, a balm to soothe the turmoil within. She lifted their entwined hands, pressing his knuckles to her lips in gratitude. In that simple touch, she felt the pulse of his earthy magic, a grounding force against her own fantastical surge.

"Thank you, Aerin," she whispered, her voice steadied by the unwavering support reflected in his stormy eyes. "For being my rock in this relentless sea."

"Always," he murmured back, his thumb brushing a tear from her cheek with a tenderness that belied the warrior's strength before her. "Together, we will protect Erenor and restore its magic. Together, we are unstoppable."

His words were a vow, a promise that spanned beyond the boundaries of the night, echoing into the uncertain dawn that awaited them. And for the first time since the demon's defeat, since the revelation of her lineage's duality, Lysandra felt the scales of her inner balance tip ever so slightly towards the light.

Lysandra's gaze lingered on Aerin, the firelight casting a dance of shadows across his chiseled features. She searched his eyes, those deep pools of conviction that pierced her soul, and she found an anchor in their depths. His belief in her didn't waver; it was as solid as the earth he commanded with his newfound powers.

"Aviara will not break us," she said, her voice no longer a tremulous whisper but a clarion call forged from the same steel that lined her spine. "We are the shield against her darkness."

Aerin's lips curved up in a smile that promised dawn after the longest night. "That we are, Lysandra. And we will triumph as long as we stand together."

The space between them charged with a current stronger than any magic they wielded. It crackled through the air, raising the fine hairs on Lysandra's arms, drawing her closer to him as if bound by an invisible force.

"Your faith in me," she started, her breath hitching, "gives me the strength I never knew I had."

"Your courage," Aerin replied, his voice low and husky. You inspire me to be more than the sum of my past sins. You awaken the best parts of me."

Their gazes locked, and in that moment, all the battles and bloodshed faded into insignificance. There was only this connection, this burning need that rose like a phoenix from the ashes of their strife.

With a shared breath, they leaned in, the warmth of the fire paling compared to the heat that sparked when their lips met. The kiss was like a storm, a clash of elements as fierce as their duels with shadow and steel. Lysandra tasted the smoky tang of the night air mingled with the sweet hint of Aerin's breath, a heady combination that left her craving more.

Aerin's hands, rough from swordplay, were surprisingly gentle as they cradled her face, rough thumbs stroking her cheeks with the softness of a whisper. Her fingers traced the taut lines of his jaw, the sensation grounding her, even as their kiss sent her senses reeling.

She felt the thrum of his pulse against her own, a drumbeat that matched the earth's rhythm. Their bodies pressed closer, seeking solace in each other, and the heat of their embrace melted away the icy dread that once gripped Lysandra's heart like frost under the morning sun.

"Stay with me," she breathed against his lips, a plea wrapped in a vow.

"Always," he promised, sealing it with another kiss that spoke of unyielding commitment—a flame that neither shadow nor time could extinguish.

The night came alive with the whispering of leaves and the distant hoot of an owl, but within the circle of light cast by the fire, another world existed.

Lysandra and Aerin moved together in a dance as old as time, their bodies speaking in hushed tones of touch and sighs. Silhouettes intertwined; they imprinted the map of their scars and desires upon one another.

"Are you sure?" Aerin murmured, his voice a low rumble against her ear, his breath a fluttering caress on her skin.

"More than anything," Lysandra replied. Her response was not just to his question but to every silent plea her heart had ever made in the night's solitude.

Their connection deepened, a cascade of fervent discoveries. Each brush of Aerin's lips against her collarbone was a spark that lit her from within, and each glide of her hands across his muscled back was a current that pulled him further into her depths. The crackling fire could not compete with the energy between them, a testament to their earth and ethereal magic finding harmony.

Fingers laced through hair as dark as midnight, pulling Aerin closer until there was no space for doubts or fears. Their kiss, a mingling of spirits and breath, was both an anchor and a storm, holding them fast even as it threatened to sweep them away.

Lysandra felt the world's pulse beat beneath them, the rhythm of Erenor itself echoing through their conjoined forms. Together, they redefined the essence of their union, their love a potent force against the encroaching darkness.

As dawn's fingers crept across the horizon, they lay in a tangle of limbs, the soft glow of embers reflecting off their entwined bodies. The air was cool, teasing the lingering heat from their skin, the shared sweat a testament to their ardor now easing into tranquil rivulets.

Their breathing slowed in unison, hearts gradually returning to a restful cadence, the once urgent beats now gentle waves lapping at the shores of their consciousness. Contentment settled over them like a blanket woven from the threads of their affection, heavy and warm.

In this serene aftermath, the world held its breath, granting them a reprieve from the chaos that awaited beyond the flickering shadows. They basked in the stillness, in the rare peace afforded to those who bore the weight of Erenor's fate.

"Tonight, we have forged something unbreakable," Aerin whispered, his voice a soft echo in the quietude.

"And tomorrow, we face what comes with hearts fortified," Lysandra added, her gaze locked on the first hint of light painting the sky.

They remained there, wrapped in each other's embrace, two souls melded into one, ready to rise with the sun and continue their fight. For now, though, they were content to exist in the simple, profound intimacy of the moment, knowing it would fuel them for the battles ahead.

Lysandra's fingers danced lightly across the contours of Aerin's chest, tracing the lines of battle-hardened muscle that had so often shielded her from harm. Beneath her touch, the rhythmic thud of his heart was a grounding drumbeat, a reminder of life amidst their relentless struggle against the encroaching darkness.

"Without you," she murmured, her voice barely louder than the crackle of the dying fire nearby, "My shadows would have swallowed me." Her eyes, reflecting the remnants of starlight, held his in a gaze as intimate as their earlier embrace. "Your strength has become my beacon."

Aerin regarded her with eyes filled with the tenderness he felt for the woman beside him. He brushed a rogue strand of hair from her face, his fingertips grazing her cheek with a devotion that surpassed mere physical desire.

"Every scar on my soul," he said, his voice steady and sure, "is a testament to my journey. But it is with you, Lysandra, that I've found a purpose beyond vengeance." His thumb lingered at the curve of her jaw, a silent promise etched in his touch. "Wherever this path leads us, I will walk it by your side."

Their exchange was a subtle dance of words and gestures, a language they had crafted together through trials and triumphs. They spoke it in the quiet confidence of their intertwined fingers and the shared glances that conveyed much more than any incantation could.

"Then let us tread that path together," Lysandra replied, the corners of her lips lifting in a smile that belied the ferocity of her spirit. "As protectors of Erenor, united."

In the silence that followed, they sealed a pact not with grandiose oaths but with unspoken understanding—an alliance of heart and soul, ready to face whatever perils awaited with the dawn.

Lysandra's eyelids fluttered as the fire's embers waned, casting their last warm breath over her and Aerin. Their limbs, a tangle of shared warmth, refused to unravel, content in their mutual embrace. The forest beyond their camp exhaled the nocturnal chorus of crickets and nightjars, while the canopy whispered secrets to the stars.

"Sleep," Aerin murmured, his voice a lullaby woven with the night's serenity. "I'll keep watch, even in your dreams."

A smile played around Lysandra's lips, fatigue pulling them into a gentle bow. "In dreams, we are both warriors and sages," she whispered back, her fingers tracing idle patterns on his arm, feeling the rhythm of his blood like a silent drumbeat against her skin.

"Then tonight, let us dream of peace," he said, tightening his hold just enough to affirm his presence, his protection.

"Peace," she echoed, a soft sigh escaping as she nestled closer. The scent of earth and pine on Aerin's skin, mixed with the smoldering wood, ground her thoughts and anchored her to this moment.

The night draped over them like a velvet cloak, rich with the promise of rest and renewal. Lysandra's consciousness wavered on the brink of sleep, her senses attuned to the steady cadence of Aerin's heart—a rhythm that beats in time with the pulse of Erenor itself.

"Will you still be here when I wake up?" Her voice was a thread of sound, nearly lost amidst the rustle of leaves.

"Always," he vowed, his breath warm against her ear. "As certain as dawn follows the night."

With those words, a tranquil assurance settled in Lysandra's heart, a counterweight to the darkness that often sought to unbalance her. She allowed the weight of her eyelids to close the world away, trusting in the bond that linked her spirit to Aerin's.

And as sleep claimed them, drawing their minds into its quiet realm, they remained a fortress of two—defiant against the encroaching shadows, bound by a love that was both their armor and their flame. Together, entwined in body and soul, they drifted into slumber. The lines between them blurred until it was impossible to tell where one ended and the other began.

Chapter 7

SPIRITS AND FORESHADOWING

The mist covered the forest, giving it the appearance of being a secret, magical place. Leading her companions through the dense thicket, Lysandra's breath formed frost in the air, and her boots were damp with dew. The gnarled branches of the trees appeared to bow down, guiding them deeper into the heart of the woods.

"Stay near," she whispered, her voice almost not audible over the rustling leaves, her hand dabbing the handle of her sword.

With a determined stride, Aerin surveyed the undergrowth with his piercing dark eyes, embodying the essence of a warrior despite his reservations about the uncertainty of magic. The wolf-like figure of Shadow, his coat as dark as her innermost desires, prowled silently, effortlessly merging with the shadows cast by the foliage.

A hush fell upon the grove. The birds ceased their singing,

and the wind held its breath. A figure, translucent and shimmering, materialized in the clearing ahead, its form flickering like the flame of a candle caught in a gentle breeze.

"By the ancients," Feyla whispered, her crossbow hanging forgotten in her grasp.

Lysandra stepped forward, drawn to the spirit as if by a force beyond her comprehension. It was an ancient being, older than the oldest tree, and its presence was a tapestry of wisdom and power woven through the fabric of Erenor.

In a soft, melodic tone, the spirit declared, "You are the Child of the First Mage, with the dual lineage flowing in your blood, and that is the key."

With a simple brush of their hands, Aerin wordlessly expressed solidarity, suggesting the shared battles and difficult circumstances that had solidified their relationship. His touch was grounding, a beacon of humanity amid the swirl of ancient forces around them.

"Will I be confronting Aviara?"

"Without a doubt," the spirit replied, its gaze delving into the depths of her being. The interwoven nature of your lineage, encompassing both darkness and light, has the potential to tilt the balance of power.

"We shall not waver," Aerin promised, moving closer to Lysandra, the unspoken commitment fueling an intense resolve in his eyes.

"Nor shall you walk alone," the spirit assured, a glimmer of approval in its ageless eyes. "For the path you tread is one of destiny, and the blood of the ancestors flows within you – a river of strength against the tide of darkness."

When the spirit spoke, Lysandra felt the conflicting forces of her dual nature fighting inside her. Yet, surrounded by her loyal companions, with Aerin's unwavering gaze locked on hers, she knew the fight for Erenor would not be hers to bear alone.

Lysandra's heart raced as the ethereal presence in front of them shimmered, shifting and transforming like fog in the early morning sunlight. The grove distorted time, holding ancient secrets that were on the brink of revelation from the being that had observed countless ages go by.

"Your ancestor," the spirit intoned, voice echoing with the rustle of leaves, "was beguiled by a demon of many faces. A creature adept in the art of deception, wearing guises as easily as one might don cloaks."

The air grew still, the earth holding its breath as the tale unfolded. The spirit's eyes, deep wells of knowledge, fixed upon Lysandra.

"This shapeshifter spoke honeyed lies, weaving illusions that ensnared your forebear's heart." The spirit's form flickered, shadows playing across its features as if to mimic the duplicity of the demon it described.

"Trust yielded to betrayal, and the noble lineage that flowed through her veins became tainted. Her fall was orchestrated by cunning and malice, leaving Erenor to teeter on the brink of ruin."

Lysandra clenched her fists, nails biting into her palms as the legacy of deceit coiled around her like a serpent. The echo of ancient wrongs clamored for retribution in her blood, the blend of darkness and light within her churning tumultuously.

"Be wary, child of both shadow and sun," the spirit warned, its form contracting slightly as if bracing against an unseen storm.

"Aviara is the tempest that seeks to unravel your will. Her power is vast, and she hungers to corrupt the strength you possess. Your dark heritage, a siren's call to her malevolence."

The words struck Lysandra with the force of a gale, yet she held fast, her resolve steeling. She could feel the gaze of her companions upon her, their silent support a bulwark against the rising tide of doubt.

"Can I wield this dual nature without succumbing to its darker half?" Her question hung between them like a blade poised over fate's thread.

You can achieve great salvation or cause profound destruction within yourself. It is a delicate balance, as fragile as a spider's web, yet as strong as the roots of the mountain pines.

Lysandra nodded, the gravity of her lineage a mantle upon her shoulders. She knew the path ahead was fraught with danger each step a dance with destiny. But within her burned the fire of her ancestors, a beacon against the encroaching dark.

"Then I shall learn to harness the storm," she declared, her voice imbued with the conviction of those who had walked before her. "For Erenor, for all who stand with me, I will not yield to Aviara's shadows."

The spirit regarded her with a timeless gaze, an acknowledgment of the warrior's heart that beat within Lysandra's chest.

The atmosphere was charged with anticipation, the silence broken by the creaking of leather and the rustling of leaves.

Each one of them observed it—the tightening grip of destiny, the pressing urgency of the war towards which they were marching. A symphony of unvoiced emotions played across their faces; determination mingled with dread; courage interlaced with the specter of despair.

Among the rustling leaves, harmonizing whispers filled the grove with ancient magic. The dancing shadows gave the impression of being alive, setting the stage for Lysandra to encounter a pure and unrestrained apparition of energy. The spirit appeared fluid, a flowing stream of light that had no limits, its voice a harmonious melody that echoed the soul of Erenor.

"Descendent of the First Mage," the spirit addressed her, "your arrival was written in the stars."

Lysandra's eyes, unwavering and mesmerizing, reflected the otherworldly brilliance of the apparition. "I seek your wisdom, Spirit of the Grove. How do I use my heritage, the blood of both light and shadow, to weaken Aviara?"

"Within you flows the power of creation and destruction," the spirit intoned. "Balance them, as the horizon marries night and day. Your relic is the key—its light can pierce through the deepest darkness."

As the deep conversation progressed, Feyla's eyes involuntarily wandered towards Eolande. His figure stood out like a stroke of a brush in the fading light, leaving her curious and eager to understand his mystery.

She noticed the slight change in his posture, the barely noticeable tilt of his head to acknowledge her focus. They chose duty over curiosity, and with some hesitation, they shifted their attention back to the importance of the spirit's guidance.

"Light alone cannot banish darkness, nor can shadow exist without its counterpart," the spirit continued, its form pulsating with ethereal intensity. "Embrace both, Lysandra, and let them guide your hand in the battle to come."

"Isn't there a clearer path? A way to ensure victory?" Lysandra pressed; her brow furrowed with the weight of her responsibility.

"Certainty is the domain of gods, not mortals. Forge ahead with courage, and let the relic unveil its power when the moment arises," the spirit replied, its voice fading like the last echoes of a dream.

Lysandra nodded, absorbing the cryptic guidance with a sense of resolve that appeared to emanate from her core. The air crackled with anticipation of what lay ahead—a confrontation with Aviara that had the potential to change the fate of Erenor forever.

On the vibrant moss, Aerin knelt, his hands poised over a wounded sparrow. Someone had twisted the wing of the small creature causing its chest to rise and fall with shallow breaths. With deep concentration, Aerin's forehead furrowed and his dark hair fell into his face as he tapped into the growing power within him—a power that used to be his enemy.

"Focus, Aerin," the spirit's voice resonated, gentle yet firm. "Healing is an extension of the life force that flows through every living being. Connect with it, become one."

Lysandra watched, her heart thrumming against her ribcage, as the air around Aerin shimmered with a subtle green glow.

She recognized the conflict brewing within him as he grappled with the clash between his former fight against magic and the growing gift he had gained. It stood as a testament to their journey, offering a glimpse into the shared complexities they faced.

"Feel the warmth of the earth, the pulse of nature," the spirit guided. "Let your essence intertwine with the bird's vitality."

Inhaling deeply, Aerin closed his eyes and allowed the raw energy to stream from his palms. The sparrow twitched, and then, miraculously, righted itself, fluttering up into the air, its wing mended. Aerin let out a breath he didn't realize he'd been holding, and a triumphant grin broke across his face.

"Your guidance... it's invaluable," he said, standing to face the spirit, the bond between him and Lysandra fortified in the glow of his achievement.

"Use it wisely, young healer. Your powers will grow, as will your need for them." The spirit's gaze held a depth that suggested it saw far beyond the grove they stood in.

Lysandra's eyes met Aerin's, her pride in his progress mingling with the warmth that had steadily grown between them.

They were warriors of different magics, yet united in purpose.

Feyla explored the perimeter of the open space, her imaginative thoughts whirring like the inner mechanisms of a clockwork apparatus. The spirit ignited Feyla's insatiable curiosity as it shared stories of ancient relics and lost knowledge, engrossing her.

In the ruins of the Silent Spires, you will discover traces of the ancient technology left behind by the Old Ones," the spirit whispered, its urgent tone tingling Feyla's sharp instincts.

Feyla's fingers danced across the leather satchel at her side, already imagining the schematics, the mechanics of what she could forge. An invention that might harness the wild energies of Erenor, channel them into something tangible, something powerful.

"Thank you," she whispered, more to herself than to the spirit, as ideas crystallized into plans. Her lack of magical blood mattered little when her mind could conjure wonders just as potent.

"Be wary," the spirit cautioned, its form waning. The power of knowledge can rival that of any weapon or spell.

"Understood," she replied, determination hardened her gaze. Feyla turned to look back at the group, her thoughts alight with possibility, ready to put her newfound insight to the test.

"Come on, let's hurry to the Silent Spires," she urged, her eyes shining with the excitement of what lay ahead.

The shape of the spirit flickered, its edges unraveling like the fading whispers of mist in the morning. Its radiant eyes locked onto each of them with a final, perceptive stare before it vanished into the lush surroundings of the secret forest.

"Thank you," Lysandra murmured, her voice steady though her heart thrummed with the gravity of their charge. "For your wisdom and for recognizing the struggle within us."

"May your guidance light our path," Aerin added, his deep voice resonating with newfound purpose.

As the last glimmer of the spirit's presence faded, silence enveloped the clearing, heavy with the weight of their destiny. They stood still for a moment, letting the serenity of the grove wash over them, steeling themselves for the battles ahead.

"We should leave," Lysandra ordered, her voice reflecting the power of her ancestry as she surveyed the line of trees.

Stepping closer, Aerin's nod expressed a deep sense of shared determination. Locking their gazes, they wordlessly exchanged a vow to support one another and recognized the obstacles they would confront as a united front.

As their gaze locked, her eyes shimmered with the lingering essence of the spirit, causing the world around them to fade away for a moment.

"Whatever lies ahead," he said in a deep voice, breaking their wordless communion, "we face it as one."

Lysandra's lips curved in a small, resolute smile. "Together," she agreed, their pact sealed not by words but by the shared fire in their veins.

With a glance at Feyla, who was already strapping on her satchel with a look of fierce readiness, a look of encouragement to Shadow, and a nod to the stoic Harrow, whose golden scales shimmered with anticipation, Lysandra led the way out of the grove.

Shoulder to shoulder with Aerin, each step took them closer to Aviara, closer to the climax of their quest to save Erenor, closer to understanding the depths of their power and the nature of their bond.

Feyla's boots crunched on the forest floor as she sidled up to Eolande. The elf stood like an ancient sentinel, his gaze lingering where the spirit had vanished, a silent testament to the gravity of their mission.

His features, appearing both stern and ethereal in the dappled sunlight filtering through the leaves, intrigued Feyla and drew her in.

"Your thoughts are loud, even in silence," Feyla ventured, her tone light yet lined with the weight of their conversation with the spirit.

Eolande glanced back, a small crease appearing on his forehead. "And yours are curious, Feyla of Erenor."

"Curiosity is a trait that has served me well," she replied, keeping her admiration at bay, though her eyes betrayed the respect she held for him.

"Indeed," Eolande agreed, his gaze shifting back to the path ahead. "But let us not dwell on mysteries when certainty is required."

Feyla nodded the inventor within her sparking with the possibilities of what they had learned from the spirit. She tucked away every detail, every syllable, knowing it could be the key to their survival—or their downfall.

"Certainty drives my inventions," Feyla said, hoisting her satchel higher on her shoulder. "It's the unknown that fuels the fire."

"May your fire illuminate our darkest hour," Eolande murmured, almost to himself, before he strode forward, joining the others at Lysandra's signal.

Against the backdrop of an awakening world, the group moved out of the hidden grove, forming a line of shadows.

The mist in the early morning stuck to their armor, with droplets shining on the leather and iron, as if they held the essence of the ancient spirit's power.

The Dragon Harrow's wings spread open, making a sound resembling the gentle rustling of leaves, creating a golden tapestry in the early morning sunlight. Shadow walked alongside Aerin, his body moving smoothly and blending into the darkness, resembling a predator about to attack.

"Aviara won't know what hit her," Lysandra declared, her voice cutting through the stillness like a blade. The staff she carried shone brightly, emanating a magical energy that rippled through the clearing.

Aerin suggested, "We should keep things as they are," as he unsheathed his sword, the metallic resonance revealing its readiness.

"Stealth and cunning," Feyla put in, checking the string of

her crossbow, her fingers deft and sure. "That's how we strike."

"Let us harness today's lessons," Eolande said, his hand resting on the hilt of his blade, his eyes reflecting the company's resolve. For our unity is our strength."

The pact was not made aloud but was as potent as any spell cast by the mightiest of mages. Each member of the fellowship knew the risks and felt the pulse of their destiny thrumming in their veins.

They stepped through the veil of branches, leaving the sanctuary of the hidden grove behind, and ventured into the heart of danger.

Aviara's domain beckoned, a land fraught with darkness and deceit, but they marched on, fueled by the power of the spirit's wisdom, the bond between them, and the unwavering determination to reclaim Erenor from the brink of chaos.

Chapter 8

ANCIENT SPIRITS

The sound of Aerin's heartbeat reverberated in his ears like war drums, shattering the stillness of the forest. He knelt on the mossy ground, the cool dampness seeping through his trousers, grounding him to the earth. The ancient spirit hovered before him, its form a cascade of starlight woven into the shape of a sage long lost to time.

"Harmony is key," the spirit whispered, a voice like wind through autumn leaves. "Your breath is the tide that guides the ebb and flow of your power."

Aerin nodded, his gaze fixed on the translucent figure. The raw magic was palpable within him, an untamed beast pacing restlessly. But now he sought to be its master, to channel it with finesse rather than brute force.

"Envision the energy as a golden light," the spirit continued, its eyes full of ancient wisdom. "See it igniting in your core, where your soul burns brightest."

Closing his eyes, Aerin inhaled, the forest's loamy scent filling his lungs. He held his breath, counting, then exhaled slowly, releasing more than just air—a torrent of uncertainty rode the wave of his breath outward.

Breath by measured breath, a warmth blossomed in his chest. The warmth expanded and grew. A faint glow, faint at first, kindled within him, the nascent light of his healing magic. With each inhale, the light intensified, spreading from his heart through his veins like molten gold, seeking riverbeds to claim.

"Feel the balance," the spirit murmured in a chant. "The tranquility that comes when power is not taken but embraced."

The tingling sensation spread through Aerin's hands, light on his fingertips, and was palpable. Even in darkness, he could almost envision it—as if they had encountered the sun's scorching rays. The glow was eager to penetrate the world and heal its fractures.

"Embrace it, but maintain your composure," the spirit warned, its voice like a gentle thread anchoring him.

Taking another deep breath, Aerin sensed the pulsating golden energy under his control, waiting for his unique guidance. Within this sacred clearing, veiled by shadows and with echoes of ancient sorcery, he contacted the threshold of controlling the life-bestowing energy within him.

Aerin stretched out his hands, the golden light shimmering on his skin as he directed it towards the twisted tree. His hands emanated a vibrant and

warm energy that flowed in shimmering waves, soothing the

rough wounds on the tree's bark. The leaves trembled like a breeze, and wherever his magic made contact, the fragmented wood started mending together, resembling healed skin.

"See how life yearns for balance." The spirit's voice flowed like wind through leaves. "Your power serves as the channel."

"Is this me?" Aerin's voice was hushed with reverence as he watched the bark mend under the glow of his touch.

"Within you lies the heart of Erenor itself," the spirit replied, its form radiating approval. "You are the vessel through which its essence flows."

"Teach me," Aerin pleaded, pulling back slightly, afraid to mar the delicate process. "How can I control it? How can I use this gift to protect those I care about?"

"Your intent molds the magic," the spirit counseled. "Anchor your will in purpose. Feel the life around you, understand its flow, and become one. That is the key to mastery."

Aerin nodded, absorbing the wisdom offered. He refocused, sharpening his determination like a blade, and directed the healing energy into the tree's deepest scars. It was more than mending; it was an act of communion between mage and nature.

"Harmony, Aerin Stormrider," the spirit whispered. "Remember always, the strongest force in this realm is not destruction, but the relentless pursuit of rebirth."

"Rebirth." The word resonated within him, echoing his desire to forge an alternative path amid the darkness threatening Erenor. "I will learn. For my friends, for Lysandra, for our future."

"Continue on, young mage," urged the spirit. "Your journey will be fraught with challenges, but as you persevere, your abilities will flourish, and so will you."

"Thank you," Aerin acknowledged, recognizing a profound connection with the spirit, a mentor beyond human comprehension. "For everything."

"Go now," the spirit faded, its last words lingering like morning mist. "Let your light shine forth, Aerin of Erenor."

With the fading of ethereal guidance, Aerin felt a keen sense of purpose take hold. With his healing magic becoming stronger, he understood that their fight against Aviara's minions had gained a valuable ally.

Feyla's fingers paused on the tree's rugged bark as a vivid memory fragment came into focus in her mind. In her recollection, she could still smell the musty scent of ancient parchment and envision the dancing dust motes in a secluded corner of an old library.

An old book lay on the ground, with a worn cover and yellowed pages. Many years ago, she stumbled upon a tome filled with cryptic symbols and intricate diagrams that puzzled her.

The recollection became more vivid, causing Feyla to feel a sense of urgency. Those symbols had suggested the existence of a game-changing invention that could turn the tables in their tireless fight against Aviara's shadowy minions. Adrenaline surged through her, intensifying her resolve as her heartbeat sped up. If she could only remember those designs and comprehend their purpose...

Closing her eyes, she whispered, "Come on, think!" as she tried to picture the page she had been reading.

When she blinked her eyes open again, they glowed with the spark of epiphany. She skillfully retrieved a charcoal piece from her pouch and sketched on a flat stone.

The lines intersected and curved like the intricate patterns she recalled from the forgotten volume. Her sharp intellect and inherent creativity guided her hand as she executed every stroke precisely, which had been helpful in previous endeavors.

She whispered, her lips curling into a gentle smile as she thought of her beloved elf. Her affection towards him gave her extraordinary patience and a gentle strength that offset her innate impulsiveness.

"Could it be?" she mused aloud as the symbols took shape, coalescing into a blueprint she could have pieced together. It appeared to be some sort of gadget created to magnify magical energies.

"Aviara won't know what hit her," Feyla said, a fierce glint in her eye as realization dawned. This invention was truly exceptional.

With excitement rushing through her veins like liquid fire, she stepped back to examine her work. With her mind buzzing, she delved into the possibilities and the practicalities of turning this theoretical marvel into something tangible.

The prospect of requiring rare materials, careful crafting, and precise enchantments did not intimidate Feyla. She had a natural talent for innovation, and adversity only strengthened her creative edge.

"Wait till Lysandra sees this," she murmured with a grin, picturing her friend's reaction. The thought of contributing such a vital advantage to their cause filled Feyla with fierce pride. This was more than just a breakthrough; it was hope—a tangible symbol of their resilience in the face of encroaching darkness.

With her plan taking form, Feyla rolled up her makeshift blueprint and tucked it securely into her belt. There was much to do, and time was always of the essence.

But first, she would share her discovery with the others, her mind already buzzing with the steps needed to forge this new weapon in their arsenal against evil.

Feyla's boots pounded the forest floor, her breath a misty cloud in the crisp morning air. Her fingers itched to touch the smooth metal and rough wood that would form the backbone of her latest creation. The clarity of her mission banished any lingering shadows from the night's rest.

"Where did Eolande say the star iron was kept?" she muttered, weaving through the trees with practiced ease.

"By the roots of the Elderwillow, guarded by a slumbering earth sprite," she recalled, the inventor's mind piecing together the puzzle of resources needed as she went.

The forest gave way to a clearing where the Elderwillow towered, its gnarled roots twisting like ancient serpents into the ground.

Feyla approached, eyes scanning for the telltale shimmer of the sprite's aura. She found it curled up and pulsating within the hollow of a root. She retrieved the precious ore with a deft hand, murmuring a word of thanks to the sleeping guardian.

"Next, the essence of dawn flower... for the enchantments," she whispered, ticking off items on an invisible list.

Amidst a clearing bathed in soft light filtered through the canopy, Lysandra stood silently. Lysandra stood silently amidst a clearing bathed in soft light filtered through the canopy, her gaze fixed on Aerin, who sat cross-legged, his face a mask of serene concentration.

A golden glow pulsed around him, intensifying with each deep breath. The sight made her warrior's heart swell—a mage in tune with the world's heartbeat.

"Focus, Aerin," she encouraged quietly, careful not to break his trance. "You've got this."

Her words seemed to drift to him on the breeze, and the glow steadied, becoming a radiant aura that spoke volumes of his control over the healing magic.

"Good," Lysandra acknowledged, feeling a surge of hope. "Our path is fraught with peril, but with power like yours, we might just tip the scales."

When Aerin's eyes opened, they met hers in a gaze filled with gratitude and determination. His voice was steady as he replied, "For Erenor, for all of us, I'll master this."

"Of that, I have no doubt," Lysandra responded, her tone imbued with unshakeable confidence. She turned her head slightly, catching the glimmer of Feyla's form before returning through the trees.

"Look at you, Feyla," she called out, noting the bundle of materials cradled in the inventor's arms. "Like a magpie collecting shiny trinkets for your brilliant contraptions."

"More than trinkets, Lysandra," Feyla shot back, a mischievous spark in her eye. "These are the keys to our victory."

"Then let's forge our fate," Lysandra declared, her hands itching for the handle of her blade as a new day dawned on their quest.

Feyla meticulously displayed her bounty, arranging a variety of metals, wires, and mysterious objects as if they were a treasure waiting to be discovered.

Lysandra leaned in, her gaze tracing the curves and edges of each piece, noting how they caught the light of the afternoon sun filtering through the canopy.

"Your mind is a labyrinth of genius, Feyla," Lysandra said, her eyes alight with respect as she observed the inventor's careful arrangement. "These inventions of yours... they turn the tides in ways Aviara's shadows can't predict."

Feyla's hands paused, a rare blush coloring her cheeks. "It's nothing," she demurred, though pride lifted her voice. "Just a bit of twisted metal and a spark of inspiration."

"Hardly just anything," Lysandra countered firmly, resting a hand on Feyla's shoulder. "You're shaping our future with every device you craft."

The inventor nodded, a smile creeping onto her lips, bolstered by Lysandra's unwavering belief. Their eyes met, an unspoken vow passing between them - they would not falter, not when so much depended on their resolve.

The rustle of leaves announced Aerin's approach, his footsteps soft upon the forest floor. The group turned, anticipation thrumming in the air as he joined their circle.

"I've communed with the spirit," Aerin began, his voice carrying the weight of newfound wisdom. "It showed me the flow of life, the pulse that connects all things." He outstretched his hands, palms glowing faintly with the remnants of his practice. "I feel it within me, ready to mend and to soothe."

"An invaluable gift," Lysandra murmured, her admiration for Aerin's dedication shining in her eyes. "To heal is to defy death itself."

"Which brings us to this," Feyla interjected, tapping a blueprint at the top of her collection. Her finger followed the intricate designs, showing the paths that would harness magical energies. "Using this harness, Aerin's ability will be amplified, and the healing will be directed to the most critical areas."

"Or restore what Aviara seeks to destroy," Aerin added, leaning over to examine the plans more closely. His face became solemn. "Her relentless pursuit is aimed at destroying the world's resilience."

"Then we'll stop at nothing to keep it whole," Lysandra declared, her voice a steadfast promise. As she glanced at Feyla and Aerin, she saw comrades in arms and dear friends with a shared purpose. "Armed with innovation and heart, we continue to forge ahead as a team."

"Let's begin," Feyla said, the fire of determination igniting within her. She picked up her tools, ready to breathe life into her vision.

"Every step forward is a victory against darkness," Aerin agreed, his own resolve hardening like steel as he prepared to refine his command of the healing arts.

And so, in a quiet clearing shielded by ancient trees, the trio set to work fervently, crafting hope from ingenuity and magic, their hearts beating as one with the timeless rhythm of Erenor.

Lysandra tightened the leather straps of her gauntlets, each movement deliberate, grounding her to the moment.

The scent of pine and earth lingered in the air, mingling with the sharp tang of metal as she slid her sword back into its scabbard. Her muscles hummed with readiness, a silent testament to the countless hours of training that had honed her body into a weapon for their cause.

"Remember, it's not just about strength," Aerin said, his voice calm yet potent with the authority of experience. His fingers ran over the embroidered symbols on the cuffs of his sleeves, feeling the dormant magic beneath. "It's also about recognizing when to use it and when to provide solace instead."

"Between your magic and my gadgets, we've got both covered," Feyla remarked, securing a newly crafted device onto her belt, confidence etched in every line of her frame. She caught Lysandra's eye, a glint of mischief dancing in hers. "But you, with that blade—and heart—of yours, bring us balance."

A genuine and light laugh escaped Lysandra, unburdened for the moment by the weight of what lay ahead. "Balance, eh?

I suppose all those drills were good for something then." She flexed her hands, feeling the familiar grip of the hilt against her palm like an extension of her own will.

"More than something," Aerin interjected, the corners of his mouth lifting. "You're the backbone of this quest, Lysandra. Your courage gives us the strength to face whatever darkness awaits."

"Your strategy keeps us alive to fight another day," Feyla added, her tone warm with respect. Your tactics have saved our skins more than I can count."

"Only because I have the two of you watching my back," Lysandra countered, her gaze sweeping over her friends. "We each bring our strengths to the table—that makes us unstoppable."

A wordless understanding passed between them as they exchanged meaningful looks. It was a bond forged through trials, a camaraderie that no shadow could diminish.

"Let's get moving," Lysandra declared, her voice carrying the weight of their collective resolve. "Aviara won't hold off her attack forever, and we need to be ready."

"Agreed," Aerin nodded, stepping forward with purpose. His hand raised, palm facing outward, and the air shimmered around them, a soft glow emanating from his skin. The golden light pooled in his hands, a visible sign of the power he was learning to command.

"Lead the way," Feyla said, eyes scanning the horizon as she activated the mechanism at her wrist, gears clicking into place with satisfying precision. A faint blue aura enveloped her contraption, merging Aerin's magic seamlessly with her engineering prowess.

They moved together, a trio bound by destiny and determination, each step taking them closer to their enemy and fate. In the shadow of the towering trees, they became a beacon of hope—a promise that as long as they stood together, Erenor would never fall to darkness.

The forest loomed with a promise of untold secrets as Lysandra led the way, her boots sinking into the loam.

Shadows danced between the trees but were benign specters under the midday sun's scrutiny. At her side, Shadow prowled, senses attuned to the hidden life around them. Behind, Harrow's immense wings folded neatly against his scaled back, his talons leaving deep impressions on the earth with every step.

"Every stride takes us closer," Lysandra murmured, more to herself than to her companions. Her hand rested on the pommel of her sword—a reassuring weight against her thigh.

"Indeed," Harrow's rumbling voice vibrated through the air. But remember, Aviara's realm is ever-changing and treacherous."

"Treacherous, yes," Eolande agreed, knocking an arrow to his bow out of habit. "But not impervious. With Aerin's healing and Feyla's devices..."

"Nothing is impervious to us," Lysandra finished, a slight smile tugging at her lips. Casting a fleeting glance at the elf, she noticed the fiery determination in his eyes, a sign of the battle ahead. In just a moment, they shared a meaningful glance that spoke volumes of trust.

With each step through the thickening underbrush, Lysandra could feel the weight of their mission as if it were a physical load. The doubts were penetrating, but she shook her head to shake them off. Through their mutual support and reliance on one another's strengths, they had made great strides, and their unity would be the key to their future success.

"Don't forget what the spirit said," she shouted as she walked away. "Balance and harmony are as powerful as a blade and bow in our arsenal."

"Speaking of the spirit," Feyla piped up from the rear, a note of wonder in her tone. Do you think we'll ever learn who he was? His knowledge was beyond anything I've seen."

"Whoever he was, he believed in us," Lysandra said, the thought warming her. "One day, we'll unravel that mystery. We owe him our gratitude."

"A debt to be repaid," Harrow nodded solemnly.

The air grew colder as they neared Aviara's domain, a chill that seeped into one's marrow. A fire was, however, burning within each of them—an ember of hope that refused to be extinguished.

Lysandra encouraged, "We mustn't stop; let's keep moving," her voice maintained its composure despite the mounting unease. "Our destiny awaits, and we will not be found wanting."

With unanimous agreement, the group pressed on, their determination becoming as unyielding as forged steel.

Although the road ahead was dangerous, their combined strength made them formidable. As they ventured into the increasingly dark woods, they held onto the spirit's wisdom like a lantern guiding them through the approaching night.

Chapter 9

AVIARA'S REALM

The entrance to Aviara's realm stood ominously, resembling a deep wound in the world, emanating dark energy from its pulsating edges.

As the group entered the territory, the atmosphere grew heavy, as if they were wading through a swamp of darkness and malevolence.

The land here, with its contorted spires and gnarled trees, couldn't be more different from the lush magnificence of Erenor.

"Stay alert," Lysandra whispered, her hand lightly touching the handle of her enchanted sword as she carefully surveyed the murky surroundings. Her sword, seemed to hum with anticipation.

Without taking his eyes off Lysandra's silhouette, Aerin nodded in agreement. A stirring sensation of magic coursed through him in response to the restless unease that filled his surroundings. A natural instinct to shield her arose, but he stifled it, understanding that Lysandra required freedom, not overprotection.

They didn't have to wait long before the creatures arrived. Out of the gloom, a horde of shadow hounds materialized, their sinewy and dark bodies forming a grotesque tangle accompanied by a deafening cacophony of screeches. They circled, red eyes glowing with ravenous intent as if the air around the group had curdled into malice.

"Let's dance," Lysandra whispered to herself as she lunged forward to meet the wave head-on. Her sword slashed through the nearest beast, its body dissipating into wisps of shadow upon contact. Each movement was a deadly dance of steel and certainty.

"Behind you!" Aerin called out, his voice cutting through the air with urgency. The sound echoed off the walls, mingling with the scent of damp earth that permeated the underground chamber.

As his hands danced through the air, the faint whispers of his movements mingled with the crackling of arcane energy.

A brilliant light erupted from his fingertips, illuminating the darkness, as bolts of pure magical essence streaked towards the advancing creature. The surge of power sent a tingling sensation coursing through his veins, fueling him with a newfound confidence and purpose.

"Trust me," Lysandra shot back between breaths, not needing to look to know that Aerin would cover her flank. She pivoted, bringing her sword in a wide arc that cleaved through another assailant. The air crackled where the blade passed, and runes glowed brighter with each kill.

"Without a doubt," Aerin answered, a faint smile playing on his mouth despite the destruction. He conjured a shielding spell in a split second as a shadowhound leaped towards Lysandra, narrowly missing her shoulder with its snapping jaws. With a forceful impact, the barrier sent the beast tumbling back into chaos.

"She said, 'Good timing,' and offered him a quick, fierce grin. The grin held the weight of shared battles and unspoken promises. They fought together, a symphony of steel and sorcery. Each spell Aerin cast, every enemy Lysandra felled, brought them closer to the heart of Aviara's corrupted sanctuary."

"Keep pushing," Lysandra grunted, her voice laced with the exertion of battle and the urgency of their quest. "Aviara will pay for what she's done."

She did not need to explain further. They all carried the scars of Aviara's wrath. The remnants of fallen comrades and shattered dreams haunted them. But they stood there, unwavering, a symbol of the indomitable spirit of those who dared to defy the darkness.

Together, they carved a path through the nightmarish assault, Lysandra's sword an extension of her will, and Aerin's magic a testament to his growth. Both knew this was merely the first challenge of many they would face in the heart of Aviara's twisted domain.

Bolts hissed through the murky air, each a harbinger of death for the malformed beasts that dared to leap from the shadows.

Feyla skillfully reloaded her crossbow with mechanical precision, her eyes narrowed, and her stance shifted. As her bolt struck, the shadow hound evaporated into darkness.

"Reckon I don't need magic to even the odds," Feyla muttered under her breath, deft fingers already setting another bolt in place. The crossbow she wielded, a masterpiece of gears and steel, demonstrated her inventive prowess and became a deadly extension of her will.

"Your aim's truer than any spell I've cast," Aerin called out, incinerating another creature with a burst of crackling energy. His trust in Feyla's abilities allowed him to focus on weaving his magic, each arc of lightning more potent than the last.

"Keep them off me!" Lysandra shouted, parrying a barrage of claws with her sword. The runes along the blade pulsed like the heartbeat of the battle itself, casting eerie light onto her determined face.

"Got your back!" Feyla replied, launching two bolts in rapid succession. One took down a beast creeping behind Lysandra, while the other skewered a winged terror that had set its sights on Aerin.

The twisted landscape around them pulsed with malevolence, trees bent into grotesque shapes. The ground beneath their feet was eager to betray them. As they ventured deeper into Aviara's domain, the nightmarish creatures grew more cunning, adapting to their tactics with terrifying intelligence.

"Circle around!" Lysandra commanded, her voice cutting through the cacophony of snarls and spells. "They're trying to flank us!"

"Brilliant observation," Feyla quipped dryly, firing off another bolt before ducking a swipe from a creature too close for comfort.

"Focus, Feyla," Lysandra snapped, though her eyes shone with gratitude. "We need you to be sharp."

"Sharp as the tips of my bolts," Feyla retorted, but she tightened her grip on her weapon, her resolve hardening. These beasts were nothing compared to the horrors they had already faced together. She would not let herself be the weak link in their chain.

"Watch out!" Aerin's warning cry came just in time for Lysandra to whirl around, her sword slicing through the air and cleaving a shadow hound that had leaped at her from behind.

"Thanks," she breathed, and the unspoken bond between them strengthened. They moved as one, a dance of destruction choreographed by necessity and survival.

"Can't stay here long," Aerin said, glancing at the encroaching horde. "We push forward or fall back, but we cannot linger."

"Forward it is," Lysandra declared. "Aviara is waiting for us."

They fought on, united against Aviara's twisted will. Their unity was a beacon in the suffocating darkness. Feyla's bolts sang through the air, Aerin's spells illuminated the path, and Lysandra's blade carved a way forward. They were an unstoppable force fueled by friendship and fierce determination.

Aerin's fingers sparked with energy, crackling and alive. The light flickered over his knuckles as he hurled power at a beast.

The creature reeled back, screeching. Aerin's breaths were rapid, his chest tight. Dread twinged each time Lysandra fought.

"Stay close to me!" he called out to her, the words shredding through the cacophony of battle.

"Trust me," she shot back without looking at him, her voice laced with steel. "I can handle this."

He looked heart lodged in his throat as a monstrous shadow hound, fangs dripping with malice, lunged towards her.

Aerin's protective instincts screamed within him, urging him to teleport to her side, but he clenched his jaw and forced his feet to remain planted. She was not a damsel; she was a warrior forged in fire and blood.

Lysandra spun her sword in a silver arc in the dark. The blade met flesh with a satisfying thunk, cleaving through the shadow hound's neck. It evaporated into smoke before its body could hit the ground, leaving behind a wisp of darkness that dissipated into the charged air.

"Nice try," she muttered under her breath, eyes narrowing as they scanned for the next threat.

Her movements were a mesmerizing dance of death, each step deliberate, each strike precise. Shadow, ever watchful, mirrored her steps, his growls punctuating the rhythm of her swordplay. The wolf moved with a primal grace, his loyalty to Lysandra as unwavering as the moon to the night sky.

"Left flank!" she yelled, and without hesitation, Shadow

leaped to intercept a creature slinking towards them from the shadows.

Aerin couldn't help but marvel at her command over the battlefield and her innate ability to observe patterns where he only saw chaos. He cast a barrier spell around them. A shimmering dome that deflected a volley of corrupted spikes sent their way. The reprieve was momentary yet vital.

"Keep pushing!" Lysandra bellowed, her voice carrying over the din of war. "We break through, or we die trying!"

With a surge of adrenaline, Lysandra thrust herself into the fray, her blade singing a deadly tune. Each enemy fell before her, their numbers dwindling beneath her relentless assault.

A flicker of awe went through him; she was an avenging angel, her heritage both a burden and a gift and at this moment, her true strength shone through.

"Can you handle a few more?" he teased, trying to mask the icy grip of fear that refused to loosen its hold on him.

"Bring them on," she replied, her voice a mix of sarcasm and confidence that sparked a grin on Aerin's lips despite the grim circumstances.

Together, they stood as bastions of hope amidst the encroaching tide of darkness, their trust in each other unspoken yet unbreakable. And as they battled side by side, their unity became an unyielding force against the nightmares Aviara had unleashed upon them.

Lysandra's boots sank into the spongy undergrowth, the twisted roots clawing at her every step. The nauseating scent of decay filled her nostrils as she hacked away at a thicket of blackened vines barring their path. She couldn't ignore the vile energy pulsating from the soil, a reminder of Aviara's ever-present gaze.

"Left flank, Lys!" Aerin's voice cut through the eerie silence that followed their skirmish with the shadow hounds.

With a spin, Lysandra brought her sword to clash with the snarling jaws of yet another creature—a monstrous combination of beast and nightmare. With a gaze full of malice, she met it with defiant eyes as she plunged her blade into its heart.

The creature disintegrated into swirling shadows that resembled vengeful spirits before fading into nothingness.

"Good call," she said, nodding to Aerin, who was already scanning the horizon for more threats. They moved forward in unison, their movements a practiced dance born of countless battles.

Harrow's colossal shape towered next to them, his scales soaking in the dim light that penetrated Aviara's territory. He released a fiery onslaught upon a swarm of creatures that dared to approach the twisted trees with a thunderous roar. The flames consumed them, and all that remained was ash swirling in the hot air.

"Your fire cleanses the darkness, Harrow," Lysandra breathed, grateful for the dragon's might.

"Fire purges, but it is your courage that sears deeper than any flame," Harrow rumbled, his voice resonating within their bones.

Eolande's bowstring sang a continuous hymn of death as

arrows found their marks with deadly precision. A whispered incantation, the elf's affinity with the forest allowing him to bend the shadows to his will and guide his arrows through the chaos, accompanied all shots.

"Keep them off me for just a breath longer!" Feyla shouted from behind a fallen log, her hands working furiously on an explosive device of her own design.

"Take all the breaths you need, Feyla!" Eolande called back, letting another arrow fly. Upon impact, it erupted into blinding light, scattering the creatures that ventured too close to the inventor.

As they pressed deeper into the corrupted woods, Lysandra experienced the tug of Aviara's magic at the edges of her mind, whispering doubts and sowing confusion. She shook her head, trying to dispel the fog that threatened to cloud her judgment.

"Stay sharp," she warned her companions. "Aviara's tricks are as dangerous as her beasts."

"Her illusions cannot deceive us if we trust in what binds us," Eolande answered, his gaze never leaving the tree line as he notched another arrow.

"Indeed," Harrow agreed, his presence a reassuring beacon amidst the encroaching gloom. "Our unity is what destroys her deceit."

"Then let's stick together and end this," Aerin declared, stepping closer to Lysandra with a determined look in his eyes.

"Agreed," Lysandra replied, tightening her grip on her sword. "Together, we'll carve a path straight to her dark heart."

Bolstered by their unwavering determination, they pressed on as a closely knit group of friends, confronting the onslaught of corruption. In the struggle against the dark deity, every companion played a crucial role, their individual strengths blending in a symphony of resistance. As they walked, their bond grew stronger, an unbreakable chain that not even magic could ever have.

Branches cracked underfoot as Lysandra led the charge, her sword a flash of steel against the dark. The air was thick with the stench of decay, and the twisted forms of Aviara's minions lurked within the shadows, their eyes glowing with malevolent hunger.

"Spread out!" Lysandra's voice sliced through the heavy silence like a command to the winds. "Eolande, high ground! Aerin, with me. Feyla, cover our flanks!"

Aerin nodded, his hands igniting with azure flames that cast ghostly light over the gnarled trees.

They moved in unison, a seamless dance of blade and fire, as creatures emerged from the darkness. Each monstrous form was an aberration of nature, their shrieks tearing at the night.

"Watch their patterns," Aerin called out, his voice steady despite the adrenaline coursing through his veins. "They're learning how we fight!"

Carving through grotesque flesh, Lysandra's blade encountered chitin and sinew belonging to a creature once a graceful forest stag. The antlers, sharp as scythes, were dripping with a poisonous gleam. She pivoted, avoiding a swipe that would have torn into her side.

"Adapting to us?" Her laugh was devoid of humor, laced instead with steely resolve. "Then let's be unpredictable."

Feyla unleashed a volley of bolts from her crossbow; each tipped with gleaming silver. One by one, they found their marks in the hearts of the shadow hounds that leaped from the underbrush. Their demise was silent, the creatures dissipating into curls of black mist.

"Unpredictable works for me," Feyla shouted back, reloading with practiced ease.

Above them, Eolande's silhouette melded with the treetops, the elf's arrows singing as they cut through the air.

A creature lunged towards him, its form a distorted echo of an owl, its eyes aglow with fury. But Eolande was quicker, his movements fluid and precise as he loosed an arrow that pierced the beast's heart.

"Keep moving!" Lysandra urged, her opinion, that their progress with every slain enemy was too slow. "Aviara's heartbeats are close—I can sense it."

"Her heart or her trap?" Harrow intoned, his scales alight with a pale glow that kept the encroaching darkness at bay. His vigilance was unwavering, the arcane symbols etched into his scales pulsating with power.

"Doesn't matter," Aerin replied, his flames scorching another creature that dared approach. "We'll face whatever comes."

The creatures grew more relentless, their assaults a testament to Aviara's twisted influence. Yet the companions did not falter.

Undeterred by the approaching threat of oblivion, they pressed on, refusing to succumb. Every incantation, projectile, and sword swing carried a resolute message—they were determined to stay united and never give up on their mission.

Lysandra said, "Let's stay true to each other," as she locked eyes with Aerin, their silent communication revealing the depth of their shared struggles and moments of tranquility amidst the chaos. "Our bond is our source of strength, and it will cause Aviara's defeat."

Lysandra swung her sword in a graceful arc, its blade glowing with a brilliant blue flame that burned both flesh and shadow.

Creatures of darkness recoiled, their hisses fading as they retreated from the blaze. With agile grace, she pivoted on her heel, scanning the battlefield with hawk-like precision.

"Left flank, Harrow!" she called out, voice cutting through the clamor of battle as another wave of twisted beings emerged from the blackened trees.

Harrow nodded, his fiery breath sweeping across the ground. The runes on his scales glowed brighter, and a barrier shimmered into existence, repelling the encroaching horde's gnashing teeth and clawing hands. He grumbled in an almost silent incantation, reinforcing their defenses.

"Feint and strike, Aerin! They're learning our patterns!" Lysandra instructed, eyes locked onto an enormous beast that had outmaneuvered one of Aerin's fiery blasts.

"Understood," Aerin responded, feigning a move to the right before unleashing a torrent of flames to his left, where the creature had expected to find an opening.

"Can't keep this up forever," Feyla muttered, her crossbow thrumming as she dispatched bolt after bolt into the fray. "They're adapting too fast."

"Then we adapt faster," Lysandra shot back, ducking beneath a swipe from a nightmarish talon and thrusting her sword into the beast's underbelly.

"Watch your six, Eolande!" she yelled as the elf spun around, letting three arrows take flight rapidly. They found their marks in the shadows that crept too close, seeking to exploit any distraction.

"Everyone, tighten the circle! Force them into the bottleneck!" she ordered, and the group converged, a united front against the relentless tide.

The creatures snarled and surged forward, but the companions' formation held strong, a testament to Lysandra's command.

She caught each friend's eye, nodding her encouragement, her confidence bolstering their spirits amidst the chaos.

Suddenly, the ground started trembling, and a thunderous roar filled the eerie forest. Out of the darkness, a massive shadow hound, larger than any they had ever confronted, emerged. Its eyes blazed with malevolent intelligence.

"Steady," Lysandra breathed, her gaze never leaving the massive form that now stalked towards them. The oppressive weight of Aviara's magic suffused the air, pressing down upon them with tangible malice.

"Stand together," she said, louder now so every companion could hear. "This is the test we were meant to face."

"I'm prepared," Harrow confirmed, inhaling deeply before unleashing a massive fire explosion.

"Let's show it what we're made of," Aerin added, flames dancing between his fingers.

"Bring it down," Feyla said, a new bolt notched and aimed.

"Strike true," Eolande whispered, an arrow already flying toward their formidable foe.

Lysandra stood her ground as the hound lunged, a blur of fangs and fury. With a flash of light, her sword collided with the charging enemy amid the darkness. Faced with Aviara's wrath, this was the moment that tested their determination.

Not meeting expectations was never an option for them.

Chapter 10

THE AFRITS

With malevolent energy filling the air, Lysandra fearlessly led the charge into Aviara's realm, her blade glinting like a shard of starlight in the darkness.

As they looked ahead, the world twisted into a macabre reflection of Erenor, where the land morphed into grotesque forms and shadowy tendrils brushed against their feet while the sky oozed shades of crimson and onyx.

"Be on your toes," Lysandra cautioned, her voice a menacing growl that mirrored the fierceness in her eyes. "Trust nothing you see."

Feyla's fingers danced over her gadgets, her eyes darting to the eerie shadows that shifted and whispered secrets of madness.

Eolande nocked an arrow, the string of his bow pulled taut as he surveyed their nightmarish surroundings, his usual calm demeanor edged with tension.

Harrow's scales shimmered with a spectral luminescence,

casting ghostly light over the group.

Aerin followed close behind Lysandra, his hands glowing faintly with the burgeoning power of his healing magic—ready to mend flesh or ward off evil.

The ground trembled beneath them, announcing the arrival of the Afrits. Monstrous silhouettes emerged, towering figures with cruel horns and hooves that split the earth with each thunderous step. Their eyes blazed with malevolent fire, reflecting a hunger for destruction.

"Demons," Lysandra hissed, recognizing the creatures from the dark whispers of her heritage. "Their hearts beat within pomegranate seeds. Find them, destroy them, and these beasts will fall."

"Seeds?" Aerin echoed, his brow furrowed, even as he readied a shield charm.

"Trust me!" she snapped, parrying the swipe of a massive claw with her sword, sparks flying.

"Cover me," Feyla said, already slipping into the fray. Her mind whirred with strategies as she dodged lethal limbs.

"Absolutely," Eolande said, releasing an arrow that found its mark in the throat of an oncoming Afrit, although the creature barely faltered, driven by a force far more potent than mere mortal existence.

"Look for the unnatural," Lysandra called out, weaving through the Afrits' vicious onslaught, her blade a blur of deadly precision. "A fruit out of place!"

"Here!" Eolande shouted, spotting a glimmer amongst the

chaos, an orb nestled within the gnarled roots of a corrupted tree.

"Keep them off me," Feyla instructed, her eyes locked onto the target as she sprinted toward it.

"Consider it done," Harrow boomed, unleashing a torrent of flame that carved a path for her.

Lysandra pivoted, severing the sinewy arm of an Afrit with a clean cut.

Aerin's spells lashed out, chains of light that bound another creature, if only momentarily. They fought in tandem, a dance of steel and sorcery.

Feyla reached the pomegranate seed, its crimson surface pulsating with dark power. She glanced back, meeting Eolande's gaze, and in that moment, they shared a silent vow—a promise of survival, victory, and returning to each other's arms.

"End it, Feyla!" Lysandra urged, cutting down another demon as it lunged for her friend.

With a deft movement, Feyla crushed the seed beneath her boot, and the world appeared to hold its breath.

A cacophonous wail tore through the realm as the Afrits crumbled to dust, their essence extinguished in a gale of dark smoke that roiled and dissipated into the cursed air.

"Move!" Lysandra ordered, already on the move. "We press on."

"Right behind you," Aerin confirmed, sparing a glance at the remnants of their enemies.

They stepped over the ashes of the fallen Afrits, heading

deeper into the heart of darkness, their resolve as unyielding as the blades and bows they wielded.

Amidst the smoldering remnants of the Afrit horde, Feyla crouched, her mind whirling with ideas for mechanisms and strategy.

She withdrew a tiny orb from her satchel, its surface lined with delicate etchings and gears. With a flick of her wrist, she spun it into the air, where it emitted a disorienting array of lights and sounds, scattering the attention of the remaining demons.

"Keep them off balance," she shouted, her voice a clarion call above the din of battle.

Eolande notched an arrow to his bow, his movements fluid like the wind through the willow leaves of his homeland.

He released in rapid succession, arrows finding their marks in the eyes of the beasts, granting precious moments for Harrow to scour the battlefield with his infernal gaze, searching for the heart of their adversary—the pomegranate seed.

"Found it!" Eolande cried out, his keen, elven sight piercing through the chaos.

"Bring it down, Harrow!" Lysandra commanded, parrying a vicious strike from an Afrit's jagged blade.

The dragon reared, his scales shimmering like molten bronze under the sickly light of Aviara's realm. He drew a deep breath, and a scalding blaze erupted from his maw, engulfing the seed in an inferno that seared the air.

The Afrits' cries tore through the realm as their own annihilation consumed them, their forms dissolving into shadows that fled from the light.

"Quickly, to the cliffs!" Feyla urged, her eyes already scouting the treacherous path ahead.

The landscape twisted beneath their feet, the ground heaving as if alive with the malice of the forgotten deity. Crumbling cliffs rose, a maze of jagged rocks and narrow ledges that dared them to falter.

"Steady now," Eolande whispered, leading the way with the grace of his kind. His hand clasped Feyla's for a fleeting second—a silent promise amidst the chaos.

"Watch your step," Aerin cautioned, his gaze locked on the unstable earth below.

"There are dangerous swamps ahead," Harrow warned, his deep voice resonating as his wings disturbed the toxic mist floating above the water.

"Excellent," Feyla murmured, getting started on a contraption made of vines and recycled metal. "We should be able to manage with this."

Step by step, they made their way across the temporary bridge, fully dependent on Feyla's creative thinking to bridge the enormous gap. Each individual plank stood as a testament to her unwavering resolve.

"Let's make our way towards the dark forests," Lysandra suggested, her gaze fixed on the tangled thicket. "Aviara's henchmen will be close behind."

"They can come," Eolande proclaimed, preparing his bow with a determined look.

"Keep close. Trust in each other," Harrow said, his presence a bulwark against the encroaching darkness.

"Without a doubt," Feyla answered, her crossbow poised as they ventured into the darkened branches, the vast unknown dangers of Aviara's realm stretching out endlessly in front of them.

Lysandra's boots sank into the mossy ground, and the forest teemed with its own vibrant energy, murmuring secrets that only Shadow appeared to comprehend. The wolf's ears perked up, and his snout trembled as he sniffed the scent. With a deep growl, he changed direction, guiding them through a maze of twisted roots and thorny bushes.

"Trust him," Lysandra murmured to her companions, her hand resting on the hilt of her blade, eyes mirroring the ghostly silver of Shadow's coat. They moved in perfect unison, the burden of their intertwined fate weighing heavily on her.

The silence was broken by the sound of a crack, leading to the cascade of rocks from a cliff nearby. With great swiftness, Aerin stretched out his hands, resulting in the formation of a luminous barrier above their heads, woven from strands of green light. The shield was bombarded by debris, which fell harmlessly to the sides.

"Stay close!" Aerin shouted, his voice steady despite the choking on the dust in his throat, his eyes reflecting the emerald glow of his magic.

"Excellent job," Feyla exclaimed, her crossbow aimed at the shifting shadows just beyond their line of sight.

"Your control is improving," Harrow noted, his massive form shifting to shield Eolande from a larger boulder.

"Needs to," Aerin replied tersely, wincing as the shield flickered before regaining strength.

Lysandra glanced back at him, a wordless nod conveying her gratitude.

She was aware of the physical toll that magic took on the body. However, Aerin possessed a natural talent, with his power increasing steadily as they explored this accursed domain.

"Is it much further, Shadow?" Lysandra asked softly, receiving a chuff in response. Shadow's sharp vision had rescued them on multiple occasions, and she relied on him more than her own instincts.

"His instincts are uncanny," Eolande observed, his bowstring tense. "He can observe things that are invisible to us."

"He feels it too," Lysandra agreed, watching Shadow pause, his hackles rising ever so slightly.

"More minions?" Feyla asked, squinting into the thicket.

"Or something worse," Lysandra said, tightening her grip on her sword as Shadow let out a low, warning bark.

"Then we face it together," Aerin said, stepping up beside her. His healing energy was already swirling around his fingertips, ready to mend flesh or bolster their defenses.

"Let's hope it's just a shadow," Harrow rumbled, flames licking at the corners of his mouth.

"Shadows I can handle," Lysandra said with a grim smile, feeling the adrenaline rush sharpen her resolve. With Shadow at her side and Aerin's magic enveloping her, she was ready for whatever horrors lay ahead.

The chasm yawned before them, a gaping maw in the twisted landscape of Aviara's realm. Feyla's eyes narrowed as she took in the expanse, her mind racing through possibilities and mechanics.

"Give me your grappling hooks," she commanded, words clipped with focus. "And any rope you have."

Eolande unhooked his gear and handed it to her without a word while Harrow watched with an impassive gaze, his scales catching the eerie light of this place.

Lysandra could only watch as Feyla worked, tying, twisting, and testing knots with deft fingers.

"Trust me," Feyla murmured more to herself than to them as she secured the ropes. With a deep breath, she launched the hooks across the divide, where they clung firm and true to the other side. Testing the tension, she gave a satisfied nod. "It'll hold. Go quickly, one at a time."

Lysandra stepped up first, heart thundering as she gripped the rope bridge. Hand over hand, foot after foot, she traversed the chasm, Shadow's soft whines urging her on from behind. When her boots touched solid ground again, she let out the breath she had not realized she'd been holding.

"Your turn, Eolande," she called, her voice steady despite the adrenaline coursing through her veins.

One by one, they crossed, with Feyla following last, her eyes never leaving her makeshift bridge until she was certain it would bear her weight. As soon as Feyla's feet hit the ground, the earth trembled beneath them, and a chorus of hisses slithered through the air.

"Minions," Lysandra said, unsheathing her sword, the dark metal gleaming with deadly promise. "Keep close."

Like specters taking shape, they appeared as a distorted mockery of life, with limbs that were too long and mouths that were unnaturally wide.

Lysandra swiftly attacked the first adversary, her sword slicing through the air with a melodious sound, piercing their flesh that instantly transformed into smoke upon contact.

Another creature lunged at her from the left, its talons poised to strike her face, but she dodged and rolled, emerging behind it to snap its spine with a single fluid movement.

"Behind you!" Feyla shouted, notching an arrow and letting it fly into the minion that had almost taken Lysandra unaware.

"Thanks," Lysandra grunted, sparing her friend a quick glance before charging into the fray again. Each cut and thrust was a dance she knew, the rhythm of survival ingrained into her muscles.

"Can't keep this up forever," Aerin panted, striking down a creature with a burst of radiant magic. His eyes were alight with the strain of battle, the glow around his hands flickering with each healed wound.

"Then we don't," Lysandra replied, slicing through another minion. "We push forward. Together!"

"Agreed!" Harrow bellowed, his fiery breath incinerating a

cluster of enemies that dared to approach him.

"Cover me!" Feyla yelled, setting up another trap with the remnants of her bridge materials. A tripwire here, a snare there; soon enough, minions were toppling into pits or being yanked into the air, flailing helplessly.

"Nice work, Feyla!" Eolande called out, loosing arrows with lethal precision, each one finding its mark.

"Move!" Lysandra ordered, and they did, slicing, burning, and trapping their way through the horde of darkness.

They were a storm raging against the night, a symphony of destruction harmonized by necessity and honed by desperation.

As the last wisp of shadow evaporated under the relentless assault, the group stood panting, surrounded by the quiet that follows a storm. But there was no time for rest — Aviara's realm waited for no one, and their quest was far from over.

Lysandra's blade danced with lethal precision, arcs of silver cleaving through the dark forms that surged around her. She moved as if one with the shadows, the dark blood of her heritage lending her an uncanny grace amidst the chaos. Yet even she could not evade every claw and fang.

"Behind you!" Aerin's voice cut through the din of battle.

In a well-timed move, she rotated her body and met the gnarled limbs of another minion with her sword.

However, it was impossible to block every attack, and she felt a sharp pain in her side—a deep wound caused by the sharp talon of a creature. The injury felt like icy flames, but she understood that any hesitation would result in her demise.

"Keep fighting," Aerin instructed, his hands aglow with a soft emerald hue. The warmth of his magic seeped into her flesh, knitting skin and muscle back together, even as he raised a hand to cast a shimmering barrier that deflected an incoming blow meant for her back.

"Thanks," she grunted, nodding to acknowledge the healing and the save. Trust was their unspoken language; he would mend, and she would fight.

"Of course," he replied, his focus never wavering from the ebb and flow of her needs in this violent dance.

With her eyes narrowed and crossbow in hand, Feyla carefully scanned the battlefield from a vantage point. With her finger on the trigger, she waited for the perfect moment, the bolt ready to be released.

As she breathed in and out, she meticulously calculated angles and trajectories, her mind filled with strategy and foresight.

Lysandra was surprised as an unseen and unheard shadow lunged at her from the side.

Feyla's response was a barely perceptible motion as she released the bolt without uttering a single word of warning.

The deadly messenger soared and settled in the creature's heart, or at least where a heart would normally be found. The shadow wavered, before eventually fading away into a mist.

"Got it," she called out tersely, already loading another bolt. Her weapon sang again and again, providing a deadly counterpoint to the chaos below.

"Your aim is true, Feyla," Lysandra called up to Feyla, her

voice steady despite the onslaught.

"Wouldn't be much of an inventor if I couldn't calculate a proper trajectory," Feyla shot back with a half-smile, her eyes scanning for the next target.

The group pressed on, a well-oiled machine of destruction.

With each fallen enemy, they delved deeper into the twisted realm, their resolve hardening like forged steel.

Eolande's arrow cut through the gloom, a silent streak of death that found its mark in the throat of an advancing minion. The beast gargled on a dark substance before collapsing, its contorted shape dissolving into the tainted earth of Aviara's domain.

"Another one to the shadows," Eolande murmured, his voice barely capable of being heard over the din of battle." He knocked another arrow with fluid grace, the bowstring humming as he released it towards a hulking figure looming over Aerin.

"Thanks," Aerin grunted, rolling away from the fallen beast and scrambling to his feet as he summoned a shimmering orb of healing energy, casting it toward Lysandra.

Lysandra sidestepped an oncoming blow, a silver blade arcing through the air, a dance of deadly precision. She caught the orb without missing a beat, the magic seeping into her skin, closing a gash along her arm. "Keep them coming, Aerin!"

"You know I will," he shot back, fingers weaving a tapestry of spells that sent bursts of light hurtling toward their enemies.

At that moment, the corrupted mage materialized, a shadowy silhouette contrasting with the chaotic scene, its hands emanating an ominous power.

Lysandra's eyes narrowed as she charged, steel meeting dark fire in a clash that reverberated through the air.

"Focus on the minions, Eolande!" she called out, parrying a vicious strike from the mage.

"Understood," Eolande replied, another arrow flying towards a lesser creature that dared creep too close.

Aerin's chants grew louder, his aura flaring with protective enchantments that enveloped Lysandra like a cloak. His hands glowed, pulling at the fabric of magic, knitting together the essence of life and mending flesh.

"Watch your flank!" Aerin warned, thrusting his staff forward to release a bolt of energy at a shadowy assailant sneaking up behind Lysandra.

She spun, sword sweeping out to send the minion headless into the abyss. "Good eyes!" she praised, feeling the rush of adrenaline fuel her movements.

"Stay alert. The Mage is gathering power," Aerin cautioned, eyes locked on their enemy as he prepared his next incantation.

"Enough games," the mage hissed, voice echoing with malice. A surge of darkness coalesced in its palm, aiming to unleash devastation upon the pair.

"Rally to me!" Lysandra commanded, stepping in to meet the challenge. She moved with lethal intent, every strike a whisper of steel that sang for blood and vengeance.

Aerin's magic responded to her summons, his offensive spells intertwining with the void to counter the enemy mage's attack. The way they fought together showed how strong their bond was, two parts of a whole uniting against the approaching darkness.

With a swift strike, Lysandra declared, "The end is near for you, servant of Aviara!" Her blade moved so quickly that it was a blur, fueled by the fury of her heritage.

"Through the light of Erenor, you shall fall!" Aerin's voice broke the silence as he bolstered Lysandra's assault with an enormous power surge.

Together, they fought, a symphony of sword and sorcery, their hearts beating as one in the fight for their world's salvation.

Lysandra's muscles screamed with each clash of her sword against the corrupted mage's shielding spells.

The air crackled with Aerin's magic, a dance of light and shadow as he cast barriers to shield his comrades from dark energy flares.

"Keep pressing!" Lysandra shouted, ducking under a whip of eldritch power that scorched the earth where she'd stood moments before.

Aerin's hands flowed through the incantations, his voice steady, "I'm with you, just a little longer!"

The corrupted mage cackled, its form shimmering with Aviara's dark power, summoning a vortex of shadows. "You cannot hope to—"

Harrow's massive silhouette blotted out the sun, cutting short its declaration. With a roar that shook the world, the dragon inhaled the glow of impending fire, illuminating his scaled maw.

"Down!" Eolande yelled, shooting one last arrow before diving for cover.

The Dragon Harrow exhaled a torrent of white-hot flame, resembling a river of fury, and surged toward the mage. Consuming the shadows, the heat became a living thing, searing away from the corruption. Huddled behind boulders, the group experienced the wash of heat roll over them.

As the flames dwindled, they rose. The mage's defenses broke, and its form flickered uncertainly like a candle in the wind.

"Strike now!" Feyla called out, raising her crossbow as she fired a bolt laced with her own alchemical concoction.

Lysandra charged, each step leaving a heavy imprint on the charred ground. She drove her sword forward, propelled by the momentum of their collective will, her blade glowing with an ethereal light.

"Your reign ends here!" she declared, the metal biting into the mage's weakened form.

"Let this be the last," Aerin added, his hands aglow as he sent a last surge of healing energy into Lysandra's strike, not to mend but to fortify.

The mage let out an unearthly wail, its existence unraveling like a thread from a spindle. It imploded with a soundless vacuum, leaving behind only the echo of its demise.

Panting, the group gathered, eyes fixed on the space where

death had claimed Aviara's minion.

They exchanged glances, nodding in silent acknowledgment of their victory, aware that this was one battle in a war for the soul of Erenor.

"By all the stars, Harrow, your timing is as impeccable as your flames are hot," Lysandra said, a small smile playing on her lips despite the fatigue that clung to her limbs.

The dragon's rumble sounded almost like amusement, his eyes gleaming with a wisdom beyond ages. "It is not timing, but trust in one another that brings us victory."

"Let's hope that trust holds," Aerin muttered, "for I fear this is merely the first layer of Aviara's web we've torn through."

"Then we tear through them all," Eolande said, nocking another arrow to his bow, ready to face whatever darkness lay ahead. "Together."

Lysandra's hands shook as she ignited the sparks from striking flint against steel, catching the dry brush they had collected.

The tiny fire flickered to life, creating an unsettling illumination on the faces of those around her. Their bodies, clad in armor and exhausted from the day's battles, slumped wearily as they settled around the fire.

"Hand me the waterskin," Feyla croaked, her voice rough from exhaustion, reaching out with a dirty, soot-covered hand. Eolande tossed it to her; she caught it, taking a long swallow before offering it to Lysandra.

"Thank you," Lysandra whispered, tilting her head back to allow the refreshing liquid to quench her thirsty throat. She handed the skin over to Aerin, who was sitting and tending to her injured arm.

"Any more of that healing magic left for yourself?" she asked, concern lacing her tone as she glanced at his wound.

He chuckled dryly, "Plenty," Aerin replied, his hands glowing faintly blue as he tended to the cut. "But I must ration my strength. Aviara's realm is relentless."

Harrow, larger than any living creature had a right to be, lay curled up like some great hulking cat, his scales reflecting the firelight in shimmering waves. His eyes were half-lidded but alert—a silent sentinel even in rest.

"Those traps you conjured, Feyla," Eolande said, nodding in approval. "They turned the tide quicker than an arrow finds its mark."

"Improvisation is the mother of survival here," Feyla replied, a wry smile tugging at her lips as she inspected her crossbow for damage. "I'll need to replenish our supplies to craft more."

"Then we should forage at dawn," Lysandra proposed. "We can't afford to let our guard down, not when surrounded by a darkness that breathes."

"Agreed," Harrow rumbled, the deep timbre of his voice vibrating through the ground. "The shadows are thick with her spies."

They lapsed into silence, each immersed in their thoughts while eating the meager provisions they had. As the light flickered, shadows danced across their faces, painting them in hues of orange and gold. Lysandra took her time chewing, her thoughts elsewhere as she held a piece of dried meat.

"Tomorrow," she began, breaking the quiet, "we delve deeper into this cursed place. We've seen what horrors she can inflict on us. "

"I agree," Eolande said, placing an empty quiver on the ground to indicate further obstacles. "Together, as we have today."

"We should keep looking for those seeds," Feyla remarked, adding a touch of humor to her tone despite the surrounding darkness.

"Absolutely," Aerin affirmed, closing his remaining wounds. "Our collective strength is what brings her down.

"Then to unity," Lysandra raised her waterskin, symbolizing their bonded resolve.

"To unity," they all exclaimed, each raising their drink solemnly toast to the bond that held them tight.

Between them, the fire crackled, providing a momentary relief from the chilling atmosphere of Aviara's twisted realm.

It would be a long night, but in this moment, there was camaraderie, hope, and the shared determination to see their mission through.

Chapter 11

AN ENCOUNTER WITH ALLIES

While Lysandra led her weary fighters through Erenor's dense forest, the shadows between the trees coiled and swirled like living things.

After days of being taunted by shadow hounds, their bodies ached, and their spirits waned with each step.

The woods opened into a clearing filled with elves and magical creatures whose eyes reflected the pale glow like ghostly lanterns.

"Lower your weapons," a voice hissed from the midst of the crowd, its command carried by the whispering wind.

A graceful elf with hair as radiant as silver thread took a step forward, extending his hand in a gesture of peace while ready to unleash the fury of the forest if they turned out to be enemies.

Coming to a sudden stop, Lysandra's hand instinctively went to the hilt of her sword, finding solace in grounding the leather grip.

"We don't intend to cause any harm," she stated, her voice remaining steady despite her weariness. We are all facing a common enemy, someone who puts the safety of Erenor in jeopardy.

Her eyes were fixated by the penetrating, scrutinizing gaze of the elf. "Convince us, humanists heritage, why we should believe you."

"I am Lysandra Aventis," she proclaimed, sensing the significance of her name and the heritage it held. The battlefields on which I have spilled my blood are the stuff of legends, whispered about in tales.

Like leaves in a storm, a gentle murmur swept through the assembly. The creatures glanced at each other, their postures softening, giving away their desperate situation.

Amid suspicion, there was a glimmer of hope in their eyes, a desire for trust in something greater and unity.

"Show us your resolve," another elf said, stepping next to the first. His voice was not unkind but carried the weight of countless battles fought in solitude.

"Very well." Lysandra nodded to her companions. One by one, they showed their prowess: incantations woven into the night air, blades dancing in deadly arcs, and elements summoned and shaped with fierce precision.

Each display earned nods from the watchers, who showed respect in the lines etched on their faces.

"Your skills are... impressive," the silver-haired elf conceded, his stance relaxing. "Perhaps there is strength to be found in alliance."

"More than strength," Lysandra replied, her heart buoyed by hope. "Unity. We have seen what Aviara can do when we are divided. Together, we can restore balance to Erenor."

"Then let us see how your strength melds with ours," a creature chimed in, its voice a chorus of harmonious tones. It shimmered with an inner light, its form fluid and ever-changing.

"Lead the way," Lysandra said, a smile tugging at the corner of her mouth despite the gravity of their quest.

The entire group moved together, with the elves moving gracefully like moonbeams.

They practiced side by side, familiarizing themselves with their movements' synchronized flow, the wordless warfare dialogue. Combat that needed no words.

The elves conjured barriers from thin tendrils of light while the creatures brought forth magic alien and marvelous.

"See? Our magic complements your steel," the silver-haired elf noted, watching Lysandra dispatch a conjured shadow with a swift, precise strike.

"Definitely," she agreed, breathing steadily and carefully. "Your wisdom guides us."

As they sparred, a camaraderie sprouted from the shared soil of necessity and the common water of purpose. Each parry and thrust, every spell cast and countered, wove them tighter together—a tapestry of defiance against Aviara's looming threat.

As dusk settled upon the makeshift camp, the echoes of laughter mingled with the crackling warmth of the fire, enveloping them in a sense of camaraderie.

In the flickering flames, they glimpsed the unity of their combined forces and the promise of triumph over the encroaching darkness that threatened their world.

The night air grew tense, its cool touch carrying a faint hum of anticipation. As the fire dwindled to smoldering embers, elongated shadows danced deceitfully, toying with vigilant eyes scanning the camp's perimeter.

Lysandra's gaze fixated on Harrow, a towering figure standing as a silent sentinel against the encroaching gloom. Sensing her unease, she whispered as she slid beside him, "What troubles you?"

Harrow's golden eyes flickered with inner turmoil. "Whispers among the trees speak of deceit," he rumbled his voice a low growl that resonated with apprehension. "An enemy is walking among us."

Lysandra's hand found the hilt of her blade, the familiar cool metal grounding her rising concern. "Have you seen anything?"

"Only shadows within shadows. But be watchful." Harrow turned his gaze skyward, nostrils flaring as he sampled the air for unfamiliar scents.

"Stay close," Lysandra instructed her companions, who nodded in silent agreement, their hands inching towards weapons and charms.

As they settled back around the dying fire, one elf, a lithe figure with eyes like polished forest leaves, approached with a smooth gait. "The night brings unease," he said, his voice melodious yet carrying an edge of warning.

"Unease?" Harrow echoed, his tone betraying a spark of aggression.

"Rumors," the elf clarified, extending a hand where a small, silver orb pulsed with light. "A gift from unknown benefactors found just beyond our wards."

Suspicion crept into Lysandra's mind as she eyed the orb. "No ally of ours would approach unseen nor leave gifts unannounced."

"Perhaps it is a token of good faith," another elf suggested, but his words lacked conviction.

"Or a beacon for shadow hounds," Lysandra countered, her fingers tracing the sigils etched into her leather bracers.

"Then we must unmask this treachery," Harrow declared, his voice rising above the murmurs of the assembly. "Before it festers."

"Who brought this into our midst?" Lysandra demanded, her stare piercing the gathered faces. Murmurs swirled through the group, but no one stepped forward.

"Trust fades like smoke," Harrow said solemnly, his tail swishing with contained irritation. Fear finds a place to grow when it is not present.

"Let us not turn on each other without cause," the silver-haired elf counseled, his hands raised in peace. "We must remain united."

"United, yes, but not blind," Lysandra retorted. She locked eyes with Harrow, silently conveying a plan of vigilance.

"Understood," the elf conceded. Our task is to stay vigilant and validate the veracity of these hushed rumors.

"Verify quickly," Harrow insisted, his scales shimmering with a premonitory shiver. "Deception is a poison, swift and lethal."

The group dispersed, each member cloaked in an additional layer of suspicion. Whispers became the wind's language, every rustle a potential threat.

The once solid alliance shook on its foundation, fragile as glass under the weight of distrust.

"Keep your senses sharp," Lysandra said to her closest allies. "We will expose this lie by dawn."

Harrow remained motionless, his confusion manifesting in the restless twitch of his wings. He had been a creature of certainty, his instincts honed over centuries. Now, he faced an enemy that used guile as its weapon, and it gnawed at his confidence.

Lysandra counseled patience, sensing his distress. The enemy may be cunning, but we are not without our own slyness."

Harrow let out a breath that stirred the ashes, reigniting a single flame that danced against the dark.

His nod to Lysandra was imperceptible, but she recognized the resolve within it. They would face this web of lies together, and they would emerge with the truth clutched in their grasp.

With her hand hovering over the sword's hilt, Lysandra's eyes scanned the shadows. Wrapped in darkness, the night concealed friend and enemy, yet the heavy tension lingered.

She whispered over the camp's murmur, sensing something

was wrong. Surrounding her, her allies stood closely together, ready with their weapons, imitating her vigilant posture.

"Don't hold back," Eolande urged, his grip on the staff tightening with lethal precision. "What are you feeling?"

Her eyes never strayed from the tree line; she replied, "There's a pattern." "The lies weave together too neatly. Deception is rarely so... organized."

"Then let's unravel it," said Feyla, her fingers playing with her satchel's edges.

"Watch them," Lysandra commanded, nodding towards a clutch of figures huddled by a dying fire. "Their stories shift like sand—never the same tale twice."

"Divide and conquer?" Harrow suggested, his voice rough with a frustration born of betrayal.

"Exactly," Lysandra affirmed. "I'll take the lead; watch my back."

With purpose in her step, she approached the group by the fire. Their conversation died as they marked her approach, their eyes wary, calculating. She met their stares with unwavering confidence.

"Your tales are as substantial as mist," she accused, "and just as easily dispersed."

"Accusations require proof," one retorted, standing to face her.

"Proof," Lysandra echoed, circling them like a predator. "Comes from action, not words."

Without warning, she struck, her blade flashing free and arcing towards the speaker.

A magical shield blocked the attack—a surprising display of unseen powers. In haste, the group rose to their feet, relinquishing their pretense to summon shadows and flames.

"Traitors!" Harrow bellowed, launching himself into the fray, his wings unfurling to their full, impressive span.

The battlefield erupted into chaos, a symphony of clashing steel, crackling spells, and primal roars.

Lysandra, graceful as a dancer, wielded her sword with precision, each swipe severing the sinister tendrils of darkness that threatened to ensnare her.

Eolande's arrows whizzed through the air, their flight accompanied by the humming resonance of his staff. The arrows unleashed shockwaves that disrupted the enemies' balance.

Feyla's inventions illuminated the sky with dazzling bursts of light, piercing through the veil of illusion.

"Flank!" Lysandra's voice pierced through the cacophony, her trust in her companions unwavering.

Harrow, understanding her command, swept wide, his tail lashing out to trip a shadow Hound lunging towards Lysandra's vulnerable back.

"Focus!" she bellowed above the chaos, her words fueling their unity.

They moved in perfect synchrony, each compensating for the other's weaknesses with their own strengths.

The unbreakable bond they had forged in previous battles held steady despite the enemy's relentless attempts to exploit their every hesitation and doubt.

"Clear!" Aerin shouted, a spell parting the darkness like a curtain, revealing the true forms of their attackers.

"End this!" he roared, and together they pushed forward, their combined might overwhelming the impostors who had infiltrated their ranks.

Amidst the chaos, Lysandra's blade sang a song of retribution, cutting through lies as easily as flesh.

With each enemy that fell, the web of deception unraveled further until the truth lay bare before them: these were no mere traitors but spies sent by Aviara herself, meant to divide and conquer from within.

"Never again," Lysandra vowed, panting as she surveyed the aftermath, her friends standing tall beside her. "We shall be wiser, stronger."

"United," Harrow agreed, his earlier confusion replaced by the clarity of battle. They had weathered the storm of deceit together, their bond unbroken.

"Let us prepare for dawn," Lysandra said, her voice steady. "For when the sun rises, we shall be ready to face whatever darkness awaits."

Lysandra's breath came in sharp gasps, the metal of her sword slick with sweat and dark ichor as she parried a shadow Hound's gnashing fangs.

Ignoring the pain in her muscles, she fought through and beheaded the beast with her sword. It turned into smoke and returned to where it came from.

She shouted, "Circle!" and her friends closed in, their backs almost touching. Their realization came through tough times, teaching them that solidarity was their shield against the unknown.

Aerin chanted, "Vines of Valora!" while weaving an intricate pattern with his hands. Ensnared by the green tendrils erupting from the ground, the assailants were pulled down, thrashing and howling.

Lysandra commanded, "Strike now!" they all charged forward with a battle cry.

Eolande shot his arrows, Harrow's fire burnt, and Lysandra's blade danced with lethal grace. Each move was a testament to their unity, their resolve galvanized by the trust forged in fire and blood.

As the last shadowy figures fell, an eerie silence descended upon the ravaged clearing.

The group stood panting, their eyes meeting as they acknowledged the gravity of their triumph.

This was more than a mere skirmish; they had struck a blow directly at Aviara's subterfuge.

One of their trustworthy new allies, an elf, stepped forward and reverently uttered, "By the Ancients," as they bowed respectfully. You have the kind of strength that becomes a legend.

Lysandra responded, her chest heaving from the effort, "Legends originate from the truth." "And ours is a truth written in unity."

The new allies—elves, fairies, and creatures of light—gathered around, their expressions morphing from awe to gratitude.

"You've shown us what it means to lead, to stand undivided," said a fairy with wings shimmering like morning dew.

"Bravery is not the absence of fear," Harrow rumbled, "but the will to act despite it. Lysandra embodies that."

"Let's all embrace it together," Lysandra proposed, scanning the group of newfound comrades with her eyes. In each other's presence, we become even more brave.

"Here, here!" Eolande roared, hoisting his bow as a sign of their shared strength.

Clasping hands, arms, and shoulders, they formed a mosaic of beings united by purpose and newfound fellowship.

Their laughter and shared relief wove a tapestry of hope amidst the ruin, the earth seeming to sigh in contentment beneath their feet.

"Tonight, we feast, for tomorrow, we prepare," Lysandra declared, her voice clear and true. "Together, we shall turn the tide against Aviara, for Erenor, and for all who call her home."

Cheers erupted, their jubilant echoes reverberating through the wounded forest, a resounding declaration of their indomitable spirit.

In the aftermath of deceit and battle, they had discovered something far mightier than any spell or steel: the unbreakable bond forged by those who had faced darkness together and emerged into the radiant embrace of light.

Silent as the moon gracefully ascended the night sky, Lysandra silently patrolled the outskirts of the camp, where smoldering embers whispered their secrets to the glittering stars above.

With each step, her boots caressed the earth, leaving no trace in their wake, as if she were a stealthy predator in her own right, a vigilant guardian cloaked in the weighty mantle of responsibility.

"Can't sleep?" Aerin's voice sliced through the stillness, his figure materializing from the shadows like a familiar ghost.

"Sleep is a rare luxury," she replied without turning, her unwavering gaze fixed upon the forest's edge, where darkness seemed to exhale and observe.

"Or a necessity," he countered, stepping beside her, his eyes reflecting the dying firelight. "Even for the savior of Erenor."

Lysandra let out a breath that carried the weight of their recent victory and the countless battles ahead. "There's no saving to be made if Aviara has her way," she murmured, her hand instinctively resting on the pommel of her sword. "Trust and unity... they're our sharpest weapons now."

"We have plenty of both, which is a good thing, don't you think?" he asked, his smile fleeting. It was a small spark against the encroaching darkness.

"Tonight has proven that," she admitted, allowing herself to remember their clasped hands and shared determination. "But it's just the beginning, Aerin. The path ahead is dangerous. Aviara won't give up until she has any power left."

"Let her come," he replied fiercely, matching her intensity. "We'll be prepared." The camp behind them stirred as the first light of dawn revived tired bodies and weary spirits.

Eolande's voice rang out, calling everyone to arms as preparations began in earnest. Their companions worked purposefully, and each task was executed smoothly.

"Sharpen your blades, check your arrows," Lysandra commanded effortlessly, taking on the role of a leader. "Pack light, but smart. We leave at dawn."

"Where are we going?" asked a pixie, fluttering its wings, its voice reminiscent of a hundred chimes. "North," she answered, her voice unwavering. "To the Splintered Mountains. If there is a way to weaken Aviara and stop her curse, it's there."

Whispers rippled through the group, a mixture of anticipation and trepidation. She knew each face masked stories untold, fears unspoken. Yet, in their eyes glimmered an unquenchable fire, the same flame that burned within Lysandra's heart—the promise of a future reclaimed.

Addressing them, she emphasized, "Let it be known that our unity stems not from blood ties but from our shared resolve to safeguard our land, our haven."

The varied gathering came together in agreement, nodding and murmuring. The elven archers assessed their bowstrings, the dwarven warriors clashed their axes against shields, and the mages prepared their sorcery by tracing arcane symbols in the air.

"Today, we forge a new destiny," Lysandra proclaimed her conviction a beacon against the uncertainty of the future. "Not as elves or humans, fairy or dwarves, but as champions of Erenor. Together, we rise."

The resounding chant, "Together, we rise!" filled the air and mingled with the emerging sunlight.

With her pack on her shoulder, Lysandra felt the weight lessen as it was divided among others. They resembled an approaching storm, a formidable energy that would cleanse the land from the oppressive shadow.

She led the rallying troops into the unknown, her heart fierce and unyielding, their battle cries a beacon of hope for all who dared to dream of peace. As if from nowhere, the menace erupted.

Evading the shadow hound's lethal jaws, Lysandra's boots kicked up the dirt as she dove, the creature's snarl reverberating in the eerie forest. She rolled, coming up with her sword alight with an ethereal flame, the only beacon amidst the creeping darkness.

"Watch your flank!" Aerin's voice cut through the chaos as he cast a shimmering barrier just in time to deflect a swipe from another beast.

"Appreciated," Lysandra panted, slashing at the hound, which dissipated into a cloud of smoke under her blade's heat.

Feyla let loose a volley of her own invention—bolts that burst into blinding light upon impact, disorienting their foes. "We could use some cover, Eolande!"

"Already on it!" Eolande loosed three arrows in rapid succession, each finding its mark in the eyes of the encroaching shadows, his precision a deadly dance.

"Stay close," Harrow bellowed, his form massive against the

dimming sky. Flames licked from his maw, creating a fiery perimeter around the group. The dragon's presence was a wall of certainty in the turmoil.

"Your fire burns brighter than ever, Harrow," Lysandra called out, her admiration clear even amidst the fray.

"Your courage fuels it," Harrow returned, reverberating with pride and warmth.

As they fought back-to-back, their bond grew stronger and more palpable than ever. Shadow darted between their legs, a silent guardian weaving protection with tooth and claw.

"Can't keep this up forever," Feyla grunted, reloading her crossbow with swift, practiced movements.

"Then let's end this now!" Lysandra exclaimed, her voice a rallying cry. With a gesture, she signaled Aerin, and he nodded, understanding immediately.

"Converge!" Aerin chanted, his hands weaving an intricate spell. The ground pulsed, roots shot up, entangling the shadow hounds and dragging them below.

"That's Good thinking," Lysandra said, panting. Let's move while we have the chance."

"Agreed," Thane, the leading Elf, chimed in, appearing out of nowhere, his staff glowing with inner light. "But remember, deception lies ahead. Trust in what you've learned. Trust in each other."

"Deception?" Lysandra's brow furrowed, but she knew better than to question the master's foresight.

"Aviara's influence runs deep," Elarion had warned when she

last saw him, his gaze piercing. "Keep your wits about you."

"Her tricks won't break us," Lysandra stated, meeting each of her companions' eyes. "We are united by more than just our cause. We're bound by the faith we have in one another."

"Indeed," Eolande agreed, unaware of her discussion with an invisible Master Elarion. She nodded with a slight smile that stitched their resolve tighter together.

"Let's make sure that faith isn't misplaced," Feyla added, a rare seriousness etching her features.

Thane's voice resonated with respect as he urged, "Please, go ahead, Lysandra."

As she clutched her sword tightly, Lysandra squared her shoulders, demonstrating her unwavering resolve to face whatever challenges lay ahead.

As she faced the daunting task ahead, she couldn't ignore the weight of expectation, but she also drew strength from the unwavering support of her friends.

The crucible of warfare hardened and strengthened their spirits, equipping them to face the hidden deceptions that lingered in the shadows of Erenor.

With each breath Lysandra took, the night air felt colder and harsher, causing her lungs to ache, yet she persisted, leading her companions through the thicket.

As they hurried through the dense underbrush, their footsteps muffled, every snap of a twig resonated loudly in her ears.

The rhythmic swaying of her sword at her side showed her readiness to strike, as it acted as an extension of her will.

"Left up ahead," Aerin whispered above the rustle of leaves. His eyes, shining with the remnants of magic, provided a faint glow that functioned as a guiding light amidst the encroaching darkness.

Suddenly, they made a sharp turn, and Lysandra could feel the ground beneath her boots sloping downwards, causing her to lose her balance.

It was not the physical strain that caused her heart to race, but the adrenaline coursing through her veins, knowing that each passing moment had the potential to erupt into violence.

Feyla, filled with concern, cautioned Eolande to be careful and reached out her hand to provide support.

Their eyes met briefly but intensely, silently communicating their commitment to stand together and shield one another from whatever obstacles may come their way.

"Quiet," Harrow's deep rumble cut through the tension like a knife. "We are not alone."

As if on cue, shadows coiled around them, writhing, and twisting into the corporeal forms of hounds, their eyes ablaze with malevolent hunger.

Lysandra's grip on her sword tightened, the familiar weight a reassurance in the unknown's face.

"Stand back-to-back!" she commanded, the authority in her voice belying the uncertainty that gnawed at her insides.

Metal sang against metal as Aerin unsheathed his dagger, runes shimmering along its blade. Shadow snarled beside Lysandra, his hackles raised, a mirror of her own readiness.

"Let them come," Eolande said tersely, arrow nocked and bowstring taut.

The hounds leaped forward, a blur of fangs and fury. Was there no end to these beasts from hell? The thought was fleeting. Lysandra stepped into the fray, her sword arcing gracefully, severing shadow from shadow.

Each movement was precise, a dance she had practiced a thousand times, yet it was always difficult against such ethereal foes.

Aerin chanted, his words weaving a protective barrier around them, the air shimmering with raw energy.

Feyla launched an intricate device skyward, which exploded into a blinding light, throwing the hounds into disarray.

"Focus!" Master Elarion's voice echoed in Lysandra's mind. "Remember, deception lies ahead."

True to his word, the hounds shifted, their forms flickering between reality and illusion. Lysandra's sword met empty air where once there had been solid flesh.

"Trust your instincts," she called out, parrying a swipe that would have exposed her.

"Can't tell which are real anymore!" Feyla shouted, frustration lacing her words.

"It doesn't matter," Lysandra grinned, sweat beading her brow. Fight them all!"

Harrow's flame-seared the night, incinerating shadows with each fiery breath. The battle raged on, a tempest of steel, magic, and cunning.

Then, as suddenly as it had begun, silence fell. The hounds vanished, leaving them in quietude so stark it rang in their ears.

Lysandra panted, trying to slow her racing heart, her eyes scanning the dark for signs of another onslaught.

"Is it over?" Aerin asked, his gaze flitting about nervously.

"Never assume it's over," Lysandra replied, her voice low. She turned to her friends, seeing the toll etched in their faces, the resolve hardening in their eyes.

"Aviara is playing with us," she stated, the truth heavy on her tongue. "This was just a taste of what she can unleash."

"Then we'll be ready for her," Eolande declared, his determination mirrored in the nodding heads of their circle.

"Whatever comes next, we face it together," Feyla added, a steely edge to her voice.

"United," Harrow affirmed, the ember glow of his eyes never wavering.

While they gathered again, the lingering scent of ozone in the air served as a constant reminder of the magic they had spent and the intense battles they had waged.

When all eyes turned to Lysandra, she returned their gaze, sensing the responsibility of leadership firmly taking hold of her.

In a gentle tone, she instructed, "It would be best if you rest now." "We move at dawn, and Aviara won't be holding back."

As they solemnly nodded, they understood and grasped the gravity of her words. In the quiet that followed, they tended to their wounds and prepared their minds for future challenges.

Erenor's fate hung precariously in the balance, and they all knew the coming days would test their unity and strength like never.

As they settled into an uneasy rest, the first fingers of light crept over the horizon, heralding a day that promised more than just the rising sun—a day of reckoning, shadowed with both peril and promise.

Chapter 12

MEETING AVIARA

As the evening air turned crisp, the unmistakable scent of pine and frost intertwined, creating a captivating atmosphere for the group as they gathered around the massive slab of rock, which had been ingeniously transformed into their impromptu council table.

Feyla, using her nimble fingers, skillfully unfurled the aged maps and scrolls from her satchel, carefully spreading them across the solid stone surface.

Both magic and time twisted the lands they depicted, but on this night, those same lands transformed into treasure maps that would guide them to a prize of utmost importance, which held more significance than any amount of gold.

"Here," Lysandra said, her voice carrying the weight of responsibility, "the Heart of Shadows, The Ouroboros. Our target."

The relic in question was no mere trinket. It was a shard of night, a piece of pure obsidian rumored to have been born from Aviara's own essence.

Etched within it was an intricate web of runes that pulsed with the potential to bind or unleash a deity's power.

According to the legend, people believed this relic possessed the power to imprison Aviara—a weapon against a goddess who could not be slain but could only be confined in eternal shadow.

"Aviara's strength wanes and waxes with the moon's cycles," Lysandra continued, tracing a path across the map with her finger. We must reach the Heart before the new moon—before she regains enough power to shroud it from us forever."

Aerin leaned forward, his dark eyes reflecting the flicker of the campfire. "If the Heart is connected to her power, my healing magic might sense its energy, like detecting a pulse." His gaze met Lysandra's. "I can guide us to its rhythm."

"Magic's good," Feyla chimed in, her hands already sketching schematics on a spare piece of parchment, "but we need certainty. I'll build a device attuned to the relic's unique signature." Her mind worked as swiftly as her hand moved, the idea taking shape. "It won't just lead us to the Heart—it'll sing when we're close."

Rolling up the scrolls swiftly and doubtlessly searching, Lysandra declared, "Then it's settled."

"We navigate by Aerin's senses and confirm with Feyla's creation. We cannot afford missteps; Aviara's minions are doubtless searching as well."

Each member's distinct display of courage characterized their camaraderie, which was a powerful but silent force.

They had experienced darkness in the past, but this time, they were embarking on a dangerous quest to find a fragment of pure darkness, a mission where every move forward was risky.

Despite this, their unspoken vow was clear in their exchange of glances and nodding at each other. They were determined to protect Erenor, to stand united, and to vanquish the looming shadow that threatened to consume their entire universe.

The night air hummed with tension as Lysandra stood rigid, her hand gripping the hilt of her sword. Her companions' eyes were upon her, a silent circle of anticipation beneath the boughs of the Whistling Woods.

She closed her eyes, drew a deep breath, and let the whispers of the forest seep into her consciousness.

The constant and watchful Shadow pressed against her leg, an anchor in the sea of uncertainty that threatened to drown her.

Aerin's presence, a warm flame beside her, flickered with shared intent.

Harrow's colossal form loomed overhead, casting a protective shadow that dimmed the stars above.

Then, in the quiet before the coming storm, the vision struck—a symbol glowing like embers in her mind's eye: a serpent devouring its tail, an ancient emblem of infinity. Its scaley loop enclosed a heart pulsing with light as dark as Aviara's soul.

The Ouroboros Heart, the relic they sought, now had a shape in Lysandra's thoughts. She snapped her eyes open, her voice a whisper of steel.

"North," she said, piercing the darkness towards the mountain silhouettes. "The Ouroboros Heart lies north, where the serpent coils around the peak."

"Then north we go," Aerin affirmed, his eyes reflecting not just the campfire but also Lysandra's resolve.

Their path was carved through the malevolent terrain, as unforgiving as the serrated edge of a blade.

Thorns lashed out like cruel whips, cutting across their skin, while the earth groaned with malice under each step.

Shadow Hounds, Aviara's spectral minions, emerged from the murk, their growls slicing through the silence like daggers.

"Execute the split formation!" Lysandra ordered, her voice resounding above the chaos. Shadow dashed ahead, guiding the way through the dense vegetation, a dark blur contrasting with the illuminated leaves under the moonlight.

"Don't stray too far from Harrow!" Aerin yelled, his hands glowing with radiant healing magic, creating a protective barrier against the creatures' threatening jaws.

During the chaos, his eyes sought Lysandra's, pledging to keep her safe.

The mighty roar of Harrow shook the leaves loose from their branches while flames erupted from his mouth, turning the advancing Hounds into nothing but ash.

The dragon's power was their shield, an unstoppable force comparable to the immovable mountains.

As the battle raged on, disharmony took hold.

Believing in their own path, the new allies left with resolute shouts, reducing Lysandra's group to a small number. However, their spirits remained strong even as their numbers declined.

Lysandra encouraged, "Have faith in our power!" as she skillfully wielded her blade, cutting through the darkness.

"Move ahead!" Aerin repeated, holding his staff up high, leading them with the radiant power of his magic.

Despite facing snaring brambles and treacherous ravines, they pressed on, propelled by an unwavering sense of urgency that pushed them forward like a relentless wind.

The Ouroboros Heart throbbed with greater intensity in Lysandra's vision as they dismantled traps and overcame adversaries, providing a beacon of hope and foreshadowing the imminent battle.

Lysandra's breath came out in quick bursts, creating a mist in the cold air as she maneuvered through the twisted trees, her boots barely touching the writhing roots beneath her. With heightened senses, she could perceive energies beyond the physical plane. This ability was a testament to her control over magic and firm determination.

"Left! A pitfall!" Her voice cut through the night. A warning flared before Aerin could enter the camouflaged trap.

Aerin avoided falling by shifting his weight at the right moment and using his staff, which he had crafted from a magic oak tree.

"You have a keen eye," he commented, briefly looking at her as they flew.

"You're being too emotional," she shot back, her words lacking fervor. She knew his intentions originated from a place of love, a love that they both shared, but that occasionally made her feel constrained.

As they raced onward, the echoes of their pursuers filled the vibrant darkness overhead.

Lysandra could not ignore the relic's call. Its constant pulsation, like a drumbeat in her thoughts, led her forward despite the doubts that threatened her confidence.

Could she genuinely conquer the darkness, or was she destined to be overtaken by it?

"Watch out!" Aerin's sudden shout brought her attention back to the present moment. Coiling tendrils emerged stealthily from the underbrush, seeking the life-giving warmth.

The flash of Lysandra's sword illuminated the darkness, cutting through it with silver arcs as Aerin's incantations closed the wounds with light, banishing the appendages back to the void.

In a brief pause during their assault, Aerin looked at Lysandra with intensity and furrowed brows, emphasizing, "You have to trust me." "Not because you need protection, but because we're stronger together."

"Strength is the least of my worries," she countered, her chest heavy with unspoken fears. The main thing I'm seeking is control.

Aerin reached out, his hand briefly brushing hers in reassurance. "And you will find it. You're not alone in this—none of us are."

The menacing growl of a larger and more ferocious beast abruptly disrupted their moment, although fleeting, surpassing the Hounds they had encountered before.

In unison, they shifted their attention towards it, their unity serving as a silent promise. By harnessing her magical abilities, Lysandra surrounded them with a shield that kept them safe while Aerin's healing powers continuously restored their vitality.

The beast towered before them, a terrifying blend of darkness and wickedness, yet they stood firm.

United, Lysandra, and Aerin battled, their blades and spells intertwining in a graceful fight for survival. Each action showcased their unbreakable connection—an alliance that served as their greatest source of power and their most delicate vulnerability.

Amidst his incantations, Aerin's eyes filled with determination as he spoke softly, "I will shield you."

Lysandra answered, her unwavering determination shining through the steely gaze, "I will be your sword."

They advanced Side by side, clearing a way toward their inevitable destiny. Their love and devotion were the driving force determining their ultimate success or complete destruction.

The air was thick with tension, an electrifying energy that enveloped every nook and cranny of the cave as Feyla devoted herself to her newest creation. With an intriguing mix of gears and shimmering stones, the device had a singular and crucial aim - to trace the energy signature of the relic.

"We're nearly there," Feyla whispered, her hands steady as she meticulously made the last modifications, delicately turning a dial engraved with ancient symbols until the gemstones glowed in perfect synchronization.

"Should this plan succeed, we'll uncover the source of Aviara's downfall before daybreak."

Lysandra looked over Feyla's shoulder, carefully examining the intricate patterns carved into the device. "What if it doesn't happen as expected?"

"Well, in that situation, we'll just have to think on our feet," Feyla replied, her attention unwavering from her work. "But it will work."

The device came alive with a gentle click, filling the air with a low hum that sent vibrations through their entire being.

A bright blue beam of light pierced through the cave's darkness, illuminating it like a guiding light. After a couple of flickers, the light stabilized and pointed them towards the north.

"With the grace of Eolande..." Feyla whispered, a smile forming on her lips, a sight seldom seen.

"It's time to go," Lysandra declared, her hand automatically settling on the hilt of her sword. Shadow padded alongside her quietly, his senses finely tuned for any potential threats.

Energized and guided by Feyla's device, the group resumed their journey, skillfully navigating the hazardous terrain. However, the journey was not without its dangers.

With the sun's setting, dusk blanketed the land like a somber veil, and from the obscurity emerged a stealthy skittering sound, a sound that held an intelligence surpassing the savage growls of the Shadow Hounds they had confronted in the past.

"There's something out there," Aerin whispered, his healing powers already manifesting in his fingertips, prepared to mend any injuries.

Lysandra replied, scanning the encroaching shadows, "It's more than just something." "A trap, perhaps?"

No sooner had the words left her mouth than the ground beneath them shifted, a pitfall disguised beneath a thin layer of earth. They sprang back, narrowly avoiding the chasm that yawned open, hungry for victims.

"Keep your wits about you," Lysandra cautioned, her voice a low growl.

"Betrayal stinks worse than a dung heap," Feyla said, bitterness lining her words as she recalibrated the device, its beam dimmed by the near disaster.

"Trust is a luxury we can scarcely afford now," Aerin agreed, though his hand found Lysandra's, an unspoken promise of loyalty amidst uncertainty.

"Move forward," Lysandra ordered, her unwavering resolve uniting them all like a strong metal cable.

They persevered, with the night filled with hidden dangers that moved and whispered just out of sight. Each step they took was a bold defiance, a statement of their refusal to be consumed by the engulfing darkness.

"Aviara's minions are desperate as hell," Aerin commented as they maneuvered around another trap.

"Desperation leads to foolishness," Lysandra pointed out, "and screw-ups."

"I'm keeping my Fingers crossed that our enemies are into both," Feyla quipped, fixing the device with her nimble fingers.

The path kept winding, taking them further into the unknown. As they overcame each obstacle, their bond grew stronger, combining trust, skill, and relentless determination.

"We're gonna find this relic," Lysandra said, her voice determined. "Together."

Lysandra's blade danced in the air, its shiny edge meeting the Aviara minion in the moonlight. The creature snarled and vanished into black mist, and another showed up.

They were getting closer to where the relic was, and with each step, the minions multiplied each one meaner than the last.

"Left flank!" Aerin yelled, his voice piercing through the chaos. Lysandra turned around smoothly, nailing every move despite her heart pounding.

She spotted a minion heading straight for Aerin, claws out and eyes glowing with evil.

She didn't think twice and jumped in between them, her sword slashing through the darkness.

The minion disappeared, but not before brushing her arm with its burning touch. Despite the pain shooting up her arm, she ignored it and focused on Aerin.

"Thanks," he uttered, a fleeting glimpse of apprehension in his stare transforming into determination.

He extended his hand, his fingers emitting a gentle blue

glow, and touched her injured arm. Lysandra's veins filled with warmth as the healing magic seamlessly knitted her skin back together.

"Be vigilant," she responded, but her voice expressed appreciation. As they danced the dance of death, their movements were harmonious, their trust in each other an unspoken promise that no obstacle could break.

"Be careful!" Feyla's cautionary words came at the perfect moment, enabling them to dodge a flurry of dark energy bolts launched by a minion on a gnarled tree.

"Cover me," Lysandra said to Aerin, who immediately erected a protective shield around them without uttering a word.

The bolts made a fizzling sound as they missed their mark, granting Lysandra the chance she had been waiting for. With deadly intent, she gracefully sprinted forward and leaped into the air.

Her sword hit the mark with a precise strike, causing the minion to lose its balance and disappear before it could touch the ground.

With a light landing, she stole a quick look at Aerin. His eyes radiated with pride and something even more profound—a love that the encroaching darkness couldn't overshadow.

"We need to stay on the move," she calmly declared despite the surge of adrenaline.

"I'll be by your side no matter what," Aerin answered, synchronizing their steps as they sprinted towards the pulsing signal emitted by Feyla's device.

As they moved, the ground turned treacherous terrain, revealing concealed traps.

However, they had become more astute to the tricks of their adversaries, their collective abilities intertwining seamlessly as they overcame every challenge.

"Almost at the finish line," Feyla gasped, her attention fixed on the device that hummed louder and louder.

"Prepare for anything," Lysandra warned, her hand squeezing Aerin's for a moment.

"Anything for Erenor... for us," Aerin whispered back, understanding the weight of their mission, and the love that gave them the courage to face it.

Their hearts beat as one, propelling them forward with unwavering resolve and unwavering passion, ready to confront whatever challenges lay ahead in their relentless pursuit of the relic, of Erenor, and of the future they dared to envision.

The cavern loomed ahead, a gaping hole in the side of the frostbitten mountain. The icy air made Lysandra's breath foggy as they got close.

Their skin felt the sting of the cold, even with layers of protective charms incorporated into their cloaks. Like a living organ, the relic's energy surged beneath Feyla's device, illuminating their path through the maze of frozen stone and ice.

"Stay calm," Lysandra murmured, bending down as they approached the entrance.

By her side, Aerin nodded in agreement, his hand firmly gripping the hilt of his sword. He was always ready to call upon his healing magic at a moment's notice.

The cave expanded in width and depth, its walls glimmering with ancient symbols pulsing with energy.

Positioned at the heart of it all, atop a platform sculpted from obsidian that seemed alive, was the ancient artifact - a shimmering orb that emitted an inner light, reverberating with the very essence of Erenor.

And then she made her presence known.

Like a mesmerizing figure born of moonlight, Aviara stepped out from the shadows, her presence silencing the whispers of the wind.

She was not the monstrous being from ancient tales but a divine figure of exquisite grace—her flawless complexion, a canvas for the flowing garments that adorned her slender figure, her eyes a captivating silver that held the wisdom of centuries within their gaze.

"Did you genuinely believe you could deceive a goddess?"

Lysandra boldly proclaimed, "Aviara, your reign of tyranny stops now," taking a determined step forward, masking the fear in her heart. We won't permit you to dismantle something that is precious to us."

"Admirable words, little one."

"Watch out!" Aerin cried, swiftly cutting through the closest tentacle with a magically enhanced blade. He stared at Lysandra, vowing to sacrifice himself for her if necessary—a promise she rejected.

"Everyone, direct your focus towards the relic!" Lysandra's

voice rang out as she harnessed her own magic to erect barriers and protect the group from the incoming assault.

"I got it!" Feyla exclaimed, operating the intricate machinery of her device, adjusting it to disrupt the relic's connection to Aviara.

"Your trinkets are no match for the power of the divine!" Aviara sneered, her form becoming blurred as she moved with an otherworldly grace. She unleashed a relentless onslaught of arcane energy, overwhelming them with its sheer force.

"A heart consumed by malice cannot embrace divinity," Lysandra countered, her spells entwining in a complex dance of defense and assault.

Darkness and light responded to her every command as her power surged, a powerful display of the determination she had sharpened in countless battles.

"Don't leave me, Lysandra," Aerin pleaded, his soothing energy enveloping her like a protective shield, warding off the exhaustion that relentlessly plagued her body.

"Never," she whispered, sensing the strength of their connection grow as they both became resolute. Standing together, they remained steadfast, confronting the storm that raged ahead.

"That's it!" Aviara shouted, her intense rage causing the cave to tremble.

With her hands held high, she caused the relic to react, its light growing stronger until it became a dazzling star amid the surrounding darkness.

"Act now!" Lysandra exclaimed, capitalizing on the distraction caused by Feyla's device emitting a pulse that disrupted Aviara's concentration.

With a swift and powerful movement, Aerin lunged forward, his sword cutting through the air like a song to break the bond between the relic and the deity.

As Lysandra gave chase, her magic surged, meeting Aviara in a clash that resonated with the primal energy of the universe's inception.

Lysandra's voice rang out amidst the commotion, declaring, "Our love for Erenor will ensure our triumph!"

When the forces of steel met the fragility of crystal, and the realm of magic clashed with unyielding rage, those who dared to challenge the might of a goddess held the very fabric of the future in suspension, with its outcome dependent on their actions.

Chapter 13

THE ORACLE OF LUMIN

Lysandra's gaze became fixed on Aviara's silhouette amidst the swirling vortex of shadow and mist.

As Aviara held the ancient object close to her chest, the forsaken deity set free an aura of darkness in the surrounding air, and something unexpected happened. She melded with the mist, exuding a malevolent hiss of satisfaction as her derisive laughter lingered in the air.

"Damn it!" Lysandra exclaimed, her grip on her blade tightening. Ragged breaths escaped her, leaving a bitter taste of defeat in her mouth.

Unable to do anything, she looked on as the mists again became dense, erasing any sign of Aviara and the relic.

"Take it easy, Lyss," Aerin whispered, gently touching her shoulder for support. Although his face displayed clear signs of frustration, his being calmed down dense Lysandra's chaotic situation.

"Standing here is not an option." "She has the relic."

"After all that, we proceed." Her inventive mind was already plotting, scheming for contingencies and countermeasures.

They withdrew to their temporary camp, a solemn silence enveloping them like morning dew. As the sun rose, its soft amber rays illuminated their weary yet determined faces, bearing the marks of battles fought.

"Make sure to pack everything.'

Lysandra skillfully sheathed her sword and started rolling up her sleeping mat with precise movements, although she knew it was wrong to make a headlong rush into the unknown and that it would serve no one.

"Lyss, this isn't on you." The voice belonged to Harrow, the dragon, whose wisdom often belied his ferocious appearance. His scales caught the dawn's light, casting colorful shadows across the ground.

"Isn't it?" There was a sharp edge to Lysandra's response. "Stopping her was my mission,"

"I intended to," Harrow growled. But not alone. We are in this together, remember?"

"Right. Together." Lysandra echoed, allowing the weight of their shared purpose to fortify her spirit.

"Here." Aerin handed her a waterskin, his fingers brushing hers briefly. The gesture, simple as it was, spoke volumes of the trust and camaraderie that they had forged among them.

"Thanks." Lysandra took a deep swig, feeling the cool water soothe her parched throat. "We have a long road ahead."

"Aviara won't make it easy for us," Feyla said, securing a pack around her back.

"Since when do we do it easy?" Aerin quipped with a wry smile that didn't quite reach his eyes.

"Never," Lysandra affirmed, her mind already mapping strategies and paths. "Let's get moving."

With their supplies gathered and their spirits bolstered by the unspoken bond between them, Lysandra led the way. Each step they took represented a silent vow to reclaim what was lost and thwart Aviara's dark designs.

The journey to find the relic had only begun, and they were ready to face whatever lay ahead. Together.

Lysandra's boots crunched on the frost-laden grass at dawn.

Shadows retreated as the sun rose, but darkness lingered in their hearts. Aviara's image, shrouded in malevolence, haunted her.

Aviara had escaped with the relic into a realm where light dared not follow.

"Feyla," Lysandra said, breaking the silence. "Master Elarion mentioned the Oracle of Lumin."

"Yes," Feyla replied. Lysandra's eyes sparked with hope. "The Oracle of Lumin could lead us to the relic."

Aerin scanned the horizon, hand on his sword. "Then let's find the Oracle."

Harrow's voice resonated deep within them. "Legends say the Oracle can see what mortals can't."

Lysandra mused, "If Lumin holds such power, it may be our

only chance."

"But there are trials," she continued, resolve to harden.

"We can handle trials," Aerin nodded. "It's uncertainty that troubles us."

Feyla checked her gadgets by adding, 'Caution keeps us alive.'

Lysandra commanded, 'Let's not waste daylight,' stepping forward. 'The Oracle is waiting for us.'

The party navigated the rough terrain, guided by their instincts and purpose. The weight of their mission grew heavier, but so did their commitment. Lysandra reflected on Master Elarion's wisdom. "Each step brings us closer to understanding our fight."

"A shadow hound's bite won't spare you," Aerin reminded her. Harrow added, "Knowledge can be a weapon." Feyla, with her keen eyes, scouted the landscape for signs of danger or guidance. "Let's equip ourselves with as much of it as possible."

Their conversation wove through the march like a tapestry, each thread an assorted color of their shared history and individual strengths. They were more than a band of adventurers; they were a force fused by fate and fire, each member essential to making the whole succeed.

As they crested a hill, the forest of Lumin sprawled before them, ancient trees standing sentinel over secrets untold. A land of enchantment and enigma. It promised both revelation and risk.

"Remember, the Oracle will not reveal itself to just anyone," Lysandra warned, her hand absently tracing the runes on her sword's pommel. "We'll need to prove our worth."

"Then let's prove it," Aerin said, his eyes reflecting a relentless spirit. "Not just to the Oracle, but to Erenor herself."

"Agreed." Feyla nodded, her collection of gadgets rattling slightly with her movement. "Our resolve is our greatest asset."

"Resolve and each other," Harrow affirmed, his massive form casting a protective shadow over his companions.

With the forest's edge drawing near, the group tightened their ranks, ready to face whatever magic and mystery awaited them. The Oracle of Lumin beckoned, and they would answer its call.

Mist curled around their ankles as they stepped into the Lumin Forest, an ethereal border that whispered secrets of ancient magic.

The canopy above was a tapestry of luminescent leaves, casting a surreal glow on the path ahead. Lysandra led the way, her sword half-drawn and her senses alert for the enchantments they were told would challenge them.

"Stay close," she said, her voice low but firm as she scanned the shifting shadows. "The barriers here are not just physical."

Aerin flanked her left, staff in hand, while Feyla and Eolande readied their respective tools and weapons on her right. Harrow's massive presence loomed behind them, a silent guardian against the unseen threats.

Without warning, the air before them shimmered, and the ground trembled. A barrier sprung from the earth—a wall of vines laced with thorns sharp enough to pierce armor.

Aerin raised his staff, murmuring incantations, blue sparks dancing at his fingertips.

"Let me," Feyla interjected, stepping forward with a device cobbled with gears and glowing stones. With a twist and a click, the contraption hummed to life, emitting a pulse that softened the vines until they parted like curtains, allowing passage.

"Nicely done," Lysandra praised, though her eyes never strayed from their path. Feyla merely nodded, holstering her invention as they continued onward.

Deeper within the forest, the air grew colder, and whispers fluttered on the breeze—voices not quite heard but felt tugging at their resolve.

Shadow paced anxiously, ears flat against his head, sensing the distress of his companions.

"Remember why we're here," Lysandra reminded them, her heart steeling against the spectral temptations. "For Erenor, for the balance."

"Nothing will sway us," Eolande vowed, nocking an arrow to his bow, his keen eyes piercing the gloom.

They finally arrived at a clearing bathed in silver light. In the center stood the Oracle of Lumin, a swirling vortex of energy pulsating with the forest's heartbeat.

The Oracle's voice boomed, resonating through their beings: "Who is out there, seeking my wisdom?"

"We seek your guidance to reclaim a relic taken by Aviara," Lysandra answered.

"Many desire power, but few are prepared for its burden," the

Oracle answered.

To prove their intentions, they must make a choice. Two specters appeared before them—one shrouded in darkness, the other radiating light. The dark figure held a chalice filled with black liquid, while the light figure held an identical cup filled with a golden elixir.

"Choose," the Oracle commanded.

"Darkness and light are intertwined, and there must always be a balance," pondered Aerin.

"Perhaps it's a trick," Feyla suggested, eyeing the chalices warily. "A riddle wrapped in a test."

"Or a test of our understanding," Eolande added, his gaze flickering between the ethereal figures.

Harrow snorted, his breath creating spirals of steam. "The answer lies within you, Lysandra. Trust what you have learned."

Lysandra closed her eyes, reaching inward to the tumultuous sea of her lineage—the constant dance of shadow and light within her soul.

Opening her eyes, she approached the figures and took the chalices with steady hands.

"Balance," she affirmed, pouring the contents of one into the other, merging darkness with light. The resulting mixture shone with a brilliance that rivaled the Oracle's glow.

"In the realm where darkness prevails, beneath the gaze of the guardian betrayed lies the hidden key, covered in sorrow and silence," the Oracle declared. The merged liquids solidified into a radiant orb, which floated before Lysandra.

"Thank you," she whispered, taking the orb and feeling its warmth spread through her fingers. It was a beacon amidst the uncertainty of their quest.

"Come," she said to her friends, her determination renewed. "The relic is waiting, and so is our fate."

Chapter 14

THE BETRAYED GUARDIAN

As the Oracle's cryptic prophecy resonated in their minds, they turned from the clearing, each step away from Lumin's enigmatic presence bringing them closer to the truth.

A powerful gust of wind suddenly swept the clearing, bringing the scent of decomposing leaves and the distant whispers of unsettled spirits.

Lysandra's hold on the hilt of her magical blade grew more potent as the intricate markings on its surface softly shimmered, attuned to the unseen energies that encircled them.

Her friends huddled around her, their determined expressions mirroring the strength in her own heart.

"A betrayed guardian," she pondered aloud, her eyes narrowing as she remembered the Oracle's prophecy. "Our journey's direction has to be toward a monument."

"Statue of the Guardian," Aerin affirmed, his voice steady despite the weight of their task. He ran his fingers through his hair, removing some stray leaves that had gotten tangled during their trip.

"I've come across a description that mentions it, describing it as a silent guardian overseeing the Dead Marshes."

As Feyla adjusted the straps of her pack that held various cleverly crafted gadgets and gizmos for whenever they were needed, she confidently interrupted, stating, "If that's the case, we have a clear path ahead."

"We will go there early in the morning."

With a nod, Eolande's face remained impassive, yet his eyes revealed a wealth of knowledge that only comes from years of journeying through the lands of Erenor. "Shrouded in sorrow, this place holds the quiet pain of those who have been let down."

"We don't tolerate trespassers either," complained Harrow, his scales glimmering in the diminishing daylight. "However, if this is okay, then I accept it."

Lysandra looked up, searching for the first stars of the evening. "We will overcome any obstacles, including darkness."

"How about we make camp?" Aerin suggested. "We'll need our strength to venture into the marshes."

"Agreed," said Lysandra, her mind dancing with strategies and what-ifs. "Feyla, can you—"

"Already on it," Feyla cut in, reaching for her tools. Moments later, a contraption unfurled, creating a protective canopy above their chosen spot. "This should keep us hidden from prying eyes."

As the sun sank beneath the horizon, casting the forest into darkness, they huddled around a small fire that Aerin had conjured. The flames flickered and danced, casting a warm and comforting glow across their faces. The crackling of the burning logs and the faint chirping of crickets in the distance provided a peaceful soundtrack to their evening in the wild forest.

Eolande stood guard during the first watch, holding his bow at the ready while his companions rested. Lysandra struggled to find sleep as the Oracle's prophecy played repeatedly in her mind until she finally succumbed to dreams.

"Where darkness dwells, under the gaze of the betrayed gua rdian..." The words twisted and turned to her slumber, a puzzle demanding to be solved, a relic waiting to be found. And she would find it for the sake of Erenor and all its people.

The sound of squelching echoed through the air as Lysandra's boots became engulfed in the mire of the treacherous Dead Marshes, her determined steps undeterred.

Her skin was moist, and a dense fog enveloped the world in an icy embrace. The smell of decay permeated the air, and the marsh appeared as a vast, desolate landscape under the hidden sky.

"Stay close." Aerin's voice pierced through the mist, guiding Lysandra as his hand gently rested on her shoulder. "The marsh tricks the senses. One false step, and you're swallowed whole."

Feyla mumbled from behind, "That's a cheerful thought, Aerin," as she heaved her pack of inventions higher onto her back. Her eyes swiftly moved towards the dancing shadows that loomed at the edge of her sight—wicked apparitions lurking, ready to pounce.

In an instant, a creature made of shadows emerged, its physical form barely discernible and its teeth displayed in a silent and menacing snarl.

Reacting with precision and instinct, Feyla swiftly produced a small and intricate device from her belt. With a flick and a twist, it expanded into a vibrant burst of energy that forcefully repelled the creature, causing it to retreat into the darkness with a yelp.

Aerin grinned and briefly relaxed as the successful repulsion brought some relief, commenting on the toy, "That's a nice one."

"It's not just toys," Feyla retorted, her pride evident even in the sad surroundings. "They are crucial for our survival."

"Pay attention, both of you," Lysandra interrupted, scanning the path ahead. "We have company here."

"Steady!" Aerin shouted, weaving a spell with deft fingers. A soft light emanated from his palms, solidifying the ground just enough for their passage.

"Couldn't you have done that sooner?" Feyla's tone was dry, but her eyes held gratitude.

"Saving the best for when it counts," Aerin replied wryly. But his gaze remained vigilant, searching the mists for the next threat.

"Remember the prophecy," Lysandra murmured, more to herself than her companions.

"Under the gaze of the betrayed guardian…" As she spoke, her voice trailed off into a whisper. Her sharp eyes caught sight of a monument in the distance, barely visible through the thick fog.

Lysandra stood there, gazing at the statue emerging before me. She couldn't help but notice its worn silhouette. The years they had left their mark on its surface, etched with lines of sorrow. It was a poignant reminder of the passage of time and the weight of the world's tragedies.

"Is that…?" Aerin began, hope shining through his words.

"It is," Lysandra confirmed, stepping forward with renewed purpose. The Statue of the Guardian loomed over them, its stone eyes etched with the pain of betrayal. "We're close."

"Then let's not keep our relic waiting," Feyla said, adjusting her pack once more and readying another device.

—⋈—

Together, they pressed on, the weight of history bearing upon them as they approached the statue's base. The air was charged with ancient power—a whisper of secrets long buried.

"Here," Lysandra whispered as she knelt before the statue.

She brushed aside layers of moss and dirt to reveal an inscription—runes of old Erenor begging to be read. Her fingertips traced the sigils, her lips moving silently as she deciphered their meaning.

"Can you make it out?" Feyla asked, crouching beside her.

"Partially," Lysandra admitted. "It speaks of darkness, guarding, and…" Her breath hitched. "Here. A hidden chamber."

"Where?" Aerin peered over their shoulders, his knowledge of the arcane seeking answers in the enigmatic text.

"Not where," Lysandra corrected, standing abruptly. "How. The relic isn't simply lying beneath our feet—it's safeguarded by the Guardian's last act of defiance against betrayal."

"Then we'll honor that defiance," Feyla stated, her hands working over her devices, ready to tackle whatever lay ahead.

"Let's uncover what's been hidden," Aerin agreed, his magic already coalescing around him, prepared to reveal the unseen.

With a shared nod, they set to work, the trials of the Dead Marshes behind them and the promise of the relic before them—an echo of hope in a land shrouded in shadow.

Lysandra's eyes narrowed as she scrutinized the towering statue, its stone surface etched with intricate runes.

The shadows of the Dead Marshes loomed behind them, but the sense of urgency propelled her focus forward.

With each rune, her fingers caressed, a fragment of ancient knowledge whispered in her mind, a puzzle demanding to be solved.

"Look for patterns," she muttered, stepping back to gaze at the larger design. "The runes are not just words; they're keys."

"Keys?" Aerin echoed, furrowing his brow. He leaned closer, the tip of his staff glowing as he traced the magical script alongside her.

"Every culture has its safeguards," Feyla interjected, her mechanical contraptions clinking as she adjusted their settings. "This is no different. Lysandra, you're our best chance."

"Not much pressure on me, is there?" Lysandra asked under her breath, though a smirk played on her lips. She appreciated Feyla's blunt confidence and Aerin's unwavering support. It grounded her when the whispers of her lineage threatened to sway her focus.

"Here," she said, pointing to a sequence of runes spiraling around the statue's base. It's a riddle wrapped in history. The Guardian was betrayed, so trust must be earned, even by those who seek to right the wrongs."

"Then earn it we shall," Aerin declared, his voice steady as the wind swept through the marshes.

With a firm yet respectful tone, Lysandra uttered the incantation, showing her deep respect for the past.

The atmosphere surrounding the statue buzzed with vibrating energy, which grew stronger and became a tangible presence.

The earth shook as soon as the last syllable escaped her mouth, and the statue shifted, exposing a hidden entrance below.

Exchanging glances, they wordlessly communicated their decision to dive into unfamiliar territory.

With her sword unsheathed, Lysandra led the way as they descended into the recently uncovered chamber. The walls emitted a faint light that reflected off her blade.

Chapter 15

THE CHAMBER OF SORROWS

The Chamber of Sorrows loomed in front of them, massive and eerily silent.

"By the gods," Feyla whispered, her voice cracking the silence like thin ice.

Ethereal energy chains trapped the spirits of the betrayed, their eyes hollow with centuries of agony, clinging to the chamber walls.

Lysandra cautiously approached, her warrior instincts balanced by the compassion that flowed within her.

"We don't approach as conquerors but as those seeking justice for your betrayal," she spoke to the spirits, her voice laden with the importance of solemn oaths.

Aerin touched his heart and said, "I can see your sorrow." "And it will not go unheeded."

Is it possible for inventions to bring solace? I am here to use my skills to pay tribute to your cherished memories.

A sense of movement and awakening spread through the spirits, causing a ripple of consciousness to fill the room while the chains that held them faded, growing weaker with every word of recognition.

In a gentle tone, Lysandra requested, "Kindly explain how we can liberate you," while lowering her sword to convey a peaceful stance.

"Revenge," whispered a spirit, its voice a faint echo of existence. "Promise... justice..."

"We promise," Lysandra swore, and with each oath they offered, the spirits' chains dissolved, freeing them from eternal torment.

Lysandra and her companions pressed on through the winding path, their hearts pounding with anticipation. They knew they were getting closer to their ultimate goal, but they also knew the journey was far from over. Finally, they reached the entrance to a dimly lit chamber that held the precious artifact they were searching for.

The atmosphere was heavy with the presence of the souls they had freed, who stood guard over the artifact. They approached cautiously, filled with a sense of reverence and awe. The artifact glowed softly in the center of the chamber, its intricate details and precious materials catching the light in a way that seemed almost magical.

As they reached out to touch it, the ghostly chains that had bound it fell to the floor with a loud clang, their links slowly disappearing into thin, melancholic wisps of mist. Lysandra knew this was a pivotal moment in their quest, bringing them one step closer to confronting the malevolent Aviara and restoring peace to the troubled land of Erenor.

Lysandra felt a tightness in her chest when the spirits, previously trapped by their own sorrow, floated in front of her, appearing translucent and eager.

Their eyes, empty but intense, appeared to probe her innermost being in search of her deepest beliefs.

"Your release is at hand," she assured them, her voice firm despite the chill that crept up her spine. The words were like an oath, a sacred promise made amidst the whispers of the dead.

Aerin stood steadfast next to Feyla, his blue cloak drifting softly in the chamber's stillness. His eyes shone with the emerging light of his healing magic. "We will hold your stories close," he announced, "and let them steer our journey."

Feyla adjusted the detailed gauntlet on her wrist, its gears ticking in agreement with her firm resolve. "Your memories will ignite our next wave of creations," she assured, sharing a knowing glance with Eolande, who gave a silent nod, his bowstring tight in a quiet salute.

Harrow, towering and dignified, bowed his head gracefully. His scales caught the light, casting a kaleidoscope of colors around the room. "The might of dragons will reflect the strength you once held," he stated, his voice deep and resonant, filled with the wisdom of eons.

Lysandra's voice was earnest and filled with a plea. "We need to hear from you," she implored. Tell us about the relic, about Aviara's fall."

An apparition, clad in the remnants of its armor, glided forward. The sound it made resembled leaves brushing against stone. "Aviara... once our protector... then our doom."

"As Erenor's magic diminished, her heart grew colder," another voice chimed in, its presence concealed by a shimmering cloak.

Harrow solemnly spoke, "Betrayal spawned more betrayal," as his eyes mirrored the ghosts' suffering.

"We found solace and inspiration in her radiant beauty."

Pointing to the shackles that bound them, the armored spirit proclaimed, "Her pain became our confinement."

Drawing nearer, Lysandra reached out her hand to touch the frigid air where the ghostly figure lingered. "Her tale is intricately connected to ours," she said.

The spirit advised, "Instead of perceiving her as the monster she is believed to be, remember her as the protector she used to be."

"I got it," Aerin said again, his determination now clear.

"Empathy," Feyla murmured, locking eyes with Lysandra as they agreed to bring harmony back to their world.

Eolande concluded with a downward salute of his arrow, saying "Unity" to honor the fallen.

"Proceed," the spirit in armor called, gradually vanishing into the approaching light. "Search for the Ouroboros, but proceed with caution."

"Thank you," Lysandra whispered, feeling excitement and apprehension as her heart filled with emotions.

The voices of her companions joined in chorus, harmonizing and merging, creating a soothing melody that eased the ache in the chamber as they all gratefully said, "Thank you."

While they moved forward, the Chamber of Sorrows metamorphosed, shedding its centuries-old despairing walls to expose mystical runes that radiated with untapped power.

Moving silently, Shadow stayed close to Lysandra, his presence offering her a reassuring weight against her leg.

"May the lessons we learn here serve as our guide," Lysandra stated, her gaze sweeping over the cryptic symbols. With Erenor in mind, in memory of Aviara, and for the future ahead.

As they got closer to the center of the chamber, they heard echoes of their past experiences. These echoes carried the weight of either unlocking their salvation or sealing their fate at the final trial set by the Guardian.

Lysandra felt the coldness of the chamber seeping into their skin as they descended, the heavy silence contrasting with the previous chaotic struggle that brought them to this point.

As the bone-chilling air sucked the life from their bodies, she clung to her sword, finding solace in the cold comfort of the metal.

"Can you feel it?" Feyla murmured, her voice barely above a

whisper as if the sorrow itself demanded hushed reverence.

"It feels like I'm wading through despair with every step," Lysandra replied, her breath appearing in the dim light emanating from the runic torches grasped tightly in Aerin's hands.

"Stay by my side," Aerin advised his eyes carefully surveying the shadows that clung to the aged walls. "This location... it is brimming with memories."

They moved in perfect harmony and formed a united front, protecting against the unseen influences of Erenor's painful history.

As they walked, the stones whispered secrets of betrayal, triggering Lysandra's own fears and doubts to resurface.

"Stay calm," she advised, speaking more to herself than to her companions. After coming so far, the ghosts of history could not undo their significant progress.

A sudden change in the air, a gentle movement that suggested hidden magic, caught her attention. Taking a momentary pause, she reached out with her finely honed senses, sharpened through years of training and battles fought in the depths of darkness.

"Magic," she declared, her voice unwavering even as doubt consumed her. Ancient and complex.

"Magic that arises from sorrow," Eolande added, his sharp Elven eyes penetrating the darkness. Its strength is incomparable.

"Then we shall meet it with the strength of our resolve." Lysandra declared her statement not just a promise but a challenge to the chamber that sought to overwhelm them.

The closer they got to the chamber's center, the more Erenor's anguish weighed upon them, a tangible force that seemed poised to break their spirits.

Still, they marched forward unafraid, carrying the flicker of hope deep inside them—hope for redemption, healing, and a future where the sorrow would become a distant recollection.

"Proceed," Lysandra directed, her voice piercing the silence like a guiding light, leading her friends through the darkness toward the trials that awaited them.

Navigating through the Chamber of Sorrows, Lysandra and her friends could hear the stones underfoot whispering ancient secrets.

The sound of each step reverberated, intensifying the profound stillness that enveloped them like a stifling cloak. Holding the sword's hilt tightly, Lysandra silently swore to eliminate the shadows that clung to their path.

"The silence," she whispered, pausing to allow the calmness to engulf her. "It's as if the air is mourning."

Next to her, Aerin scanned the rocky surroundings, his hands shimmering with a subtle touch of magic, ready to be summoned. "Keep your wits. Sorrow can be as dangerous as any wild animal we've ever encountered."

In unison, they pressed on, sensing the surrounding space contract and expand with each inhalation. The chamber appeared to be alive, responding and almost breathing in a painful rhythm synchronizing with their hearts beating.

Lysandra could sense it—the sorrow was so strong that it felt like a tangible presence, a mournful reminder of every act of betrayal embedded in Erenor's essence.

Despite her despair, a blazing resolve grew within her, fighting against the tide.

As she struggled to make sense of her emotions, she sifted through her memories: her mother's gentle warnings, the loud clash of steel in her first battle, and the bittersweet taste of victory and heartbreak.

Every memory served as a building block, a valuable experience gained on the path that brought her to this point.

"Keep your attention on why we're here," she said, her voice piercing through the heavy sadness. "On what lies ahead, not what lies behind."

Aerin nodded, his face displaying intense focus. He was acutely aware of the consequences of being distracted in a location filled with enchantments.

With a surge of energy, his fingers twitched, harnessing his growing healing abilities, a stark contrast to the suffocating atmosphere of the chamber.

"Balance," he murmured, repeating the word like a sacred chant. "Amid the sadness, we still manage to achieve harmony."

The moment their eyes connected, a wordless agreement formed between the warrior and the mage, a deep understanding of the intricate interplay between light and dark.

Giving a slight nod, they pushed forward, Lysandra at the forefront, moving with the grace of a dancer. Her sword held steady—not merely a weapon but a manifestation of her un-yielding resolve.

Moving through the chamber, they took measured steps, each an act of resistance against the grief that threatened to consume them.

Amid the despair, they brought hope and defied the sorrow that tried to trap them. The silence persisted, watchful and witnessing their unwavering resolve, their refusal to surrender.

With history's specters as witnesses, Lysandra and her friends pressed forward in the depths of the Chamber of Sorrows, their resolve unshaken and their spirits undaunted.

They waited eagerly for the ancient relic, just like the trials that would put their souls to the test.

They prepared themselves for the grief, the fights, and what-ever lay ahead beyond the chamber's suffocating stillness.

The glow of the chamber cast an otherworldly pallor over Lysandra's face as she stepped forward, her boots barely making a sound on the cold stone floor.

Before her, spirits shimmered like mirages, their chains clink-ing in the stifling silence. Each link seemed to pulse with their heartaches, a haunting melody of betrayal that clawed at the edges of her resolve.

"By the Ancients," Eolande muttered, his bowstring tensing unconsciously.

"Stay close," Lysandra commanded, her voice grounded de-spite the spectral tableau unfolding around them.

She could feel the sorrow pressing against her, a tangible force that threatened to sap her strength. The air was a morass, dragging at her limbs, whispering despair so deep it could drown even the bravest soul.

But Lysandra was no stranger to darkness; its tendrils had long entwined with the light within her, and she wielded both with equal finesse.

"Shadows and sorrow," Shadow growled lowly beside her, his fur bristling as if to ward off the gloom.

"Indeed," Harrow rumbled his massive form a comforting solidity amidst the ephemeral wraiths.

Aerin's hand found hers, a lifeline in the mire of despondency. She squeezed back, grateful for the connection, for the shared strength that thrummed between them.

"Focus on the living, not the lost," he said, his eyes scanning the spirits, searching for the key to freedom—for them and the souls bound to this place.

Feyla stepped up beside them, her gadgets clicking quietly as she adjusted settings, tuned to detect any shifts in the magical spectrum. "We need to break the cycle," she determined, her voice steady but tinged with an edge of urgency.

"Then let's start by breaking these chains," Lysandra replied, her sword gleaming with a light that defied the encompassing gloom.

Together, they moved among the spirits, each step a deliberate defiance of the chamber's oppressive will.

As Lysandra approached the first spirit, she locked eyes with the specter, its gaze hollow yet flickering with the embers of long-smoldering injustice.

"Tell me your tale," she said, not as a command but as an offering—a chance for the spirit to unburden its eternal vigil.

The spirit's lips parted, and a voice as thin as a dying breeze spilled forth the story of a warrior betrayed and abandoned to darkness by those sworn to fight alongside him.

Lysandra listened, not just with her ears but with her heart, her empathy a balm to the raw wounds of the past.

"Your valor remains undiminished by treachery," she whispered, her words carving hope into the air. "Let go of the chains. Let us carry your legacy."

The specter's eyes brightened, a flicker of peace smoothing the etched lines of suffering, and one by one, the chains dissolved into motes of light that danced away like freed fireflies.

"Move to the next," she instructed, turning to her companions. Her voice carried the weight of command and compassion intertwined.

Aerin nodded, stepping toward another chained spirit as Shadow paced protectively nearby. The mage's presence was a soothing warmth against the chill of the chamber, his healing magic a silent promise of renewal.

"Share your burden," Aerin offered his voice a gentle undercurrent in the stillness.

With each spirit's release, the air grew lighter, the ethereal glow more vibrant. They were not just freeing the trapped souls; they were liberating the chamber from its own sorrow, unshackling the future from the tyranny of the past.

As the last chain fell away, the transformation of the Chamber of Sorrows was complete.

Chapter 16

OUROBOROS, THE HEART OF SHADOWS

The glow intensified, coalescing into a path that beckoned them forward. At its end, the relic awaited—guarded by the spirit of the ultimate guardian, his visage a testament to the trials they had overcome and those yet to come.

"Brave souls," the Guardian intoned, his voice resonant with the wisdom of ages, "you've shown compassion where others would show fear. The relic you seek was never truly lost, only waiting for something worthy of its power."

Lysandra came forward, accepting the responsibility with the respect it deserved. In front of her was the Ouroboros, the Heart of Shadows, an emblem representing the past and the future.

"Remember her beauty," the Guardian implored, echoing Aviara's untainted past.

With her eyes illuminated by the relic's reflection, Lysandra made a determined pledge, saying, "We will." "And we'll remember the lessons learned in this chamber, too."

They secured the relic and recognized the weight of its historical importance before turning around to depart, with each footstep echoing with determination as they ventured toward their next test.

The upcoming quest to locate Aviara was daunting, but they were well-prepared—connected, compassionate, and motivated to bring balance back to Erenor.

The chamber's glow pulsed like a living thing, its rhythm coordinated with the spectral chains that bound the spirits to their eternal torment.

Lysandra and her companions edged forward, the heavy air pressing against them as if urging them back.

Yet, they persisted, the glow from the Heart of Shadows, The Ouroboros, a beacon in their hands casting elongated shadows on the walls.

A spirit before them writhed, the clanking of its chains a cacophony that pierced the silence. Feyla, with furrowed brows, moved closer.

Her nimble fingers, which usually danced with tools and gadgets, hovered over the luminous bindings, hesitant but drawn by compassion that bridged the realms of the living and the dead.

"Can we not provide them with some solace?"

The mystical communication device, a sphere made of intertwined metals that hummed with energy, sparked into existence.

The image of Master Elarion appeared momentarily, his eyes reflecting the prevailing solemnity that had taken hold of the group.

"Understanding and acknowledging their sorrow is key," he advised, his image blurring at the edges as if struggling against the chamber's oppressive aura. "Their chains are of their own making, a result of unresolved anguish."

Feyla nodded, unable to tear away from the spirit's twisted countenance—a reflection of a tormented soul, forever denied tranquility.

Empowered by Elarion's words, she extended her hand, encountering not human skin but the icy grip of despair that bound the soul to its suffering.

"Let us be the source of your comfort," she murmured, her innovative mind racing to solve the puzzle of their anguish. The restraints that confine you originate from your inner self, yet we are standing beside you at this moment.

The spirit, once consumed by betrayal, now had a glimmer of consciousness in its hollow gaze. The chains made a gentle sound, a melodic note within a mournful song, as they loosened.

Lysandra's hand tightened around the relic, reinvigorating her purpose. This went beyond a mere pursuit of power.

"By understanding them, we liberate them," Lysandra spoke, her voice steady and clear. "And in their liberation, we find our own path towards what we must become."

A collective sigh seemed to emanate from the chamber, as

if the walls were resonating with the spirits' liberation, their ethereal shackles breaking apart piece by piece.

Silently, Shadow glided through the Chamber of Sorrows, his steps making no sound on the frigid stone floor.

Beside him stood the majestic dragon Harrow, its scales glistening softly in the ethereal light.

With her hand on the pommel of her sword, Lysandra followed closely, her eyes carefully surveying the spectral figures that lined their route.

"Stay nearby," she whispered, and Shadow's ears perked up. His yellow eyes reflected the eerie light.

Harrow tilted his gigantic head towards the first spirit, a shade floating just above the ground, its face marked with centuries of deceit. With an air of authority mixed with gentleness, Lysandra approached and humbly kneeled down before the spirit.

"Please share your story," she pleaded, her voice providing comfort in the suffocating quiet.

As the spirit spoke, its chains rattled, creating a haunting sound similar to the wind passing through decaying leaves. "I served as a guardian, with a solemn oath to defend the realm of Erenor."

With a compassionate expression, Lysandra listened intently, her brow furrowed. When the spirit paused momentarily, she vulnerably shared a part of her story, her voice reflecting her emotions. "I know what it is to feel the weight of responsibility, to fear the darkness within me could one day overshadow the light."

The spirit's essence emitted a soft glow, transitioning into tranquility. The chains turned into tiny specks of light, swirling around Lysandra and whispering their thanks before disappearing.

Expressing gratitude, the spirit found solace in their shared confession.

With his wings gracefully folding, Harrow moved closer, meeting the eyes of another tormented soul. The spirit hesitated, unused to encountering such a commanding presence.

Harrow's voice echoed through the chamber as he said, "Speak, I am here to listen."

The spirit mourned, expressing that betrayal came from an unexpected source—its own family. "They coveted my power, my station, and so they took it all, leaving me but a shadow in these forsaken halls."

With a gesture of respect, the dragon inclined its head. "Throughout my extensive lifetime, I have witnessed much deceit."

Harrow's words of wisdom had a calming effect on the spirit, softening its features and replacing the sadness in its eyes with understanding. The chains broke apart and disappeared as the spirit rose towards the unknown peace outside the room.

As Aerin advanced, his mage's robes swept the ground. Standing before him was a young spirit, its essence flickering with instability, much like a candle swaying in the wind.

With a hand enveloped in a calming aura of restorative magic,

Aerin extended his arm and said, "I am willing to bear your pain, even if only temporarily."

Whispering, the spirit revealed that it was a mere apprentice who had been abandoned and considered too weak to engage in combat. "Abandoned by my master, I met my end in the shadows, helpless and alone."

"Power can take on numerous shapes," Aerin replied, his own uncertainties creeping into his statement. "The actual source of power stems from having the courage to confront our darkest moments rather than shying away from them."

His touch ignited a newfound brightness in the soul, an expanded warmth until the ethereal figure stood complete and liberated. With a thankful nod, the spirit faded away into the lingering light.

Each person faced the spirits individually, revealing their vulnerabilities and fears while seeking solace.

Lysandra and her companions broke the chains of eternal torment for each spirit by showing them empathy and forgiveness.

With the clattering of the last chains hitting the ground, a shared sense of accomplishment swept through the chamber.

They successfully completed the Trial of Empathy, not by exerting force or power, but by connecting through the universal language of emotions.

United, they turned towards the rest of their path, their relationship fortified by their hardships.

Lysandra's breath fogged before her as she stepped forward,

drawn by a spectral figure that shimmered with the muted light of a dying star.

The spirit, a soldier garbed in ethereal armor, paced restlessly, its translucent sword cleaving through the silence with every stroke. Chains rattled from its form, binding it to the sorrow-drenched stone.

"Your comrades left you to face darkness alone," Lysandra said, her voice steady despite the tightness in her chest. Her fingers curled around the hilt of her own blade, a weight familiar and comforting.

The spirit stilled, turning hollow eyes upon her. "Betrayal cuts deeper than any blade," it rasped. "My trust was my undoing."

Lysandra understood and empathized with the sorrowful spirit before her. Fate gave him his namesake, separating him from his loved ones.

A flickering spirit floated before her, a lost soul. The spirit whispered, "So you understand the weight of my shackles?"

"Better than you might realize." Lysandra took another step, her boots whispering against the stone floor. Her hand stretched out, palm facing up, a gesture of solace. "However, unity cannot be achieved by standing alone."

A shiver passed through the soul, momentarily bringing a renewed presence. "Finding trust again... Maybe unity holds the key to strength."

"Together, we are strong enough to overcome even Aviara," Lysandra affirmed, thinking of her companions, who had become her chosen family. Together, we can mend what was broken."

With a clink like ice breaking upon a winter lake, the chains fell away, and the spirit saluted Lysandra with its sword before dissolving into the healing light.

As Aerin took center stage, his flowing robes mirrored the storm clouds that gave him his namesake, creating a dramatic presence. A spirit floated in front of him, its flickering form showing a lost soul on the brink of being snuffed out by the overwhelming despair that filled the Chamber of Sorrows.

"None remembered my name when I fell," the spirit murmured, its voice barely carrying over the thrum of magic in the air. "I was but a shadow among many, and shadows are so easily forgotten."

"Yet here you are, remembered now," Aerin said, meeting the spirit's gaze. "Honor doesn't reside in renown or tales sung by bards—it lives in the heart, in the deeds that outlast us."

"Can honor restore what was lost?" the spirit questioned, a skeptical undertone to its wavering voice.

"Perhaps not," Aerin conceded, a wistful sadness in his eyes for all the friends he could no longer laugh with, their memories a tapestry woven through his being. "But memory is the ground upon which we build the future. We honor the fallen by carrying them with us as we forge ahead, ensuring their sacrifices were not in vain."

"Then let my memory be a beacon," said the spirit, a newfound determination in its stance. "One that guides you through the darkness ahead."

As if summoned by the spirit's conviction, the ghostly light around them brightened, the shadows retreating to the corners of the chamber.

With a nod akin to respect, the spirit unfurled its chains, and they dissipated into motes of light that rose like stars ascending to the night sky.

Aerin declared, "We must press on, upholding the honor of those who have preceded us," as he turned back to the group, his eyes gleaming with a newfound sense of purpose.

"Certainly," Lysandra concurred, sheathing her sword as they prepared to continue their mission. In unity, we find both strength and hope— and it is hoped that will illuminate our journey to Aviara.

Feyla moved ahead, her boots scraping on the aged stone below. The spirit, resembling a ghostly figure draped in translucent gray, had a face twisted in a perpetual grimace of self-doubt as she approached it. A thousand regrets hung in the air, creating a palpable hum.

"Hello," Feyla started, her voice remaining calm despite her inner trembling. My name is Feyla Swiftshadow."

Their hollow eyes connected, and in that instant, the room fell into a deafening silence, save for the faint echoes of their breaths.

"I was... I am Orrick," the spirit murmured, its voice a mere thread of sound. "In life, I was never enough, always overshadowed by mightier warriors and more powerful mages."

Feyla nodded, understanding creeping into her gaze. "Magic," she scoffed gently, "has always been the currency of worth in our world. But it isn't the only one."

"Easy for you to say," Orrick countered. "You stand here among heroes, your name woven into their tapestry of valor."

"Stand, yes, but not without my own shadows." Feyla's gaze drifted down to the intricate devices strapped to her belt, her lifeline in a world that often felt like a puzzle missing half its pieces. "I'm no mage, Orrick. My mind and hands are my only allies in this dance of magic and power."

"Is that not a magic of its own?" Orrick's form flickered, drawing closer to Feyla.

"Perhaps," she conceded, "but the fear of inadequacy gnaws at me. Whenever I see a spell cast or a curse broken, I wonder if my inventions will ever measure up."

"Yet here you are," Orrick whispered, his form becoming clearer and less fragmented. "Facing the trials of Erenor with nothing but your wit and your will."

"Because I have to believe that there's a place for me here," Feyla confessed, her words carving out a space for herself in the silence. "That my strength lies not in the magic I wield but in the problems I solve."

"Then let us solve this together," Orrick said, his chains beginning to shimmer with a light that hadn't been there before. "Let my inadequacy meet your ingenuity, and together, we'll forge a fresh path."

Feyla reached out, her hand passing through Orrick's spectral form yet somehow touching something deeper. "Your story won't end here, bound by chains of doubt. Together, we'll rewrite it."

A soft glow enveloped them both, and the chains broke away, dissolving into nothingness as Orrick's spirit smiled—a genuine smile, free from the burdens of his past.

"Thank you," he whispered, fading into the ether.

"Thank you," Feyla echoed, turning back to her companions with a small, triumphant smile playing on her lips.

Harrow, the dragon, watched Feyla's exchange thoughtfully. His trial would be different, not a battle of physical might, but one of wisdom and age-old knowledge.

"Come then, wise Harrow," beckoned a spirit of regal bearing, its own chains a heavy mantle around its neck. "Share with us the breadth of your years."

"Time is a peculiar master," Harrow rumbled, his voice resonating through the chamber. "It grants us the illusion of wisdom, yet the greatest lessons are often learned in moments, not millennia."

"Speak to me of these moments," the spirit urged, leaning forward.

"Of fire and ash, of empires rising and falling," Harrow began, closing his reptilian eyes. "Each moment is a spark catching the wind. Each decision, courage or cowardice, shapes the world."

"Yet here I remain," the spirit lamented, "a relic of a forgotten age, unable to move beyond this moment of betrayal."

"Even relics have stories to tell," Harrow replied, opening his eyes to gaze upon the spirit. "Yours is not over; it merely awaits the next chapter."

"Then let us turn the page together," said the spirit, a sense of anticipation lighting up its age-worn features.

"Indeed," agreed Harrow, his presence alone seeming to lift the weight of centuries from the room.

As the last chains evaporated, the elf stepped forward, taking his turn to face the trial. His light footfalls were nearly silent, his expression serene yet focused.

"Who speaks for the trees and the stars?" asked a lithe spirit, its form barely more than a whisper of leaves and moonlight.

"I do," the elf answered, bowing his head slightly. "For they are kin to me, as much a part of my being as the blood in my veins."

The spirit suggested, "Then let us speak of nature's resilience, its endless cycle of death and rebirth."

"Nature does not yield to sorrow," the elf replied. "It takes the fallen leaf, the extinguished star, and weaves it into new life. It knows no betrayal, only transformation."

"Teach me this transformation," the spirit pleaded, its chains echoing the rustle of dying foliage.

"Embrace change as you would a trusted friend," the elf counseled, reaching out to touch the spirit's heart. "For in it, you will find renewal."

The spirit's chains crumbled with those words, turning to dust that glittered like dew in the morning sun.

The Elf nodded respectfully as the spirit found peace, becoming one with the forest of spirits around them.

"Change," the Elf murmured, "is the only true constant."

"Change," echoed Lysandra, her hand resting on her heart. "And hope."

Lysandra's eyes reflected the wavering forms of the lingering spirits. She could feel the chamber's heaviness recede like a tide pulling back from the shore with each whispered promise and shared tale of woe.

It was Harrow's turn, his massive form dwarfing the ethereal figure before him. The ancient and wise dragon bowed his head to the level of the spirit, an act of humility that belied his imposing presence.

"Speak, a creature of flame and scale," the spirit commanded its voice, a hiss of steam over hot coals.

"Power, I wield, and destruction I have brought," Harrow rumbled, the language of dragons flowing like molten gold from his maw. "But through the ash, life rises anew."

"Show me this life," the spirit demanded, its chains clinking with the heat of rekindled embers.

"Life is the spark after the inferno, the seedling in the charred ground," Harrow said, smoke curling from his nostrils. "From my fire, let warmth foster growth, not decay."

As Harrow's words filled the space, the spectral chains disintegrated into a cloud of soot that danced away on an unfelt breeze.

The spirit nodded, its form glowing brighter before dissipating in a final exhalation of release.

"Renewal," Harrow whispered, his eyes meeting Lysandra's. "Even for those who have scorched the earth."

"Renewal," Lysandra echoed, her voice steady despite the tremor of awe at the dragon's wisdom.

Finally, it was Lysandra's turn to step forward. She approached the remaining bound spirit, feeling the air lighten further as the soft glow intensified, pushing back the darkness.

The specter before her bore the regal countenance of a warrior wronged, its visage etched with noble suffering.

"Who will hear my story?" the spirit asked its voice, a lament that held the echoes of countless battles.

"I will," Lysandra vowed, holding her sword hilt in her hand to symbolize her oath, not as a threat but as a promise.

"Then speak, child of fate," the spirit urged its chains a dull shackle of remorse.

"Destiny is neither kind nor cruel," Lysandra began, her gaze unwavering.

"It is the path we walk, paved with choices made and unmade. Yours was nobility; mine, a balance between light and dark."

"Balance," the spirit murmured, considering her words. "A burden and a gift."

"Both," Lysandra agreed, her voice softening. "But within it lies the power to change our course, to find honor even in the shadow of betrayal."

The spirit regarded her solemnly and then slowly nodded understanding. As it did, its chains shattered, falling away like shards of a broken mirror, reflecting not what was but what could be.

"Freedom," it whispered, and then there was nothing left but a whisper of gratitude that brushed past Lysandra's cheek like a benediction.

"Freedom," she breathed out, feeling the last vestiges of constriction around her heart loosen.

As if summoned by the liberation of the spirits, the center of the chamber illuminated, revealing an altar where no altar had stood before.

Upon it rested an ancient tome, its pages aglow with the same healing light that now suffused the room. A voice, deep and resonant, filled the chamber—the Guardian's blessing granted at last.

"Chosen ones," the voice boomed, "you have borne witness to sorrow and offered solace to the forsaken. Thus, you are deemed worthy."

"Guardian," Lysandra called out, stepping toward the altar, "we seek the Heart of Shadows to mend what has been torn asunder."

"True power lies not in dominion but in harmony," the Guardian intoned.

"Take this tome—within it, the knowledge to heal the rifts of Erenor. But remember, the greatest challenges lie not within these pages but within yourselves."

"Thank you," Lysandra replied, her hand closing around the tome. Its warmth seeped into her skin, a promise of trials yet to come but also of hope—a hope that they might bind what Aviara sought to unravel.

Lysandra's hand rested on the hilt of her blade, the cool metal a silent oath as she stepped forward, the tome clasped in her other hand.

The chamber's transformation unfolded before them like the blooming of nightshade at dusk—mysterious and laden with portent.

"Something's happening," Aerin murmured, his voice a low thrum in the charged air.

The ground shook beneath their feet, and a shimmering silver path appeared, guiding them to the center of the room. Before the altar, a radiant entity manifested its fleeting and authoritative shape.

Chapter 17

HEALING WOUNDS

Lysandra calmly addressed the spirit as "Guardian," her voice remaining steady even as her heart pounded. "We have noted the difficulties you have experienced."

"Without a doubt, Lysandra of Erenor," came the reply from the spirit of the Guardian, its ancient voice resonating with the accumulated knowledge of ages. "Your ability to remain strong amid despair is admirable. One test remains, though."

"Say it," Feyla commanded, her eyes steady as she adjusted her pack, filled with untested inventions against the power of such ancient magic.

"Aviara fled, leaving behind that which she could not carry," the Guardian intoned, gesturing towards an obsidian pedestal veiled in shadows. "The relic you seek rests there, but it demands a custodian whose heart is clear of vengeance."

"Vengeance..." Lysandra echoed, feeling the weight of the word. The need to restore balance had fueled her quest, but was it untainted by the darker thirst for retribution?

"Look within," the spirit prompted, its visage softening like moonlight filtering through clouds. "Can you wield power without being consumed by its lure?"

"Her darkness will not taint us," Lysandra vowed, stepping closer to the pedestal. "We seek to heal, not to harm."

"Prove this to me," the Guardian challenged its form blurring at the edges, becoming part of the very fabric of the chamber.

Lysandra approached the pedestal, her companions' eyes upon her, each carrying the echo of their own trials. She reached out, her fingers grazing the surface of the relic—an orb pulsing with an inner light that seemed to dance with her touch.

"By my blood and bone, I swear to uphold the unity of Erenor," she whispered, the relic resonating with her pledge.

"Then take it," the Guardian said, its voice now a fading whisper, "and let your actions reflect your words."

As Lysandra lifted the Heart of Shadows, the Ouroboros, its energy surged through her, a confluence of power and responsibility.

The chamber brightened further, casting away the last vestiges of shadow as if in approval of the new bearer.

"Let us depart," Lysandra announced, facing her comrades. "Our journey does not end here. We must find Aviara and heal the wounds of our world."

With the relic secured and the Guardian's spirit appeased, they retraced their steps through the Chamber of Sorrows, their resolve strengthened and their purpose clearer than ever.

The trials endured within these ancient walls were but a prelude to the greater battle that awaited them beyond.

Lysandra tightened her grip on the Heart of Shadows. Its surface was cool and smooth, like a night untouched by dreams.

The relic's dark sheen reflected their circle of weary but resolute faces, each marked by the trials they had undergone.

The Guardian's spirit hovered before them, its form diffused with light yet commanding an unspoken reverence.

"Brave souls, you've shown compassion where others would show fear," it began, its voice echoing through the chamber like a long-forgotten melody. "The relic you seek was never truly lost, only waiting for something worthy of its power."

Aerin stepped forward, his brow furrowed in thought. "And we have proven ourselves worthy?"

"Indeed." The Guardian's form flickered as if caught between realms. "The Heart of Shadows, the Ouroboros—our target—is not a binding instrument. It embodies hope, a chance to mend what has been torn asunder within Erenor and its children."

Lysandra felt a pang of sadness woven with determination. "Hope is a fragile thing in these times," she murmured.

"True strength lies in nurturing that which is fragile," the Guardian responded.

Feyla tilted her head, her mechanical contraptions clinking against her belt. "Aviara's tale... it was different once, wasn't it?"

"Ah, Aviara," the spirit said, and a wistfulness in its tone seemed to caress the air. She wasn't always malevolent. When the world was young, when magic flowed unabated through the veins of Erenor, she was one of the revered. Remember her beauty, for it is crucial to understand what happened afterward—that which warped her essence."

"Betrayal," Lysandra breathed, the knowledge settling in her heart like a stone dropped into deep waters.

The Guardian solemnly declared, "Her pain transformed into her fury, an eternal cycle."

"So, we shall bear this symbol of hope and confront whatever awaits," Aerin proclaimed, his hand placed on the hilt of his sword—a solemn promise to safeguard their newly entrusted responsibility.

"However," Feyla reminded us, adjusting her goggles as if seeking a clearer glimpse of the future, "we must not overlook the fact that hope alone cannot protect us from Aviara's darkness."

The Guardian's form shimmered and faded away. "You have all the resources—tools, knowledge, and determination. Move forward and, if possible, bring healing to the land and the hearts of its people, including Aviara's."

Lysandra nodded, sensing the merging of the relic's weight and the weight of their quest. Taking a deep breath, she prepared herself, sensing the support of her friends behind her and their strong bond.

"I'm grateful, Guardian," she said, her voice unwavering. We will remain resolute.

With the spirit's light fading into the surrounding glow, the group made their way toward the exit, their steps resounding with determination.

While the Chamber of Sorrows was now in the past, the path ahead would present challenges they could hardly fathom.

Together, they walked, their shoulders touching, while Lysandra held the Ouroboros delicately in her hands—a symbol of hope shining through the shadows, ready to confront whatever darkness lay ahead.

The Ouroboros felt cool and smooth as Lysandra's fingers wrapped around them. Not only was the Ouroboros heavy in Lysandra's hand, but it also carried a rich history and significance, giving it a sense of vitality.

The Guardian's words stayed in her thoughts like a reverent echo, compelling her to advance. She could sense the relic's rhythmic pulse, which seemed to align perfectly with her own heartbeat.

"Are you prepared for this?" Aerin's voice was hushed, his gaze mirroring the seriousness of their mission.

"I'm as prepared as I can be," she responded, although her voice revealed the whirlwind of feelings inside her—fear, excitement, and resolve.

The Guardian's words echoed through the air, his ethereal form shimmering like the mist they had crossed. "Remember, Lysandra, the Heart of Shadows holds immense power, but your unity and compassion will restore what has been fractured."

"Compassion," she whispered, the word echoing in her

mind, settling in with the fragments of hope and strength she held onto.

Her gaze met those of her companions, and in each set of eyes, she saw determination and unwritten commitments.

"Guardian," Lysandra started, taking a deep breath and tightening her hold on the Ouroboros. "We understand."

The Guardian started to vanish, giving a last nod that expressed approval and trust. When his light faded, the room breathed, freeing them from its solemn grip.

"Time to move," Feyla declared, shattering the respectful silence. With skillful hands, she neatly stored her tools, each one a testament to her creativity.

We must find our courage quickly because Aviara won't wait for us.

Lysandra responded, "Nor should she," as she ensured the Ouroboros were safely stored in the leather pouch beside her. With Shadow faithfully by her side, she turned towards the chamber entrance, her determination mirrored in his unwavering stare.

"The end is not in her binding," she declared, her voice resounding through the ancient stones. The healing process involves addressing the internal rifts within us and the hearts of the people of Erenor.

"Then we should bandage those wounds," Aerin suggested, unsheathing his sword. The gleaming blade reflected the faint light, guiding their way forward.

"United," Lysandra confirmed, guiding them out of the

Chamber of Sorrows. She walked carefully, silently promising to use the Heart of Shadows not for revenge but to bring much-needed healing to Erenor.

The narrow hallway from the Chamber of Sorrows was so tight that even Shadow had to squeeze himself against Lysandra.

As they ventured away from the stagnant air within the chamber, the heavy weight of betrayal that had haunted them for centuries appeared to dissipate, leaving a growing sense of resolve.

"It seems like we're leaving behind our old selves," Feyla whispered, her voice soft yet distinct within the small area.

"Like emerging from a cocoon," Eolande chimed in, his bow secured on his back while the feathers of his arrows delicately brushed against the walls.

"Pain is an inevitable part of transformation."

Looking over her shoulder at him, Lysandra added, "Or if we suffer a loss." His eyes met hers, sharing an unspoken understanding of the sacrifices they'd already made—and those yet to come.

"Indeed," Harrow rumbled from their rear, his voice echoing like an age-old entity that had observed the triumphs and downfalls of innumerable champions. However, it is also where strength originates.

The passage led them into the enchanted forest of Lumin, where the mystical barriers they had passed through now stood silently guarding their way out.

The atmosphere in this area was invigorating, mingling with

the smell of pine and the hope of sunrise filtering through the majestic trees.

Feyla adjusted her hood and remarked, "Every spirit behind us held onto their pain until it consumed them."

"Yet they found release in our empathy," Eolande pointed out, his hand finding Feyla's. Their fingers entwined, a visible sign of the bond that had grown stronger within the haunted depths of the chamber.

"Empathy... and action," Lysandra corrected gently, her gaze sweeping over her companions. They were battle-worn, each scar and bruise a testament to their courage. But the inner battles they had faced, the trials of the soul, marked them just as deeply.

Harrow snorted, a plume of smoke rising from his nostrils as he stretched his vast wings. "Words are wind without conviction to anchor them."

With his hand resting on the pommel of his sword, Aerin proposed a silent vow to fight until peace had been restored. "Then let's suggest that we be the gale that uproots the decay Aviara has sown."

"An uprooting followed by renewal," Lysandra resolved. She turned to face the path ahead, the first rays of sunlight filtering through the leaves to dance upon her blade. Shadow stood alert, his ears perked forward, ready to leap into the fray at her command.

"Renewal," she repeated, more to herself than to the others, a whisper of hope that threaded through the fabric of their shared determination.

"Let's move," she commanded then, her tone brooking no argument. But there was no need for an argument.

"Into the light, then," Eolande said, stepping forward with a grace born of the wilds.

"Into the future," Feyla agreed, her inventive mind racing with strategies and mechanisms to aid their quest.

"Into battle," Harrow declared, his voice a deep thunder that seemed to shake the earth beneath their feet.

"Into healing," Aerin concluded, the mage within him reaching out to the potential of what lay beyond the horizon.

As one, they stepped from the shadowed confines of the past, their journey through the Chamber of Sorrows not an end but a beginning—the forging of a new chapter in the tale of Erenor.

With a firm step, Lysandra led her companions away from the Chamber of Sorrows, the echo of their footsteps mingling with the chorus of dawn.

The oracle's words resonated within her, an ancient melody that haunted and guided them.

Once thick with despair, the air felt lighter, as if their presence had lifted a curse from the forest of Lumin.

"Fresh paths aren't forged by might alone," she murmured, her gaze on the horizon where light battled the retreating darkness.

"Nor by magic," Aerin said, his staff pulsing with a soft glow, a beacon against the shadowy remnants clinging to the underbrush.

"Or by clever contraptions, though they have their place," Feyla added wistfully, her fingers absently twirling a gear salvaged from her latest invention.

"Strength of heart, then," Harrow rumbled, his scaled hide shimmering with a spectrum of colors as the first sunbeams kissed his wings. "And unity."

"Exactly." Lysandra nodded, her sword reflecting the nascent light as she sheathed it. "The sorrow we witnessed; the chains we helped break are reflections of Erenor's bondage."

"Then let our empathy be the key," Eolande said, his voice serene yet laced with a fierce determination. His connection to the land hummed around him, an unspoken vow to heal the scars wrought by centuries of strife.

"Empathy... and action." Lysandra's resolve hardened like steel tempered in the flames of adversity. "We've delved into the depths of grief, but now we rise to challenge fate itself."

"Aviara and her shadow hounds will not relent," Harrow growled, his scales bristling with anticipation. His loyalty was unwavering, his readiness to protect his allies clear in every line of his muscular frame.

"Neither shall we," Lysandra declared, her eyes bright with the fire of her spirit. "Let our deeds honor those who suffered; let our courage mend what has been broken."

"Through shadow and flame, through tempest and trial,"

each voice joined the pledge, their words weaving a tapestry of conviction that would cover the wounds of their world.

"Then onward," Lysandra called, lifting her hand to signal their advance. For Erenor, for the light, we can bring it to its darkest corners. We leave behind the sorrows of the past but carry forward its lessons. Together, we'll forge a fresh path for Erenor."

With the promise of dawn at their backs, they moved as one toward whatever awaited beyond the sheltering boughs of the enchanted forest.

Each step was a testament to their shared will, each breath a defiance of the encroaching darkness that sought to claim their home.

In this moment, they were more than a band of weary travelers; they were the harbingers of hope, the architects of a future written not in sorrow but in the resolute lines of unity and the undying light of empathy.

Branches whipped at Lysandra's face as she led the way, her boots sinking into the loamy soil of the forest floor. The air here was thick with the musk of ancient trees and the distant, unsettling murmur of creatures lurking in the underbrush.

A dense fog clung to the towering trunks, turning the woods into a labyrinth of shadows and half-seen shapes.

"Keep close," Lysandra murmured her voice a low thrum that seemed to blend with the heartbeat of the forest itself. Her hand tightened around the hilt of her sword, its runes humming softly, resonating with the latent magic that saturated the land.

"Damned brambles," grunted Aerin, trailing just behind her, his eyes scanning the canopy for signs of danger. "Feels like every thorn seeks flesh."

"Focus on the path," Lysandra shot back without looking over her shoulder. "Aviara thrives on our frustration."

The sunlight that dappled through the foliage played tricks on their vision; casting illusions of movement that kept their nerves frayed.

However, Lysandra's heightened senses cut through the deception, guiding them with an unerring instinct that years of survival and battle had honed.

"Are you certain this is the way?" Feyla asked, her voice tinged with doubt as she adjusted the straps of her satchel, laden with inventions yet to be tested against their foe.

"Trust her," said the Elf, his bow at the ready, his gaze lingering on Lysandra with a mixture of admiration and concern. "She sees what we do not."

"Whatever lies ahead," Lysandra replied, "we'll face it together. Remember the Chamber of Sorrows; those spirits found peace because we stood united."

"United, then," Harrow rumbled, his dragon body a silent shadow weaving between the trees, his scales glinting briefly where the light broke through.

They pressed on, breaking the oppressive silence with the whisper of leaves and the occasional snap of a twig beneath their feet.

With each step, they delved deeper into the unknown. The air seemed to thicken as if the forest resisted their passage through it.

"Aviara's presence lingers here," Lysandra said, touching a tree trunk blackened by dark magic. "We're on the right path."

"Let her come," Aerin growled. "I have a score to settle with that one."

"Patience," Lysandra warned, sensing the tension coiling within him. "Our battles are chosen with care, not rage."

"Words of wisdom," Feyla added, clasping Aerin's shoulder. "We'll need clear heads and sharp wits."

"Clear heads," echoed Harrow, his voice a deep rumble that vibrated through the earth.

"Then let us move with purpose," Lysandra concluded, pushing forward again, her determination undiminished by the darkness that sought to swallow them whole.

In the forest's heart, where the sun rarely touched and the shadows danced with secrets, they continued their quest, bound by their shared destiny and the knowledge that the fate of Erenor rested upon their shoulders.

Their journey was fraught with danger, but the lessons of the past blazed within them, lighting their way with the promise of unity and the strength of their unbreakable bond.

The forest seemed to convulse, dark energy pulsing through the gnarled roots and into their legs. Without warning, shadows detached from the underbrush, coalescing into sinister forms with razor-sharp claws and glowing red eyes.

Chapter 18

AVIARA'S SORCERER

Lysandra's sword was in her hand instantly, its silver blade gleaming as if to scorn the darkness surrounding them.

"Circle formation!" she barked, the practiced command ringing clear above the snarls of Aviara's minions.

Aerin moved fluidly at her side, her blades flashing with deadly precision. The creatures leaped forward, a whirlwind of malice, but met the cold bite of steel instead.

Feyla's mechanical contraptions whirred to life, launching a volley of arrows that found homes in the twisted flesh of their assailants.

"Keep them at bay!" Lysandra called her voice a beacon amidst the chaos.

Countless battles refined the skill of each strike and lunge. Despite their proficiency, the enemies were, without end, an ocean of malevolence with the sole purpose of submerging them.

"Retreat!" Lysandra's order sliced through the clamor as she realized the futility of their stand.

"To the cliff's edge!"

They retreated, taking desperate yet calculated steps, while the minions relentlessly pursued them.

The ground abruptly disappeared from the edge, revealing an unfathomable darkness below, with depths shrouded in shadows deeper than the night.

On the verge of collapse, they found themselves surrounded by the enemy, a relentless force fueled by animosity and an insatiable hunger.

Drawing from her inner well of magic, Lysandra said, "I need a protective cover." "I have an idea."

Her friends stood together, forming a barrier with their bodies and determination, fighting not for a win but for every precious second. Lysandra's surroundings buzzed with energy as she skillfully maneuvered her hands, creating elaborate designs that pulled light strands from the dark woods.

"Stay near," she commanded, projecting the spell outward. Illusions appeared within their group, projecting light and sound that imitated their every action, confusing an otherwise calm situation.

"Over here!" Harrow's voice resonated, pointing to a concealed pathway covered in vines and darkness, a hidden staircase carved into the side of the cliff.

Quickly descending, they used the false echoes of their battle above to cover their escape.

"Don't stop," Lysandra urged, being the last person to depart from the edge. With a brief glance over her shoulder, she witnessed the minions viciously attacking the luminous specters, momentarily fooled by her sorcery.

"You did it," Aerin exclaimed, out of breath but grateful, as they huddled beneath the protective cover of an overhanging ledge. "But Aviara won't be fooled for long."

"We won't be long," Lysandra stated, sheathed her sword, its enchanted inscriptions still emitting a soft hum. "We just need to stay one step ahead."

"Rather than spending time appreciating the view, let's keep going."

"I agree," Lysandra nodded, guiding them further into the unknown, towards the relic, Aviara, and the fate that awaited them all.

Lysandra's boots slid on the loose stones as the path in front of her collapsed, revealing a deep ravine. Darkness clawed at the edges of the yawning abyss that lay before them. Her companions suddenly stopped behind her, panting as they gazed into the shadowy chasm.

"Are there no limits to these challenges?"

"There is just a single route," Lysandra announced, unsheathing her runic sword. The archaic engravings on the blade shimmered as if they had an appetite for darkness. She lifted the weapon into the air with a single fluid movement, and its runes blazed with energy.

The sword shone with a brilliant light, its luminescence flowing through the void like delicate threads of morning sunlight. It hardened into a bridge, a delicate yet resilient structure. "Hurry before it disappears," she urged.

Trusting in Lysandra's magic, the group moved swiftly and without hesitation. Whispers emerged from the depths as they crossed, suggesting hidden observers lurking in the shadows.

Despite everything, the bridge stayed strong, gently carrying them across with its glowing light until they reached their destination.

"We shouldn't stay here for gratitude," Feyla remarked, glancing over her shoulder at the fading ephemeral creation. It's possible that the beings living here won't be happy about us intruding.

"Alright, let's move forward," Lysandra responded, putting her sword back into its sheath as the remaining traces of its radiance faded away.

The earth beneath them moved, exposing a vast desert. The scorching heat dominated the horizon, causing it to ripple, while the never-ending stretch of sand resembled a golden sea, eager to consume everything within its reach.

Waves of intense heat shimmered above the sandy dunes, warping the air and threatening anyone brave enough to venture across this scorching desert landscape.

"Don't wander off," Lysandra commanded, struggling to see through the glaring light. "And keep an eye on your water."

As they made their way through the sandy terrain, a gust of wind howled, pelting their skin with stinging grains.

The sandstorms emerged like vengeful ghosts, obscuring the sun and transforming daylight into a hazy twilight.

Lysandra yelled, "Form a circle!" above the deafening storm. They gathered together, their backs hunched against the strong winds, each protecting the others with their bodies.

"Can we withstand this storm of fury?"

"We can only make progress if we continue to push ourselves! With instincts sharpened by numerous battles, she pressed forward. They defied the desert's fury with every step, refusing to give in.

Their strength derived from their unity, and their shared resolve acted as a beacon of hope amidst the swirling chaos. Side by side, they fought their way out of the storm, exhausted and covered in dust but undefeated.

"Are we all here and accounted for?"

"I'm in top form," Aerin said, his smirk not quite perceptible behind the grime.

With sand falling from her hair, Feyla quipped, "That's something we should avoid doing again."

In that fleeting moment, their laughter provided a much-needed respite from the difficulties of their quest.

It reminded them of the unbreakable bonds that held them together, the unshakeable friendships forged through shared experiences of danger and darkness.

Lysandra solemnly vowed that Aviara would cover all the expenses, her eyes becoming intense as she gazed towards the horizon, where peril and fate awaited.

With its vast rolling sand dunes, the desert seemed to go on forever. Peering into the horizon, Lysandra squinted as her eyes caught a peculiar irregularity in the sand—a faint contour that held whispered secrets buried within.

With a gesture, she directed the group toward the partially revealed archway, the entrance to a forgotten temple.

Noticing the absence of Aviara's minions, Eolande remarked, "It appears as if this place has remained undiscovered by them," as he instinctively readied his arrow.

"Or maybe they never actually left," Feyla remarked, her hand subtly inching towards the array of gadgets attached to her belt.

"Remain vigilant," Lysandra directed, assuming the role of leader and brandishing her sword, its magical markings shimmering with a sense of imminent power.

They entered the dark depths of the temple, feeling the temperature drop as they escaped the blazing sun.

Lysandra's blade illuminated the corridors, where hieroglyphs and statues of deities decorated the walls. Their watchful eyes carefully tracked the intruders' every move.

Shadow emitted a warning hiss while maneuvering through the intricate passages.

As the first trap was sprung, the room echoed with a lethal click, followed by arrows swiftly shooting out from secret alcoves.

Aerin cast a spell, creating a protective energy dome that shielded them just in the nick of time.

"Great job," Lysandra complimented, sharing a swift, affirming glance with Aerin before continuing.

"Mind your footing," Harrow cautioned, "this place is filled with trickery."

Ahead of them were more traps, such as unstable floors that could collapse under their weight, walls that posed a threat of crushing them, and ghostly whispers that aimed to ensnare their minds.

Every attempt required precise coordination and teamwork, like a delicate dance where a single mistake could lead to disaster.

"I've got it!" Feyla exclaimed, swiftly disabling a complicated lock with her agile fingers, granting them entry to the inner sanctum.

"Quick thinking," Lysandra acknowledged, impressed by Feyla's ingenuity.

They faced the last puzzle in the temple's heart—a mosaic spanned the floor, depicting scenes of ancient battles and alliances.

It was a riddle written in stone, and the solution lay in the footsteps of history.

"Remember Master Elarion's teachings," Lysandra murmured, her mind racing through lore and legend.

With a careful eye, she traced a path across the mosaic, each step unlocking a piece of the past until the floor shifted, revealing a stairway spiraling downwards.

"Down we go then," Aerin said with a wry smile, leading the descent into the depths.

They emerged not into darkness but a burst of life at the foot of the stairs—an oasis that defied the barren world above.

Palm trees clustered around a serene pool, their leaves whispering secrets to the wind.

Ripe and inviting fruits hung heavy on the branches, while clear water promised relief from their parched throats and dusty skin.

"Is this real?" Eolande asked, awe coloring his voice.

"It feels like a dream," Feyla agreed, her guard lowering momentarily as she reached out to touch the cool liquid.

"Let's restock and replenish," Lysandra suggested, her leader's mantle never fully slipping as she watched their surroundings. "But stay vigilant. This could still be another test."

The group dispersed, tending to their needs while maintaining readiness. Harrow bathed in the pool, his scales gleaming under the filtered sunlight.

Eolande plucked fruit from the trees, his movements graceful and precise. Shadow lapped at the water's edge, his senses ever alert.

"Thank you," Lysandra whispered to the oasis, feeling a rare moment of peace settle over her. Here, in this unexpected sanctuary, the weight of destiny felt lighter on her shoulders.

They would face Aviara soon enough, but for now, they could breathe.

"I'm Ready to leave when you are," Aerin declared after a while, his eyes meeting Lysandra's with renewed determination.

"Then let's move out," she responded, rising to her feet.

"Erenor awaits its saviors."

Together, they stepped back into the desert's embrace, the memory of the oasis lingering like a promise—a fleeting taste of what could be if they prevailed against the encroaching darkness.

A black-robed sorcerer emerged from the gathering darkness at the center of the oasis, disrupting its calmness.

Lysandra instinctively reached for her sword, her heightened senses honed by countless victorious battles.

Malevolent energy filled the air while the sorcerer's eyes shimmered with a cruel anticipation.

"Aviara sends her regards," he hissed, his voice a serpent's whisper.

Aerin's staff shimmered with powerful runes of protection.

His face became stern, lines forming on his forehead as he warned, "Don't take another step."

"Save your breath," the sorcerer sneered, raising a gnarled staff adorned with dark crystals. Shadows writhed around him, answering his call.

"Attack formation!" Lysandra's authoritative voice rang out, prompting the group to unite and move as a cohesive unit, seamlessly combining their magical abilities and strength.

Harrow spread his wings, using them as a protective barrier against the dark magic, as Feyla prepared a variety of enchanted devices, her creative thoughts racing.

Dark tendrils erupted from the sorcerer's fingertips, lashing out violently as if they were seeking living flesh.

Lysandra's blade intercepted the dark energies as she engaged in combat, causing the light to dance off the metal in a dazzling display.

Using their magical abilities, Aerin cast spells and conjured radiant barriers to enhance their defenses in the sweltering desert.

"Concentrate on where it all begins!"

"I understand!" Feyla shouted, propelling a mechanical contraption into the air, where it twirled before bursting into a brilliant explosion of light.

The sorcerer hesitated; his concentration shattered.

Taking advantage of the moment, Lysandra lunged forward, her sword moving with expert precision. The staff's integrity gradually deteriorated as the metal and dark crystal clashed.

Retaliating, the sorcerer unleashed a wave of corruptive magic, striking Lysandra and causing her to stagger back.

Aerin's commanding voice boomed, "Hold your ground!" as he unleashed his magic to counter the attack.

Harrow roared with a fiery rage, releasing a torrent of flames that scorched the sorcerer's cloak. With agility, Shadow weaved in and out of the commotion, a silent avenger delivering swift strikes from the darkness.

Despite having been injured in the battle, Lysandra rose to her feet with a determined and unyielding expression.

Each member's strengths compensated for their teammates' weaknesses, resulting in cohesive teamwork.

With a powerful cry that resonated throughout the desert,

she forcefully drove her sword into the sorcerer's staff, causing it to break apart into a myriad of dark fragments.

The sorcerer let out a scream that echoed through the air, his power fading away like mist when exposed to the sun until all that remained was a withered husk that crumbled into dust.

Lysandra panted heavily as she wiped the blood off her brow, the sensation of her recent wounds adding to her discomfort.

"Hurry, deal with your injuries," she commanded, her voice filled with the gravity of their unspoken voyage.

Despite the adrenaline rushing through her veins, Feyla skillfully made salves and bandages with steady hands.

"Is there a chance we'll reach our destination before the deadline?"

Meeting everyone's gaze, Lysandra saw her own resolve echoed in their expressions. "We must," she stated simply. "Erenor depends on us."

Bandaging their wounds and emboldened by the victory, they pushed forward, the desert sands erasing any trace of the oasis and the conflict that took place there.

Every move was a declaration, a solemn oath to fix the fragmented land that awaited them.

"Aviara will not succeed," Lysandra vowed, her words carried away by the wind. "While we remain united, it won't happen."

Lysandra's breath formed visible puffs in the cold air as she climbed the steep cliff, her fingers gripping the sharp ice cautiously.

Above them stood the grand mountain range, a massive presence crowned with snow and bearing the weathered marks of countless centuries.

Every grip required a quiet struggle, every step a defiant act against the unyielding force of gravity.

"Don't stop," Aerin grunted from beneath, the sound of his ice axes striking steadily, marking his own ascent.

With a hint of both exhaustion and wonder, Feyla called out, "We're getting close." The inventor's gadgets, usually full of life and motion, hung dormant against the mountain's chill embrace.

Despite the cold, the dragon Harrow climbed resolutely, demonstrating the immense challenge ahead.

Closer and closer, the summit loomed, a vigilant figure against the painted sky. The high altitude burned Lysandra's lungs, but the weight of their mission weighed heaviest on her shoulders.

The hidden relic, positioned on the other side of the precipice, held the key to Erenor's uncertain fate.

"Behold!" Harrow exclaimed triumphantly as they reached the highest point of the last ridge.

They witnessed a breathtaking world unfurling beneath them, a masterpiece crafted from the very fabric of existence—mountains, and woodlands seamlessly interwoven with shimmering rivers of precious metals.

However, it was not the beauty that took their breath away.

"By the stars..." Feyla murmured, her usual rapid flow of speech reduced to a mere dribble in the presence of such a magnificent sight.

Lysandra moved ahead, her boots crunching on the fresh snow, until she reached the precipice.

The cold bit through her cloak, but the anticipation sent shivers down her spine. Aviara's shadow spread across the land, an indelible mark that no amount of light could remove.

"No matter what lies ahead," she declared, turning towards her comrades, "we will confront it as a united front."

As one, they echoed the words, their voices merging into a sacred oath that held them together with a strength surpassing any incantation.

From the depths, a gust of wind emerged, bringing the fragrance of pine and the faint thunder of hidden waterfalls.

The mountain seemed to recognize their presence, allowing them to proceed to the upcoming challenges.

Aerin, his eyes gleaming with a resolute resolve that had guided them on their journey, suggested, "Then it's time to put an end to this."

"For the fallen, for the future, for all we hold dear."

Giving a nod, Lysandra led them down the hill. Their descent wasn't solely about reaching the relic but an expedition into the core of their own hopes and fears.

The shadows lengthened with every step they took, the day grew darker, and the decisive battle loomed closer.

Chapter 19

DOPPELGÄNGER

Lysandra's breath created a cloud of mist in the dimly lit arena, her heart racing in a chaotic beat as she confronted the menacing figure before her.

The minion resembled her so closely that it seemed like a perfect reflection—an evil twin born from darkness and malevolence. Its eyes emitted an eerie glow that sent shivers down Lysandra's spine.

Lysandra drew her sword from its sheath, and it emitted a melodic hum. The blade shimmered in the dull, murky light. With grace, she executed a well-practiced dance of movement, honed through countless battles.

But this was no ordinary enemy. It matched her strike for strike, parry for parry. The clash of metal and the soft whispers in the shadows created an eerie silence.

"Is this what scares you, Lysandra? Fighting yourself?" The minion hissed, its voice a distorted echo of her own. Lysandra gritted her teeth, refusing to yield to its words. She swung her sword in a wide arc, forcing the creature back step by agonizing step. Sparks erupted where their blades met, casting fleeting glimpses of light over the creeping darkness.

"Or is it the fear that you'll never be good enough?" The doppelgänger taunted, a cruel smile twisting its features as it sidestepped her thrust.

The words struck a chord within Lysandra, a vulnerable point she kept buried deep beneath layers of resolve and determination. Her grip on the hilt tightened until her knuckles whitened, and the strain in her arms reminded her of the physical toll this battle was taking.

"Silence!" she spat, launching herself at the minion with renewed vigor. Each swing of her sword was an attempt to silence the creature before her and the insecurities that gnawed at her spirit.

"Face it, Lysandra," the mimic jeered, fading into the shadows only to reappear behind her. "You can't escape who you are."

She whirled around, barely blocking a vicious strike that sought to end her.

Ghostly apparitions swirled around them, manifesting her deepest fears—her friends lying broken because she couldn't protect them, her own hands tainted with the blood of innocents because of choices she made.

"Stop!" Lysandra shouted, each illusion piercing her heart like shards of ice. She had to remind herself they weren't real, just twisted conjurations meant to break her will.

"Can you save them, hero?" the voices whispered, filling the arena with doubt.

Lysandra's chest heaved, and her breathing labored under the weight of her armor and the crushing pressure of her thoughts. No, she wouldn't let these phantoms undermine her. They were all lies.

With a defiant cry, Lysandra charged, her sword a blur of motion as she fought through the pain, the fatigue, and the assault on her mind.

This battle was more than a test of skill; it was a crucible for her soul, a challenge she could not afford to lose.

"Enough!" she roared, her voice rising over clashing swords and spectral murmurs. With one final, great effort, she summoned every ounce of her strength and plunged her blade into the heart of the shadowy fiend.

The minion screamed—a sound both alien and eerily familiar—as it disintegrated into motes of darkness that dissipated like smoke on the wind.

Heavy and absolute silence fell upon the arena, leaving Lysandra standing alone, victorious yet shaken to her core.

She knew this was just the beginning. Lysandra took a deep breath and sheathed her sword. She resolved to face whatever lay ahead, knowing that her true enemy was not the darkness around her but the doubts within.

Aerin's voice interrupted her, urgent and sharp. "Lysandra! Stop this madness!"

Lysandra turned to face him, her eyes blazing with intensity, matching the flickering shadows around them. "I have to keep going, Aerin. There is no turning back."

Aerin argued, his robe swirling as his healing magic emerged. "Your strength is limited. You can't keep fighting these nightmares on your own."

"Then step back and let me finish it!" Lysandra snapped, her sword still humming with the remnants of the battle.

"By the gods, Lysandra, you're not invincible!" Aerin's hands trembled, whether from fear or anger, she could not tell.

"Neither are you," she retorted, tightening her grip on her sword. "But I don't see you backing down from a fight."

"Because my fights don't threaten to tear you apart!" His words echoed off the stone walls, mirroring their clashing wills.

"Enough!" Lysandra shouted, stepping closer, her face inches from his. The air crackled with unsaid truths and unyielding stances.

"Is this what it comes to? You are doubting me at every turn?" Her voice was a low growl, each word accusing.

"Of course, I doubt you when you're reckless!" Aerin shot back, his eyes reflecting his tormented thoughts. "Isn't it my role to protect you?"

"Protect me?" Lysandra laughed bitterly, devoid of humor. "Since when does protecting me mean undermining my every decision?"

"Stop twisting my words!" Aerin's control slipped, and a gust of wind rose, stirring the dust at their feet. "I'm trying to save you from yourself!"

"Save me?" The notion fueled her anger, as the shadows had empowered her adversary. "Or save yourself from the pain of watching me fight my battles?"

"Damn it, Lysandra!" Aerin yelled; his restraint shattered like glass. "Can't you see I'm doing this because I—"

"Care?" she interrupted, her voice icy. "Or is it that you can't bear the thought of being left behind?"

Their breaths mingled in the air, warm puffs in the chilling void of the arena. For a moment, neither spoke, their harsh pants the only testament to their raging emotions.

"Alright, go," Aerin finally whispered, but his words hit Lysandra with more force than any unseen attack. Chase after your achievements. Chase after your mortality.

He walked away from her, leaving her standing in silence, burdened by the weight of their argument, which felt heavier than the armor on her body.

As Lysandra watched him leave, her heart raced like the beat of war drums, bracing herself for the conflicts ahead, both inside and outside.

With a graceful arc, Lysandra's blade sliced through the air, a shining silver streak contrasting the approaching darkness.

Exhausted, her muscles trembled as she deflected yet another fierce attack from her shadow, gasping for breath.

The minion, a grotesque copy of her appearance, replicated her every move, its eyes hollow where her own fears shimmered in response.

"That's it!" Aerin's voice broke through the whirlwind of enchantments and machinery, his silhouette blending with the shadows that threatened to engulf him.

Lysandra snapped, "Don't get involved in this," as she swung her sword in a wide arc, forcing the minion to retreat. "I have to put an end to this!"

"By taking your own life? Is that your definition of victory?"

Amid the turmoil, their glances intertwined like two storms merging. She glimpsed more than just fear in his eyes; she saw an unfiltered and desperate plea.

A fracture formed within her, extending through the fortress she had erected to guard her emotions.

"Curse you, Aerin," she murmured, feeling her determination weaken as she realized his true feelings.

"Curse me, then," he retorted, advancing closer, his hands quivering yet steadfast as they extended towards her.

"However, please do it with the knowledge that my love for you is stronger than any war ever fought."

With a resounding clatter, the swords slipped from their hands, hitting the stone floor and creating an echoing surrender.

As everything fell silent, Lysandra was overwhelmed by the burden of everything she had fought against—the darkness, the minion, and her own stubborn pride.

Aerin stood before her, radiating warmth that cut through the arena's coldness. Gently, he touched her cheek with his fingers, filled with a longing that matched hers.

Their lips collided in a passionate kiss, culminating in all the suppressed emotions, disagreements, and instances in which they had avoided facing the truth.

Gripping his tunic, she pulled him closer as if she wanted to fuse their beings together. With each passing moment, their kiss grew deeper, eradicating any hint of darkness and revealing only the passionate intensity of their bond.

"I'm sorry," Lysandra whispered as she pressed her lips against his, her voice filled with resilience and fragility.

"There is no need for forgiveness," Aerin whispered softly, kissing her jawline. I only need to understand and be with you against whatever darkness comes."

In that embrace, the world beyond ceased to exist. The whispers of the arena, the clash of swords, the encroaching threat—all faded into insignificance.

There was only them, Lysandra and Aerin, their hearts beating a fierce rhythm that promised they would face the coming dawn as one.

The world around them ceased to exist as they held each other tightly with raw passion. The sounds of the arena, the taste of metal from swords clashing, and the overwhelming threat—all fade into a blurry haze.

Lysandra and Aerin were the only ones in their reality, their hearts pounding with a fierce rhythm mirrored their intense desire for each other—a promise to face the morning together.

Lysandra was held tightly by Aerin, their bodies glistening with sweat after their intimate moment. His powerful chest's rhythmic movement contrasted with her heart's rapid beating.

They paid no attention to the chill of the night, as it had no significance in this location. With a delicate dance, her fingers glided over his desire-sculpted skin; each touches an unspoken testament to their possessive union.

As the fervent union ended, Lysandra found herself cradled in the comforting embrace of Aerin, his chest rising and falling in a soothing cadence that eased the rapid fluttering of her own heart.

The warmth they shared protected them from the surrounding darkness. She traced aimless patterns on his skin, each touch silently reinforcing their deep connection.

"Do you feel afraid?" she murmured softly in the silence, her tone lacking the usual resoluteness of a skilled swordswoman.

With a tremor in his voice, Aerin confessed, his breath lightly ruffling her hair. Losing you is my greatest fear, not the battle itself.

"Then we fight. We survive." Lysandra's tone hardened with resolve, even as her fingers trembled slightly against his flesh.

"Until the very end," he agreed, sealing the vow with a kiss pressed to her forehead, a mage's promise mingling with the warrior's oath.

The encroaching dawn crept upon them unaware, a stealthy harbinger of the struggles. Its first light pierced the veil of darkness, casting shadows that retreated like vanquished enemies.

Lysandra felt Aerin's reluctant shift beneath her as the silvery glow intensified.

With a regretful voice that mirrored her own silent sadness, he murmured, "The morning has come."

"It's too quick," she replied, though they both acknowledged that time was a luxury they couldn't indulge in. They had an unspoken agreement: the peaceful moments were rare and valuable.

Lysandra sighed as she lifted herself to a sitting position, feeling Aerin's hands gently slip away from her despite his firm grip. Their eyes locked, and the intensity of their stare communicated a silent exchange filled with promises that words could not express.

Lysandra's voice was intense as she started, "No matter what happens, always remember that we are greater than what Aviara molded us to be."

"We determine our own fate," Aerin interjected, his hand finding hers. Their fingers were entwined, symbolizing their unity.

The cave came into sharper view as they rose, and the harsh reality they faced replaced the peacefulness of their embrace.

Awaiting them were armor and weapons, silent protectors of the day's solemn responsibilities. However, they stayed motionless momentarily, two individuals trapped in the center of the approaching storm.

Lysandra was determined. She said, "Let's demonstrate the intensity of our passion." She squeezed Aerin's hand briefly before releasing it.

"Let's do it then," he replied, his voice bearing the weight of absolute certainty.

With a sense of expectation, they wordlessly prepared themselves, each motion intentional, their fluid movements a testament to the countless battles they had fought together.

They frequently made eye contact, each glance as a reminder of the strong connection they had built through challenging times.

By the time they finished dressing, the sun had risen, erasing any trace of the previous night. Side by side, they stood at the entrance, prepared to enter the illuminated path that marked the beginning of a long-awaited judgment.

"Don't forget about our night," Aerin whispered gently, giving her a final, lingering gaze.

"How can I ever let go of the memories we created together?"

United, they faced the day with unwavering defiance, knowing that their fate awaited them.

Lysandra's fingers wrapped around the sword's hilt, finding solace in its familiar heaviness as she surveyed the individuals standing alongside her.

The atmosphere is filled with the hushed sound of armor clinking and boots shuffling, foreshadowing the impending symphony of war reverberating throughout Erenor's fields.

Aerin stood next to her, making slight adjustments to his gauntlet straps. Their eyes briefly met before they glanced away.

"Is everyone set?"

She responded, "We're as ready as we can possibly be," her voice not showing the inner storm.

The rest of their friends created a tableau of quiet determination in their presence.

They all inspected their weapons, running their fingers along the sharp edges of blades and securing small vials of potions to their belts. There was no need for words.

With the break of dawn, the eastern sky blushed, casting strokes of gold and crimson on their faces. It was finally the right time.

With a confident and commanding tone, Lysandra ordered, "It's time to leave."

They exited one by one, stepping out from the darkness of their camp and into the welcoming light of day.

Bathed in the morning sun, their armor blazed with a fiery glow, mirroring the intense determination that fueled them. Through achieving victory or facing defeat with courage and determination.

"Don't forget our true identity!" Aerin chanted, casting a protection spell that glimmered like a shield of pure optimism.

"We won't forget," they all solemnly chanted, a united voice of resistance against the looming darkness that threatened to invade their land and existence.

As they progressed, their path converged towards an inevitable destiny: a climactic battle that would seal Erenor's fate. They would engage in combat, giving it their all.

Lysandra's muscles tensed, mirroring the tension of a drawn bowstring. Her breaths were in perfect sync with the pounding of her heart.

She surged ahead, the weight of her sword familiar and reassuring in her grip. Memories of her shadow-doppelgänger, defeated by her own hand, infused her limbs with an unyielding fortitude.

"Today, we reclaim our world," she roared over the clamor of armored bodies moving as one behind her. Their footsteps thundered across the barren landscape, a drumbeat heralding the onset of war.

Aerin flanked her, his features etched with grim resolve. "Aviara's darkness will yield to our light," he promised through gritted teeth, the air around him crackling with the latent power of his spells.

Around them, their companions' faces were stone-carved replicas of determination. Everyone had been scarred by battles past, yet alight with the fire of those to come.

Each warrior's gaze held the reflection of Erenor's fate, and they would not look away.

"Her minions are nothing but shadows," Lysandra called out, her voice slicing through the tension. "We are the dawn!"

"Shadows fade!" echoed a chorus of voices, their conviction piercing the looming dread.

Chapter 20

THE ARBOREALS

Lysandra's grip tightened around the hilt of her sword as the group trudged through the dense undergrowth.

She secured the relic, a stone of pulsating energy and ancient inscriptions, to her belt, and its weight reminded her of their mission.

It was a mission to find Aviara, not as the malevolent force they had all feared but as a deity who had suffered at the hands of cosmic misfortune.

"Keep your senses sharp," Harrow's voice rumbled like distant thunder, his massive form casting a protective shadow over them.

His scales shimmered with an inner fire, a testament to his power and ancient wisdom. "The fracture has turned a friend into an enemy; don't trust what you see."

"Aviara," Lysandra whispered, more to herself than anyone else. She tried to reconcile the image of the ruthless deity with that of a being once harmonious with nature.

But it was arduous, feeling the imbalance in the air they breathed, tasting the bitterness of corruption that now plagued the land.

"Even the mightiest can fall," said Eolande, his eyes scanning the horizon. It's tragic to lose oneself so completely."

"Tragic, but we mustn't forget the danger she presents now." Lysandra's words were firm, though the knowledge of Aviara's past gnawed at her resolve.

Their journey brought them to a clearing where the Moon-fire Foxes appeared as if summoned from the essence of night. With fur aglow, they moved with ethereal grace, circling the group before darting ahead, beckoning them to follow.

"Beautiful," Feyla breathed out, her hand reaching futilely as one fox danced beyond her touch.

"More than beauty, they are a sign," said Eolande, his eyes reflecting the foxes' luminescence. "The Arboreals are near."

And indeed, as they followed the foxes' lead, the trees changed. The bark seemed to pulse with a life of its own, and soon, they stood before the Arboreals—sentient beings as old as time, their limbs intertwined with wisdom and magic.

"Heroes of Erenor," a group of Arboreals, spoke harmoniously, mimicking the rustling of leaves.

"The fracture has unbalanced the elements, twisted the creatures, and left our goddess isolated in her despair."

"Can she be saved?" Lysandra asked, stepping forward. "Can we restore what was lost?"

"Balance can be regained," someone else added. There are many dangers along the path.

"We're ready to confront any danger," Aerin declared, sharing a determined look with Lysandra.

"Pay attention to our help," the Arboreals said in unison. Magic is known for its instability.

Lysandra's fervent voice matched the situation's intensity as she replied, "Let it be a test for us." "We'll prove ourselves worthy."

"Be cautious," Harrow interrupted, his attention drawn to the horizon, where shadows gathered. "Not all conflicts are resolved through physical combat."

Feyla declared, resting on the relic beside Lysandra, "We will fight with all our heart and soul."

The Arboreal gently whispered, "Truly, the heart often perceives what the eye cannot see," as a soft breeze carried its words.

Empowered by newfound knowledge and the mysterious blessings of the Arboreals, the team continued their journey, guided by the waning radiance of the Moonfire Foxes.

Every stride they made brought them closer to Aviara, closer to healing a broken world, and closer to the intertwined fate that bound them all.

Guided by the moonlight, the Moonfire Foxes gracefully led the way, their urgency hidden beneath their elegance.

Their coats sparkled like liquid moonlight, illuminating the forest's undergrowth with an otherworldly luminescence, turning the world into a captivating blend of fantasies and darkness.

The whispers of the ancient trees danced across Lysandra's skin, a language she knew in her bones, even though it remained unspoken.

Soft whispers of the leaves suggested secrets meant for the daring listeners as the air buzzed with enigmatic knowledge.

"Pay attention to where you're walking," Aerin murmured softly from behind, his voice resonating like the forest's pulse. They were getting near; he could sense it—the thrill of discovery that sent shivers down his spine like electricity.

The foxes came to a halt at the edge of a glade, and there they found a pool that perfectly mirrored the expanse of the cosmos above. Standing at the water's edge, Lysandra's reflection shimmered alongside the stars. Her thoughts were filled with the enormity of the sight before them.

She whispered, "Aviara was once connected to this." Her words were intended more for her own ears than for anyone else's. The artifact beside her throbbed in accord, its existence a constant reminder of the burden they all bore.

"Without a doubt, child of nature," a voice resonated through the clearing, its depth and timelessness mirroring the ancient roots of the earth. Emerging from the shadows, the Arboreals presented themselves with towering shapes adorned in intricate patterns, narrating stories of life, death, and the ebb and flow of existence.

Their eyes, old and filled with centuries of wisdom, locked onto the group with an intense and kind gaze. "Much of what we knew has been destroyed by the cosmic fracture," an Arboreal whispered, each word landing like a leaf on calm water.

"The peaceful beings have transformed into feral creatures, unleashing their fury as the land wails in torment," another voice chimed in, its tone blending with the rustling leaves.

"So it's happening just as we feared," Feyla remarked, moving forward with clenched hands. "What can we do to fix what has been damaged?"

"Those who will arrive to restore harmony are mentioned in the prophecies," growled the first Arboreal. Emerging from struggle, heroes bring the bravery to restore Aviara's broken heart.

"Us?" Lysandra's voice quivered, filled with astonishment and doubt. Are we the ones spoken of in prophecy?

"Only if you choose to be," the Arboreal replied, a knowing look passing between them. "Your journey to find Aviara is also a journey to restore balance. She is the key, as are you."

"Then let us begin," Eolande declared, his resolve hardening like steel tempered in fire. "Tell us what must be done."

"Seek the heart of Aviara's realm, but be warned," cautioned the Arboreal, its branches swaying as if caressed by an unseen wind. "The path ahead will demand everything of you—strength, unity, sacrifice."

"Whatever it takes," Lysandra vowed, her eyes alight with the flame of purpose. "We will bring back the harmony that was lost."

"May the elements guide you," the Arboreal blessed, bowing

their colossal heads as the Moonfire Foxes silently slipped away, their task complete.

"Come," Aerin urged, taking Lysandra's hand and squeezing it with quiet reassurance. "Our destiny awaits."

Together, with hearts braced against the unknown, they stepped into the night, leaving the glade and its guardians behind.

The cosmic fracture had taken much from the realm, but with every stride, they pledged to reclaim it, piece by piece.

Aerin's boots crunched on the gravel, each step a syncopated beat in harmony with Lysandra's beside him.

The path before them twisted like the serpentine back of some magnificent beast, nature itself warped by the fracture's cruel hand—the once serene landscapes now twisted, the fabric of reality unraveling at its seams.

"Look there," Lysandra whispered, grabbing Aerin's hand and her other arm outstretched to point out where ruins rose from the earth, their stones etched with the weight of history.

With a reverent hush, they passed under a broken archway, glyphs humming with residual magic.

The carvings depicted Aviara in her prime, arms outstretched as if embracing the sky. They felt the echo of her former glory, a deity connected to every root and branch.

"Aviara wasn't always a harbinger of decay," Aerin mused, tracing a line over the cool stone with his fingers. "Once, she was part of a balance we can scarcely comprehend."

"Then it's balance we must restore," Lysandra replied, her

gaze reflecting the conviction that had brought them this far.

They ventured further, and the air was filled with the fragrance of moss and the memories of long-past rain. Colorful waterfalls cascaded down from gravity-defying islands, creating a symphony of vibrant hues. Mist in the air transformed into beautiful rainbows. Before their eyes, a breathtaking spectacle unfolded, both tangible and achingly beautiful, reminiscent of a storybook myth.

"It can't be," Aerin exhaled, his senses captured by the sight.

"Nothing is impossible anymore," Lysandra countered, her voice laced with the wonder that danced in her eyes. "Not with what we've seen."

As birds with radiant plumage soar, their songs resonate through the forest. Each note is tuned to evoke deep emotions within the soul.

Aerin diligently tried to commit every detail to memory to hold onto the fleeting beauty amidst Aviara's chaos.

"Remember why we're here," he reminded himself, just as much as Lysandra. "Aviara's heart..."

Finishing his sentence, she added, "It has the power to save us or destroy us," as she held his hand, her touch anchoring him against the overpowering enchantment.

"Let us not be swayed by beauty alone," Aerin urged, though the determination in his words fought the awe overflowing from his heart. "We have a guardian to face, a realm to save."

"Lead the way, hero," Lysandra teased, but her smile belied the steely determination that shone in her gaze.

"Only if you promise to keep me from getting lost in all this splendor," he quipped back, the momentary levity a balm against the gravity of their quest.

The laughter they shared was a fleeting respite, a spark of light in the encroaching gloom of their task.

The crumbling ruins transitioned into a landscape that urged them to stay alert, reminding them that although the world possessed its share of beauty, it was also accompanied by its own inherent risks.

"Stay on guard," Aerin warned his hand automatically finding its place on the hilt of his sword. "We don't know what lies ahead."

"Except for one thing," Lysandra added, squaring her shoulders as they approached the unknown. "We face it together."

Thus, they pressed on, their fates and passions intertwined, walking through the shattered world toward the core of Aviara, where their destiny awaited.

Stepping on frosted leaves, Aerin's boots made a crunching sound as he led Lysandra through the enchanted forest. The cold air bit his face, but he pressed on, navigating the dense underbrush.

As they ventured further, the night embraced them more tightly, and the nearby trees pulsated with an otherworldly glow. Instead of relying on the sun, they followed the Moonfire Foxes, mystical creatures that weaved through the trees like ethereal specters, their presence resembling stardust.

Brushing her hand against the fox's ethereal coat, Lysandra

whispered, "Beautiful." Beneath her touch, the fur gleamed, creating a mesmerizing light pattern in the clearing.

"Keep your concentration," Aerin reminded her, although he couldn't help but watch the creatures with awe and caution.

The foxes paused, their tails flicking in a silent exchange before swiftly resuming their journey, guiding the pair deeper into the heart of the grove. In that location, the Arboreals stood tall, reminiscent of ancient sentinels. Their limbs reached for the sky, adorned with glowing symbols that shone in the darkness illuminated by the moon.

"Welcome, travelers," a voice echoed, its depth resembling the earth's. A majestic tree, with bark more twisted and detailed than its relatives, emerged from the shadows, its amber eyes glowing.

Aerin respectfully bowed his head as he expressed, "Our goal is to seek the Heart of Aviara." "We wish to mend what has been broken."

"Ah, but the fracture extends beyond a mere tear in the land," the Arboreal solemnly declared, its leaves whispering secrets untold. "By tearing apart the essence of our magic, it has made it uncontrollable and chaotic."

Is there a chance that the magic can return to its original condition?

"Possibly," the Arboreal responded. "However, the path ahead is filled with danger, disrupting the equilibrium of power."

"In that case, we must continue," Aerin declared, his determination evident in his hardened expression. Aviara may have experienced a downfall, but we won't leave her to face the darkness alone.

"You won't be left on your own," the Arboreal said, offering them aid by extending a branch down to them. A seed on the tip of the branch was illuminated with a pulsating light.

"Please accept this."

"Thank you," Lysandra murmured, her voice filled with reverence as she accepted the gift. Her fingers were enclosed around it, and she could feel a pulsating energy that carried hope and danger.

Before leaving, the Arboreal warned the heroes, "Always remember that balance is the key."

As the Moonfire Foxes reappeared, they nodded with resolute determination, ready to be led away from the Arboreals' sanctuary.

Echoing a foreboding message, the whispers of the leaves behind them would persist as they journeyed into a realm desperately crying out for deliverance.

Aerin's boots lost traction on a patch of grass that inexplicably sloped upwards, causing the ground beneath her to contort as if gravity had undergone a strange transformation.

With roots exposed and hanging like peculiar aerial serpents, a grove of trees spiraled towards the sky. Grunting, he braced himself against the otherworldly landscape that unraveled before their gazes.

"Mind your footing," he called out to Lysandra, who skillfully traversed the intricate terrain with a balance of grace and caution. The Arboreal's seed pulsed in her hand, offering a glimmer of hope in this twisted reality.

"It feels like we're venturing through a chilling nightmare," she replied, her eyes focused on the horizon, where the air shimmered with an eerie glow.

"Without a doubt, this is Aviara's doing," Aerin said, his jaw clenched. The bitterness she felt had spread and affected the entire area.

The Moonfire Foxes continued, their glowing tails illuminating the path and casting eerie, dancing shadows over the twisted scenery.

The foxes effortlessly adapted to the new reality, bounding from floating stones to upside-down hills, skillfully guiding the group through the tumultuous scene with their innate understanding and agile bodies.

Lysandra asked in a hushed tone, "Do you feel it? "The magic, it's almost like it's screaming."

A powerful gust of wind, filled with whispers of mystical rage, rushed by them, causing Aerin's hair to become tousled and tugging at the edges of Lysandra's cloak. She was right; the magic here was alive, tormented, lashing out in its pain.

"The power that Aviara once had over this realm is now completely lost," Aerin remarked. "We need to find her and confront the source of this fracture."

Lysandra's features hardened with determination as she warned, "We need to do something before there's nothing left to save."

Unfazed, they continued their march, encountering rivers that flowed in reverse and trees whose canopies seemed to disappear into the ground. The cosmic fracture completely unraveled the fabric of nature, leaving behind a tangible wound on the earth.

"Watch out!" Aerin exclaimed as a boulder, hanging in the air, suddenly dropped towards them.

He swiftly protected Lysandra from danger using his sharpened reflexes from many fights.

"Thank you," she exhaled, pushing herself up. "Seems like even the laws of physics have turned against us."

"I agree. Things are completely topsy-turvy around here," he said, extending his hand to her. "However, we will fix it."

Locking eyes, they silently communicated their resolve before proceeding forward again. While journeying through the chaotic wilderness, their determination to restore Aviara and the realm to its former glory motivated them to keep going.

Despite the ground rebelling and the sky swirling with abnormal colors, they stood unwavering in their determination. Recognizing the enduring hope amidst the fragmented landscapes and the altered enchantments, they understood they were tasked with restoring what had been broken.

Aerin's hand hesitated above the ancient stone tablet, the carvings emitting a subtle golden glow as he touched them.

The ancient power resonated in the air while traces of potent spells clung to the deteriorating walls. With her silver hair flowing down her shoulders, Lysandra scrutinized the runes, her forehead wrinkled in intense concentration.

"Can you decipher anything?"

"Symbols of harmony... unity," she murmured, tracing the lines. "It speaks of balance and a time when magic flowed unimpeded through Aviara's veins."

He looked at the remnants of machinery strewn about like the bones of a long-deceased creature and concluded, "Before it was corrupted." Gears intertwined with vines, crystals flickering weakly with residual energies.

"That's right," she nodded, her mouth forming a tight line. "The civilization here understood the land's heart. They were its keepers."

Aerin moved closer to a device that challenged the usual boundaries of design with its blend of organic and engineered elements. "If we can decode their knowledge, perhaps—"

"Maybe we can mend what's been shattered," Lysandra finished, hope dancing in her eyes like the soft glow emanating from the artifacts.

They exchanged a meaningful look, feeling the gravity of their mission, before refocusing on the artifacts.

Aerin's curiosity was aroused as he suggested, "Let's find out what other mysteries this place holds."

As they continued their journey, the dense forest cover gave way, exposing a serene grove illuminated by a mystical glow.

The sight appeared to twist and shimmer, creating a distorted effect like looking through water.

At the heart of the area stood a magnificent tree embracing the sky with its branches. The roots, thick and powerful like serpents from another era, burrowed into the ground, anchoring the impressive and regal trunk.

"By the gods," Lysandra whispered, her hand finding Aerin's as they stepped forward.

"Is that—?"

"The Heart of the Realm of Aviara," she confirmed, her voice filled with awe. "The source of all magic here."

Chapter 21

THE HEART OF THE REALM OF AVIARA

Bathed in a soothing, warm glow from the pulsating light of the tree, they could feel the grove come alive with the echoing rhythm of a heartbeat.

Aerin extended his hand, half expecting resistance from the air, yet his touch encountered nothing but the sleek texture of the tree's bark. Under his touch, it hummed, a reminder of life's presence amid desolation.

"See?" Lysandra directed attention towards the base, where the roots created a beautiful archway. "I see a message or symbol etched onto this."

They both bent down to study the ancient symbols that encircled the arch. Unlike any writing they had encountered previously, the carvings quivered with an urgent message, compelling them to grasp its meaning.

"Assuming our hypothesis is accurate," she mentioned, her

finger floating over a detailed symbol, "these glyphs could hold the answer to reversing the fracture."

"We shouldn't waste any more time," Aerin said, his words filled with determination. If we must, we'll study these until the stars fade."

"Aviara must be liberated first," Lysandra emphasized, her hand gripping his tightly. As their eyes connected, a mutual resolve surged between them, evoking the energy of sparks flying from striking flint against steel.

"Until the realm is healed," he vowed, their promise hanging in the air as potent as the magic surrounding them.

Aerin's breath was thick in the electrified atmosphere, his heart pounding in his ears as he stood side by side with Lysandra.

The grove, previously a sacred place of ancient enchantment, now appeared more like a battleground as the ground trembled beneath them.

The guardian, a colossal combination of stone and cosmic energy, emerged with a deep rumble—a massive gatekeeper protecting the Heart of Aviara's Realm.

"By the ancients," Lysandra murmured, her hand reflexively reaching for her blade's hilt.

The creature's powerful roar echoed, resonating with the ages. With its eyes filled with the brilliance of stars, it focused on the group, appraising their strength.

Aerin felt the weight of their quest settle on his shoulders, understanding the gravity of the challenge they faced.

"Stand firm," he said through gritted teeth. "Remember

what we've learned. Aviara's heart is not just a beacon of power; it's a reminder of who she was—of the balance she once brought."

Lysandra responded, her voice soft but filled with unwavering determination, "Then we should make sure to remind her."

The entire group spread out, with each person taking their designated position with a unanimous nod. Shifting its form, the guardian moved, becoming a mountain with purpose and fury. With a mighty swing, a massive limb moved towards them, making the air howl in protest.

"Divide and conquer!" Aerin exclaimed, rolling away as the ground beneath him splintered from the forceful strike.

Lysandra launched herself forward, her sword singing as it sliced through the tendrils of shadow that leaped from the creature's form.

Every strike held a deeper meaning, representing their unwavering commitment and a heartfelt appeal for Aviara's redemption.

"Don't forget the person you are protecting!"

The rest joined in, casting spells and intertwining blades in a defiant dance. They had become more than just warriors.

Mystical light enveloped their arms, with ancient symbols glowing on their skin as they channeled the pure energy of Erenor into their attack.

With a mighty roar, Aerin impaled the enchanted dagger into the guardian's core, calling out, "Aviara, heed our call! The blade went deep, a symbol of hope piercing through despair.

The guardian reeled, its form wavering as though struck by the truth in their words. And within that moment of faltering, the group found their opening.

With one final, unified effort, they struck as one, their voices rising in a crescendo of resolve.

"Return to the balance you were sworn to protect!"

A blinding explosion of light engulfed the grove, the shockwave sending them sprawling.

Silence fell, oppressive and thick, as the dust settled and the light dimmed.

The guardian stood still, its towering figure now silent and watchful. A sentinel returned to its original purpose.

Panting, the group rose unsteadily, gazes locking onto the Heart of Aviara's Realm.

The pulsing light beckoned them closer, approval radiating from the ancient tree.

"Is it over?" Lysandra asked, her voice tinged with hope.

"For now," Aerin replied, offering her a weary smile. "But our task has only just begun."

With each step closer to the Heart, they understood that the real challenge was yet to come.

Despite this moment of victory, they could feel the shattered realm finally taking a breath of relief.

"We shall repair what has been shattered," Aerin murmured as they advanced together, bracing themselves to confront whatever lay ahead in Aviara's concealed recesses.

The gardens on Tyrannis became a tranquil oasis as the sun set, with the soft glow of twilight casting a golden light and the refreshing coolness of evening replacing the earlier heat.

With her silver cloak billowing behind her like a whisper of mist, Lysandra moved along the cobblestone path.

With every step, the resounding clink of her sword at her hip reminded her of the battles she had already endured and the ones that lay ahead.

Walking beside her, Aerin's mage's robe gently swayed, its intricate embroidery shimmering in the fading light.

His eyes, which typically sparkled with arcane energy, now exuded a peacefulness that matched the serenity of the gardens.

"Beautiful, isn't it?" "The way the light plays upon the leaves, it's almost as if they're dancing."

Nodding, Lysandra took a moment to enjoy the uncommon peace and quiet. "Yes, it is," she replied, aware they had the luxury of experiencing such calmness.

Without saying a word, their presence alone provided a soothing comfort that words couldn't match.

Aerin reached out and took her hand as they walked along the path adorned with blooming wisteria.

Their hands intertwined, fitting together like a puzzle. The gesture symbolized the shared experiences, trust, and unspoken bond they had forged through their journey of conflict.

Lysandra stole a quick look at him, her eyes following the

lines of his face—the firmness of his jaw, the tenderness in his eyes saved for moments like these.

She sensed a deepening connection between them that went beyond mere friendship or the adrenaline rush of fighting.

"Lysandra," Aerin's voice shattered the quiet, filled with deep emotion. Coming to a standstill, he gazed at her, reaching up with his free hand to tuck a loose strand of hair behind her ear. The lingering touch sent a warm sensation that radiated to the depths of her being.

She locked eyes with him, witnessing the vulnerability he only revealed.

"There's something I've been wanting to tell you..." he started, his thumb gently tracing the contour of her jaw, a wordless expression of his longing. "My feelings for you have grown deeper than I ever thought possible." His words were an offering, laid bare in the dying light.

In the space between heartbeats, Lysandra felt a surge of courage. In the last embrace of the sun's rays, guarded by ancient stone and whispering flora, the truth hung palpable and heavy in the air.

With their hands still intertwined, a powerful symbol of solidarity in the face of impending darkness, they stood on the edge of an uncertain future, strengthened by a love they hadn't expected but which they had grown to treasure.

As Aerin's confession hung in the air, Lysandra let out a breath, feeling a mix of emotions flood over her.

The quickening of her pulse reminded her of the challenges

they had confronted, but this confrontation was unlike any other—they relied solely on the truth living in their hearts, with no need for physical weapons.

Her voice remained steady as she spoke, yet there was an undertone of emotion that quivered just beneath the surface. "I feel the same way, Aerin," she said.

"Being with you gives me a sense of peace and strength I've never known." Her words carried the weight of her warrior spirit yet revealed the blossoming tenderness only he could awaken.

The gardens blurred into a tapestry of color as Aerin's gaze held hers. There was magic in his eyes, not of incantations or spells but of something more potent. A silent understanding passed between them, a recognition of souls intertwined by fate and choice.

Without warning, the space between them vanished as Aerin drew her into a kiss. It was gentle—recognition of the fragile state of their world—and passionate, a defiance of the darkness that crept at the edges of Tyrannis.

Lysandra's hands instinctively grasped the coarse texture of his tunic, her slender fingers tightly gripping it as if clinging to the vibrant pulse of existence.

She could feel the fabric's rugged fibers against her skin, hear the subtle rustle as her hands moved, and catch a faint whiff of the scent lingering on the tunic's surface, all while holding onto the precious essence of life.

As they parted, a breathless moment lingered. Aerin's hands cradled her face, a mage's touch that now sought not to wield power but to memorize the contours of her skin. His thumb swept across her cheek, a soft caress that spoke volumes in the quiet dusk.

"Your courage inspires me," Aerin murmured, his voice barely above a whisper yet resonant with the depth of his conviction. "It's like a beacon, guiding me through shadow and turmoil."

Lysandra leaned into his hand, relishing the touch that brought her solace amidst the chaotic world that lay beyond.

The soft whisper of the wind carried the scent of rain, mingling with the lingering fragrance of blooming roses. Her eyes, reflecting the last slivers of daylight, shimmered with a mixture of longing and gratitude.

"And your unwavering faith in me," she replied, her voice gentle yet resolute, "it's the shield that guards my back, the spell that fortifies my spirit."

As they shared a tender smile, it was also a defiant rebellion against the encroaching night. It was a silent vow, a declaration that even as the world braced for the tempest, they had found sanctuary in each other's arms.

Aerin's declaration echoed through the corridors of Lysandra's heart, resonating like a steady drumbeat against the chaos that threatened to engulf them.

His fingers caressed her skin, tracing the delicate line of her jaw with a reverence that sent shivers down her spine. It was a promise, binding and unbreakable, surpassing any spell she had ever known.

"No matter what challenges lie ahead, I will always be by

your side," he pledged, his voice brimming with unwavering conviction.

The weight of his vow settled over her like a comforting cloak, wrapping her in a warmth that banished all doubt. Lysandra's smile, a testament to the battles they had fought and the ones that awaited, curved softly.

Her hand rose to cover his, their fingers intertwining, forming a knot as strong as the roots of an ancient tree, capable of weathering even the harshest storms.

"Together, we can face anything," she whispered, her voice resonating through the serene stillness of the twilight, filled with love.

As the sun dipped below the horizon, casting elongated shadows from every corner of Tyrannis, their eyes locked in a profound connection, holding a truth that transcended words.

They were warriors, bound not only by the blood they had shed but also by the profound understanding that their unity was their most formidable weapon.

"Let the shadow hounds come," Aerin said with a half-smile, the light of battle already igniting in his dark eyes like sparks in a dark sky. "We'll reduce them to mere whispers and dust."

"Until the very end," Lysandra added, her grip tightening on her sword, an unspoken oath radiating from her, a pledge to wield her weapon for him, for them, until the stars themselves faded from the heavens.

Their embrace was a silent chorus in the encroaching darkness, two souls intertwined, ready to dance with destiny once dawn broke the horizon.

The horizon bled into a canvas of twilight, a masterful blend of oranges and pinks that seemed to herald the close of one chapter and the promise of another.

Lysandra felt the pull, an invisible tether that guided her steps.

"Beautiful, isn't it?" She murmured, standing beside Aerin, her voice barely above the whisper of the leaves in the gardens.

"Nature's last act before night takes the stage," Aerin replied, his gaze never leaving the distant mountains that pierced the sky like jagged crowns.

She followed his gaze, finding solace in the steadfast peaks. The breeze, a gentle caress laden with the perfume of night-blooming flowers, wound its way around them. It was a reprieve, a momentary breath caught between the constant beats of their warrior hearts.

Without thinking, as if drawn by some magnetic force, Lysandra reached out, her hand hovering shy of Aerin's. His fingers twitched ever so slightly before he turned his palm upward, allowing her touch to complete the circuit of their connection. A quiver raced up her arm, setting her very soul aquiver.

"Did you feel that?" Aerin asked, his voice a low rumble reverberating through the growing darkness.

"Every time I touch you," she confessed, turning to him, their hands still intertwined.

She found herself lost in the oceans of his eyes, dark, velvety depths that held storms and serenity in equal measure. "It's like... magic, but more."

"More," he echoed, stepping closer. The words hanging between them were heavy with unspoken promises and shared experiences.

"Your strength," she began, shaking her head slightly. "No, our strength... it's here, in these quiet moments, just as much as it is on the battlefield."

"Maybe even more so," Aerin agreed, releasing her hand only to brush a loose strand of hair from her face, tucking it tenderly behind her ear.

"Because here, in this stillness, I remember why we fight."

"Tonight, let's not think of battles or shadow hounds," Lysandra said, her decision firm yet laced with an earnest plea.

She leaned into his touch, allowing herself the luxury of vulnerability. "Just this... us, the twilight, and the peace it brings."

"I agree," he whispered, his breath warm against her skin.

Their lips met, a confluence of all they had endured and hoped for—a kiss that spoke of shared burdens and intertwined fates.

"Tomorrow, we plan, we strategize," Aerin said when they finally parted, his intense gaze unwavering. "But tonight, this night is ours alone."

The stars pricked the sky's fabric, bearing witness to their resolve.

They would fight and bleed, but for now, they stood still in the embrace of dusk, two souls bound by a love as fierce as the battles they faced and as gentle as the breeze surrounding them.

As the twilight deepened, casting a velvet cloak over the castle of Tyrannis, Lysandra felt the day's tension ebb away.

Her fingers grazed the stone balustrade, which was cool and rough under her touch.

The tranquil garden below starkly contrasted the chaos that had preceded their arrival. The echoes of clashing steel and dark magic were replaced by the symphony of night creatures, rustling leaves...and their love.

With Aerin by her side, she felt a sense of peace and security; their closeness was a silent reassurance of their deep connection.

He stood like a figure sculpted from the depths of darkness, his outline merging with the advancing shadows, while his gentle gaze remained untarnished by the approaching evening.

"Lysandra," Aerin whispered in a tender, hushed voice. "I've never felt this way about anyone before. You've become my strength, my reason for fighting."

The words caressed her wounded spirit, offering solace and comfort. Lysandra paused, allowing herself to fully absorb the essence of the man who had become her unwavering support and guiding force.

The intensity in his gaze matched the ferocity of his arcane powers, creating a storm of emotions within him.

Her heart throbbed, syncing with the rhythm of his heartfelt confession. Her fingers reached up, delicately tracing the contour of his jawline, brushing against the rough stubble on his skin.

"Aerin, you've been my unwavering support through every hurdle, every fight."

A palpable energy filled the space between them, transcending the physical realm, a powerful link forged during times of war and cemented by a deep mutual respect and an undeniable surge of desire.

The tether between them was both unbreakable and fragile. They could endure the chaos of their lives but still shivered at the slightest touch.

"Every scar we share, every whisper of doubt we silence together—it's all woven into this," Aerin said, his hand gently cradling hers against his cheek, savoring the warmth of her touch.

"Then let's agree on this," Lysandra's words carried an unexpected strength, even to herself. "No matter how dark the path may be, we will walk it hand in hand, guiding each other along the way."

He whispered "More," and the word seemed to vibrate in the space between them, charged with anticipation.

In the hushed declaration, they discovered a silent promise of togetherness amidst the ominous yet captivating beauty of a world caught between light and darkness.

Aerin's whispered words sent shivers down her spine as his breath gently grazed her cheek. "Tonight, we are not saviors or soldiers." "We are simply two souls seeking refuge in each other."

She softly repeated the word "refuge" as understanding slowly dawned upon her, like the first glimmer of sunrise. "Yes, tonight we find solace within these walls and in the bond between us."

The garden below lay serene, its vibrant colors and delicate fragrances a testament to the natural balance they fought so fiercely to protect.

The stars shimmered into existence above them, dotting the night sky like beacons of hope as they navigate not only the battlegrounds but also the intricate maze of their own feelings.

Aerin's fingers delicately explored the contour of Lysandra's jaw, their touch filled with both hesitation and longing, like a wanderer discovering a hidden paradise.

As the moonlight spilled across the garden, it transformed the surroundings into a dreamlike oasis, where shadows mingled with their silhouettes.

"Are you sure?" Aerin's words were weighty, each syllable laden with the gravity of their situation.

"More than ever," Lysandra affirmed, her voice steady despite the tempest raging in her chest.

The space between them evaporated like morning mist under the sun's caress.

Drawn by a force more potent than magic coursing through their veins, their lips collided, a maelstrom of need and desire. A surge of electricity, raw and untamed, sparked at the contact, pulsing through them with a life of its own.

Lysandra's hands, calloused from years of wielding steel, now wove into Aerin's hair, tugging gently, urging him closer.

His scent, a fusion of ancient tomes and the wild tempests he so loved enveloped her, intoxicating in its familiarity.

Aerin responded, his arms banding around her waist, holding her like the anchor in his storm-tossed sea.

"Magic," he breathed against her lips, the word vibrating through their entwined forms.

"Passion," she countered, her teeth grazing his lower lip provocatively, eliciting a sharp intake of breath.

Their kiss deepened a dance of tongues and shared breaths. It was a declaration, a silent vow made flesh.

In the garden, amidst the beauty wrought by nature and spell craft, they found solace in each other's embrace, an oasis in a desert of uncertainty.

———— ✦ ————

Meanwhile, beyond the hedgerow maze, Feyla and Eolande strolled hand in hand, their steps unhurried.

The clink of Feyla's tools mingled with the rustling leaves, a symphony of the night coming alive around them.

Eolande's gaze lingered on how the moonlight played off Feyla's hair, weaving silver threads into her dark tresses.

"The stars are particularly bright tonight," Eolande observed, his voice soft as if not to startle the tranquility of their surroundings.

"Tools for navigation," Feyla quipped, her mind never straying far from her inventions, "but also reminders of the light in the darkness."

"Poetic," Eolande teased, squeezing her hand, feeling the calluses that spoke of her tireless work, each a testament to her dedication.

"Realistic," she corrected, but there was no bite to her words, only the warmth of shared understanding.

———— ✦ ————

Back on the balcony, the world narrowed to the heartbeat they could each feel, thundering beneath skin and bone, a drumbeat calling them to war, love, and life.

With each shared kiss, they armored each other against the battles to come, forging a bond not even the darkest magic could sever.

"Stay with me," Lysandra whispered, pulling back just far enough to take in the sight of him and etch this moment into her memory.

"I'll never leave you," Aerin vowed, sealing the promise with another kiss—a harbinger of dawn in the heart of the night.

Sometime later, they were walking in the garden again, seeking its coolness.

Lysandra's breath formed a mist in the cool air as she and Aerin strode through Tyrannis's lush gardens, their hands clasped tightly.

A canopy of stars unfurled above them, casting an ethereal glow on the path ahead. The night was alive with whispers of wind and the distant murmur of the city beyond the castle walls.

"Look," Lysandra murmured, pointing toward a secluded corner where Feyla and Eolande sat closely on an antique stone bench.

Their heads were bent closely together, and their conversation was a private dance of words and gestures only they understood. Feyla's fingers animatedly sketched invisible diagrams in the air while Eolande watched, his eyes reflecting a soft light that only affection could kindle.

Aerin followed her gaze, and the corners of his mouth lifted slightly. "They've found something rare," he said, his voice laced with admiration. "In times like these, love is both a shield and a sword."

"Very poetic," Lysandra teased, but her smile faded as gravity settled over her features. "We won't have many moments like this once we set out searching for Aviara."

Holding onto Aerin's hand, she paused for a moment. The journey ahead will be dangerous, challenging our determination.

"Perhaps," Aerin agreed, turning to face her. His dark eyes held a stormy intensity that mirrored the uncertainty of their quest.

"But remember, Aviara once stood for equilibrium—nature in perfect harmony. We need to remind her of who she was... of what she protected."

"Can we bring back that part of her? After all that she's

done?" Doubt shadowed Lysandra's eyes, yet the set of her jaw spoke of an unyielding spirit.

"Aviara's heart must remember the call of the wild, the serenity of the forests, the balance she once cherished." Aerin's words were fervent, a vow against the encroaching darkness.

"Then we'll make her remember," Lysandra stated, her voice firm. "For the sake of Erenor, we cannot fail."

"Failure isn't in our destiny, not while we stand together." Aerin pulled her into his arms, the strength of his embrace a testament to his words.

"Together," she echoed, resting her forehead against his.

They stood there, two warriors bound by purpose and by something much deeper—an unspoken promise that transcended the chaos of the world around them.

In the silence that followed, the couple on the bench rose, Feyla's hand lingering on Eolande's arm. Their silent exchange carried the weight of unsaid pledges, each look and touch fortifying them against the unknown. Slowly, hand in hand, they wandered back to the Castle.

"Let's not think of what tomorrow holds," Lysandra whispered to Aerin. "Tonight, the battle is far, and we are here, together."

"I can't agree more," Aerin replied, capturing her lips with his again—a kiss that sealed their shared resolve and rekindled the flame of hope in their hearts.

Seeking respite from the world's challenges, Lysandra and Aerin withdrew to a secluded corner of Tyrannis' historic ramparts. Jasmine and wild sage scented the evening air, and the stones they treaded upon were still warm from the day. Settling down, they found comfort against the sun-warmed stone, their bodies touching intimately from shoulder to hip.

"Look," Aerin murmured, pointing to the heavens where the first stars twinkled in the dusky sky. "Even the cosmos seems to conspire to give us respite."

"Or perhaps," Lysandra replied, her gaze following his, "they are but silent sentries watching over us." She turned her head, catching the soft gleam of starlight in his eyes. "Tonight, the constellations will be our guardians."

Their conversational dance skirted around the unspoken fears of tomorrow's endeavors, each word a delicate step taken in tandem. While they were talking, a silhouette separated from the fading garden and silently moved away. Shadow, sensing the deepening connection between his companions, sought solace elsewhere.

The wolf moved through the silver-streaked gardens with grace, heading towards the Dragon Harrow's resting place.

The magnificent beast lay coiled atop a craggy outcrop, scales glimmering like obsidian under the crescent moon.

Shadow approached with deference, finding comfort in the dragon's steady breath, a reminder of the enduring strength surrounding them.

"Tomorrow will come with its own shadows," Aerin whispered back at the rampart, intrinsically aware of the approaching darkness. "But tonight, let's just be Aerin and Lysandra, not mages who carry the weight of Erenor on their shoulders."

"I agree. Tonight, I am not the savior, nor you the healer. We are just..." She trailed off, searching for the words.

"Us," he finished for her. It was a simple affirmation, but it filled the space between them with an electric charge.

"Us," she echoed, letting the simplicity resonate within her.

They shifted closer, their movements synchronized like they had done this many times before.

Her head found a natural resting place on his shoulder, and she inhaled the scent of earth and magic that clung to him—a contrast to her own aroma of steel and resilience.

"Tell me," she whispered, "what you dream about when the night is still, and all battles are distant memories."

Aerin looked down at her, his fingers tracing idle patterns on her arm. "I dream of places untouched by war. Of laughter that echoes through halls without fear of being silenced by anything. And often, I dream of you—free from your burdens, dancing."

Her smile was wistful, yet it reached her eyes, igniting a spark within them. "And you're there with me, aren't you? In these dreams?"

"Of course," he affirmed, his voice a low rumble that vibrated through her.

"Then, may we dream together tonight," she proposed, lifting her face to meet his.

"May we dream, indeed." He accepted the invitation, sealing their pact with a kiss that spoke of shared dreams and quiet defiance against the encroaching darkness.

As the night deepened, they found a shared rhythm in each other's arms, a silent promise woven through every caress—a bastion against the tempest that awaited them with dawn's light.

Chapter 22

THE ENCHANTED FOREST

The Enchanted Forest enveloped Lysandra and her companions, surrounding them like living beings.

With each footfall, they seemed to tap into the forest's concealed life force, and Lysandra could feel it resonating through her boots, a constant and delicate pulsation against her flesh.

"Remain on your guard," she murmured, her resolute voice contrasting with the wonder that passed over her face as she looked up.

The trees seemed to go on forever, with branches intricately woven together like a tapestry, capturing the sunlight and creating a mesmerizing display of flickering shadows.

With his eyes wide awake beneath the brim of his gray hood, Aerin responded, "I can sense the magic here."

Lysandra nodded, her hand gently resting on the handle of her sword—a familiar weight, silently assuring protection.

She could feel the pull of her own magic strength, a faint

darkness that always hovered on the fringes of her awareness, waiting to emerge if provoked.

In a comforting gesture, Shadow bumped into her.

Feyla pointed at something ahead and murmured, "I see something."

Almost as if in response to her words, a gentle flicker of light appeared between the tree trunks—a captivating radiance that seemed to beckon from another realm.

The trees became a stage for the enchanting dance of the Ethereal Wisps as they weaved their way through the forest. Their radiant glow had a mesmerizing effect, luring the gaze and comforting the tired mind.

"Beautiful," Lysandra whispered, captivated by the orbs' elegant movements, momentarily forgetting her guard.

"Be careful, Lyss," Aerin warned, gently extending his hand to pull her back. "In these areas, danger is often hidden behind a veil of beauty."

"That's true, but they appear friendly," she replied, stepping forward to greet the wisps halfway. The frigid forest air gave way to a pleasant buzzing sound that harmonized with the melodic chiming of their voices—much like the delicate hammers of mystical blacksmiths striking their anvils.

"Can you understand them?" Feyla asked, tilting her head in curiosity.

"Not quite," Lysandra replied, her attention fixed on the melodic harmonies surrounding them. "But I think they're trying to tell us something important."

"Or lead us somewhere," Eolande added, his tone cautious yet intrigued.

"Then we should go after them," Lysandra resolutely said. "We came here seeking answers, and this may be our best chance at finding them."

Walking alongside her companions, she followed the wisps as they guided them into the innermost part of the Enchanted Forest, where mysteries awaited and fate summoned them. The pull of her lineage, the balance she fought to maintain between light and shadow—all converged in this place where magic reigned supreme.

The Ethereal Wisps closed their distance, the forest's whispers rising into a symphony of anticipation.

Lysandra's breath hitched as the floating orbs encircled her, their radiance casting dancing shadows upon the foliage.

"Greetings, Savior of Erenor," the wisps sang in unison, their voices a delicate harmony that seemed to resonate with the essence of the world around them. "We have been waiting for your arrival."

Lysandra stepped forward, her heart hammering against her ribcage, each beat echoing the ancient rhythm of Erenor itself.

Her gaze locked onto the shimmering lights, and she felt a connection as if these creatures' held answers to questions buried deep within her soul.

"You know me?" she asked, her voice soft and trembling, betraying the tempest of emotions roiling inside her.

"Indeed," they replied, swirling about her like leaves caught in a gentle breeze. "The blood of ancients flows through you, child of both shadow and light."

Her mind raced, piecing together fragments of lore she had learned from dusty tomes and cryptic tales.

Could these ethereal beings truly recognize the duality of her heritage? Could they recognize the internal conflict she faced between her inherent darkness and her pursuit of a righteous life?

"If you are aware of that, then you must also understand the motivation behind our presence," Lysandra pushed, endeavoring to mask any hint of fear in her voice with resolute determination. She needed to assert dominance in this encounter, concealing her awe and preserving her warrior spirit.

The wisps chanted "Seeking truths, challenging fates," intensifying their dance, mirroring her sense of urgency. "The journey you choose is filled with danger, yet it's the sole path that can lead you towards daybreak."

With her jaw clenched, Lysandra's hand instinctively found its place on the pommel of her sword—a clear sign of her unwavering readiness to confront the unknown darkness ahead. She was aware of the consequences.

"Lead us," she commanded, channeling the ancestral power within her words, infusing them with an undeniable authority that even the forest spirits could not disregard.

"Follow us," they chimed, their luminosity piercing through the ambiguity of the enchanted forest.

Her resolve solidified as she nodded, taking a deep breath

with hints of moss and the mystical.

The companions behind her created a solid formation, symbolizing their shared victories and unspoken support.

With their every movement, the forest came alive, its rhythmic breath echoing through the veins of Erenor.

Lysandra could not discern if the shadows she noticed in her peripheral vision were potential dangers or the forest's response to their movement.

Still, she moved forward, embracing the amalgamation of fear and exhilaration that accompanied walking on the precipice of fate.

The ethereal light from the wisps danced upon Lysandra's face, casting her features in a gentle glow that softened the hard lines of battle etched into her skin.

She felt the weight of their gaze, the gravity of their words anchoring her to the moment.

"We have seen the threads of fate that bind you to this world," they sang, their voices merging into a melody that hummed with the power of prophecy.

"Your destiny is intertwined with the fabric of Erenor's existence."

From the forest's dappled shadows, a Spirit Stag appeared as if out of nowhere, its presence commanding yet serene.

The creature's coat shimmered like woven beams of starlight, embodying the magic in these woods. Its grand and arching antlers bore a delicate filigree that glinted as if forged from the night sky.

"An omen," Aerin murmured, his gaze locked onto the eyes of the stag with a mixture of awe and understanding.

"Of what?" Lysandra's voice was steady, though her heart raced with the anticipation of ancient knowledge about to unfold.

"Change," whispered Feyla, never taking her eyes off the mystical creature. Her hand found Eolande's, their fingers intertwining instinctively.

"Strength," Eolande added, his voice carrying distant thunder's soft resonance.

"Guidance," Harrow rumbled, his draconic intuition sensing the deeper currents at play.

"Or peril," Aerin cautioned. His voice was tense, and he kept close to Lysandra. Whether she wanted him to protect her or not, he would see to it that she stayed safe.

"Speak, spirits," Lysandra asserted, her resolve steeling against the veils of vagueness. "What does the appearance of the Spirit Stag signify for our quest?"

"Paths will converge, light and shadow clashing," the wisps sang, their chorus more fervent, as if reflecting her own urgency. "The path you walk is fraught with peril, yet it is the only one that leads to dawn."

Lysandra clenched her jaw, her hand instinctively resting on the pommel of her sword—a reminder of her readiness to face whatever darkness lay ahead. She understood the stakes and witnessed the terror that shadow hounds could unleash upon her world.

The Spirit Stag moved gracefully through the dense under-growth, its steps almost soundless among the rustling leaves.

Lysandra followed in its wake, her senses on high alert for any signs of danger. Her comrades kept pace behind her, their weapons ready.

As they traveled deeper into the forest, the air grew thick with otherworldly energy that prickled against Lysandra's skin.

The spirits' words echoed in her mind, reminding her of what was at stake—not just for herself and her companions, but for all of Erenor.

After hours of trekking through the ancient woods, they finally emerged into a clearing.

In its center stood a massive tree unlike any Lysandra had ever seen. Its trunk was wide enough to wrap three dragons around, and its branches stretched upwards forever.

The Spirit Stag stopped at the tree's base and looked back at Lysandra with eyes glowed like stars.

Without a word, it disappeared into thin air, leaving Lysandra and her companions alone in front of the magnificent tree.

"This must be it," Aerin said in awe as he stepped closer to examine the tree's bark.

"It feels...powerful," Feyla whispered, running her hand along one branch.

Lysandra approached cautiously, feeling a sense of reverence wash over her. She placed a hand on the tree's trunk and closed her eyes, allowing herself to become attuned to its essence.

Images flashed before her eyes–memories from generations past. She saw great battles fought beneath this tree's canopy, powerful magic wielded by ancient mages, and moments of peace when Erenor was still young and untouched by darkness.

Opening her eyes again, Lysandra knew what she needed to do. "We must perform a ritual," she announced to her comrades.

"A ritual?" Eolande questioned, raising an eyebrow. "What kind of ritual?

Lysandra took a deep breath, trying to explain the ritual touching the tree had revealed to her.

She began, "We must use our magic and other abilities and energy to connect with the ancient magic of this tree."

Aerin looked skeptical, but Feyla nodded in understanding. "And what will that do?" she asked.

"It will awaken the true power of this tree," Lysandra answered. "It is said that this tree holds the key to defeating the darkness that threatens Erenor. With our combined magical energy, we can unleash its full potential."

Eolande's expression remained doubtful, but his curiosity was piqued. "How do we begin?" he asked.

Lysandra closed her eyes again and focused on connecting with the tree's magic.

She felt a surge of energy flow through her as she grasped onto it, sending out waves of power to her companions.

They joined in one by one, their bodies glowing with their unique magical energies.

They formed a circle around the tree's base and channeled their energy into it.

The chanting voices swelled as the circle of companions swayed.

Lysandra's upturned palms were pulsing with growing power. Goosebumps prickled her arms as the clearing filled with the electric tang of magic.

The ground rumbled, dust rising between stones as the wind whipped her robes and tore leaves from the surrounding trees.

A thunderous crack resounded through the glade as a blinding pillar of light erupted from the carved oak.

Lysandra shielded her eyes, blinking away purple afterimages as the glare faded.

The ancient tree now shone with ethereal radiance, its leaves glittering as if dusted with stars. Smooth bark rippled with currents of mystical energy so palpable Lysandra could feel it thrumming in her chest.

The spirits' promise rang in her mind—together, they could achieve anything. United by this ritual, their shared power hummed within the living wood.

Lysandra smiled, magic and purpose surging through her veins. Whatever darkness lay ahead, they now stood ready to face it as one.

Her companions stood in awe, bathed in the glow of the awakened tree. Lysandra could feel the energy coursing through her, filling her with newfound strength and purpose. But there was still a pressing matter at hand — finding Aviara.

"Where do we start looking for Aviara?" Aerin asked as if reading her mind.

"We should search for any clues nearby," Eolande suggested, scanning the area. "Perhaps there are traces of her magic."

Lysandra nodded in agreement and walked around the glade, inspecting the ground for any signs. She noticed faint traces of dark magic scattered around, leading towards a path deeper into the forest.

"This way," she called out to her companions, following the trail.

They walked silently, keeping their eyes peeled for any sign of Aviara.

The trees seemed to grow thicker and taller as they ventured deeper into the forest, casting ominous shadows over them.

Lysandra could feel a sense of foreboding growing within her as they pressed on.

After hours of searching, Feyla suddenly stopped in her tracks. "Do you feel that?" she asked, turning towards Lysandra.

Lysandra closed her eyes and focused on her surroundings. There was an intense surge of dark magic nearby.

"It's coming from over there," she said, pointing towards a large clearing ahead.

As they approached the clearing, they saw Aviara standing in its center. Her once vibrant blue robes were now tattered and stained with dark energy. In her hands was a pulsating orb of blackness that seemed to draw energy from everything around it.

"Aviara!" Lysandra called out to the deity.

Aviara turned towards them slowly, an eerie smile playing on her lips. "Ah...my dear friends," she said in a hollow voice. "How kind of you to join me."

Chapter 23

REDEMPTION

The last traces of twilight held onto the horizon while Lysandra and her group stood in front of the imposing gates of Aviara's sanctuary. The atmosphere crackled with untapped energy, a soft vow of the coming challenges. Shadow prowled at Lysandra's side, his fur bristling, sensing the tension coiled in his mistress's stance.

The air grew tense as Lysandra's blade sliced through the darkness.

Shadows clung to the ancient stone walls like cobwebs as they entered Aviara's inner sanctum.

The stale, oppressive air pressed down on them, saturated with the metallic scent of corrupted power.

The clearing stretched before them, resembling a deep wound in the earth, radiating a sinister and unsettling energy. At its heart stood Aviara, her form both majestic and terrible, the orb in her grasp casting undulating shadows that seemed to drink the light from their surroundings. Once resembling a clear summer sky, the deity's robes now displayed a tapestry of melancholic twilight.

"Aviara!" Lysandra's voice cut through the oppressive air. Her hand rested on the hilt of her sword as if it were an old friend offering silent strength.

The deity's gaze met hers—an abyss peering back into the soul of Erenor's savior. Her eyes, once a gentle cascade of sparkling blues, now swirled with the obsidian tide of the orb's influence.

"Have you come to join the darkness, child of both worlds?" Aviara's voice was the whisper of leaves in a dead forest, chilling despite the lack of wind.

With every step forward, Lysandra felt the pull of the orb, an invitation to let go or to be consumed. Yet she anchored herself in the here and now; her tightening grip resolved a bulwark against the enemy or to be consumed.

"I've come to free you from it," she declared, her grip tightening.

"Free me?" a hollow laugh escaped Aviara's lips, a sound devoid of warmth. Or bind me to your will as the others have tried?"

"Neither," Lysandra replied, steadily. "To remind you who you once were—the Aviara who nurtured this land and its people."

"Pretty words for such a bleak end," Aviara retorted, tilting her head with mock curiosity. "Do you believe your purity can cleanse my corruption?"

"Her heart is pure, but it is not she alone that stands before you," Aerin interjected, stepping alongside Lysandra, his presence counterpointing the darkness.

"Indeed," Feyla murmured her voice a melody that weaved threads of light into the murk. "We all carry pieces of what you've lost, Aviara. Let us help you find them."

"Help?" Aviara's sneer was a gash across her ethereal beauty. "You think yourselves capable of restoring what has been sundered?"

"More than capable," Eolande added, her assurance grounding them like the deep roots of ancient oaks.

"Your arrogance will be your downfall," Aviara warned, yet there was a flicker—of doubt—in the storm of her eyes.

"Arrogance?" Harrow's rumbling voice shook the surrounding leaves. "Or faith in our companion, in the bond we share?"

"Faith..." The word lingered between them, a single note holding the potential of a symphony.

"Remember the life you breathed into Erenor, the joy in creation," Lysandra implored, her words imbued with the weight of their shared history.

"Let us bring you back to that."

"Back?" For a moment, the veil of darkness seemed to waver around Aviara, a crack in the armor of her fury. "Can one truly return from the precipice of oblivion?"

"There is only one way to find out," Lysandra said, her hand leaving the comfort of her sword hilt and reaching out—not in the challenge but in the offering. "Together."

The air crackled with the tension of an impending storm as Aviara's hollow voice sliced through the silence.

Her eerie smile, a harbinger of the chaos threatening to consume them all, sent shivers down Lysandra's spine.

The deity's once brilliant aura was now a swirling miasma of darkness, corrupting the clearing that had been sacred.

"Aviara," Lysandra started, her tone steady despite the pounding in her chest. "This isn't you. Let us help."

"Help?" Aviara repeated, mockery lacing her words. "I am beyond your feeble aid."

Lysandra exchanged a glance with Aerin, whose fingers danced with the beginnings of a spell.

His eyes narrowed in concentration.

Shadow growled low, the sound vibrating through the ground like an ominous warning, while Harrow's scales shimmered with a light that seemed to fight back the encroaching shadows.

"Your power once nurtured this land," Eolande said, his bowstring taut, an arrow ready. It can again."

"Power..." Aviara mused, the orb in her hands pulsing faster. "What do you know of power?"

"More than you think," Feyla interjected, her hand resting on an array of gadgets at her belt, inventions she hoped might bridge the gap between them and Aviara.

"We've seen strength in unity, in the bonds you seek to sever."

"Unity is a facade," Aviara spat, but the slight falter in her voice betrayed a seed of uncertainty planted by their words.

"Facade or not, it's real for us," Lysandra declared, stepping forward.

The relic hanging around her neck—a symbol of her dual heritage—glowed softly, its warmth seeping into her skin.

"Our bond... our faith in each other... It's why we're here, facing you together."

"Faith," Aviara whispered, her gaze flickering to the relic before meeting Lysandra's eyes. "You wield it as a weapon."

"Only against those who have lost sight of its true purpose," Lysandra replied, her conviction unwavering.

She held Aviara's stare, seeing past the corruption of the deity that once cherished life more than anything else.

"True purpose..." Aviara echoed, her tone less certain, more reflective.

For a moment, a softness touched the cruel lines of her face—the briefest glimpse of the deity they knew lurked beneath the surface.

"Aviara, remember who you are," Lysandra urged, taking another step.

"Remember the good magic you shared, the wonder you sparked in the hearts of Erenor's children."

"Good magic..." Aviara's voice wavered, the orb's pulsation slowing as if responding to her inner turmoil.

"Let us remind you," Aerin said, lowering his hand as the spell's light dimmed, signaling his trust in dialogue rather than force.

"Remind me?" Aviara's stance softened, and the orb's blackness receded slightly, the first sign of their words reaching her.

"Allow us," Lysandra said again, her hand extended, not in defiance, but in a silent promise of redemption.

And in that moment, as the group stood united in the face of darkness, a palpable sense of hope filled the air—a belief that they could lead even a corrupt deity back to the light.

Lysandra's boots sank into the soft earth as she advanced, her eyes fixed on Aviara.

The deity's corrupted aura gnarled the air around them, turning the clearing into a battlefield of shadow and malice.

"Aviara," Lysandra called out, her voice steady despite the tremor in her heart. "This isn't you. You were once the guardian of all that is pure in Erenor."

"Pure?" Aviara spat the word like venom. "Purity is a myth, child. Power is the only truth."

Shadow growled at her side, sensing the darkness that clung to the deity like a shroud.

Aerin's fingers danced with the beginnings of an incantation, blue light flickering between his fingertips, while Eolande's bowstring hummed taut with readiness.

"Power unchecked will consume you," Feyla chimed in, her ethereal beauty marred by the grim set of her lips. "It devours what it must to grow, even if that means devouring yourself."

"Your platitudes bore me," Aviara sneered, raising the orb high. Shadows coalesced into hounds, their eyes glowing with malevolence as they circled the group, snarling.

"Fight, my friends!" Lysandra commanded, drawing her sword, its blade gleaming with a pale light against the encroaching dark. "Protect each other!"

The clash was immediate and ferocious; Shadow pounced at a hound, his jaws closing on the shadow stuff that dissipated and reformed.

Aerin wove spells of binding and barrier, his chants rising above the din of battle.

Eolande's arrows found their marks with deadly precision, each shaft bursting into radiant energy upon impact.

Harrow, the dragon, reared up, his scales catching the dim light, casting prisms across the field.

With a bellowing roar, he unleashed a torrent of fire that swept through the ranks of shadow beasts, incinerating them into wisps of smoke.

"Aviara, you must see reason!" Harrow boomed. "The cosmic fracture has poisoned your essence, but we can cleanse it!"

"Silence, worm!" Aviara's retort was a blast of dark energy that sent Harrow staggering backward, his wings beating frantically to regain balance.

"Aviara, listen to us!" Lysandra pressed forward, ducking beneath a swipe from a hound.

"You nurtured this land. You shared in our joys and sorrows. Don't let this fracture define you!"

"Define me? It freed me!" Aviara's eyes blazed with fury as she fought back against their words as fiercely as their magic.

"Remember the connection you had with everything that

grows and breathes," Lysandra pleaded, parrying another attack.

"You are not alone. We are here with you, for you."

"Your heart knows the truth, Aviara," Eolande added, releasing another arrow into the fray. "Let us help heal what's been broken."

"Enough!" Aviara's command echoed, and the orb pulsed violently, sending a shockwave that knocked them to their knees.

But they did not yield. They rose, each feeding strength into the other, their resolve crystallizing into a force as potent as any spell.

Together, they stood against Aviara's tempest, their unity a beacon in the darkness.

"Look at us, Aviara! We fight not just for Erenor but for you," Lysandra said, her voice cutting through the cacophony.

"We believe in who you were... in who you can be again."

"Believe in..." The deity's voice cracked, the orb's blackness flickering uncertainly.

"Believe," Lysandra repeated, her conviction a bright flame in the encroaching night.

"Believe," they all intoned, a chorus of faith amidst the chaos.

And as their voices melded, the orb's pulsation slowed, the shadows retreated, and Aviara's figure wavered—caught between the abyss and the dawn of redemption.

The air crackled with the charged energy of battle as Harrow's massive form swooped down from the sky, his wings casting a momentary shadow over the clearing where they faced

Aviara.

Lysandra stood her ground, sword in hand, her gaze locked on the deity who seemed to balance on the knife edge between destruction and salvation.

"Aviara!" Harrow's voice boomed, resonating with the ancient power that hummed beneath his scales. "Listen to me!"

The corrupt goddess turned her gaze upon the dragon, the darkness of the orb she clutched swirling ominously.

"Once, I was shackled by chains stronger than the hardest steel, my will siphoned away by those who would use me for war," Harrow began, his voice a deep thrum that vibrated through the very soil of Erenor.

"Lysandra freed me, not for her own gain but because it was right."

Lysandra nodded, stepping forward with the confidence that came from knowing her soul's intentions.

"I couldn't stand by while another suffered under the yoke of oppression. You were not meant to be caged, Harrow, just as Aviara was not meant to be forgotten."

"Forgotten," Aviara whispered, the word escaping like a sigh carried away by the wind.

"Her heart saw the spirit within me, mighty Aviara. Her blade shattered my bindings, and her courage gave me back the sky," Harrow continued, fixing his ancient, wise eyes onto the deity.

"Your pain and anger are significant, but so are the hearts of those who stand before you now."

"Greatness... once I knew of such things," Aviara murmured,

her fingers tightening around the orb.

"Remember who you were, what you represented," Aerin interjected, stepping beside Lysandra with unwavering support.

"You were the light in every dawn, the whisper in the leaves. You are still cherished, still needed."

"Needed..." The word seemed foreign on Aviara's tongue, yet it sparked a glint of something old and powerful in her eyes, something beyond the reach of the shadows that embraced her.

"Look at us, Aviara," Eolande said, bowstring taut, another arrow ready. We each have felt the icy touch of loneliness, the sting of being cast aside. We don't claim to understand all your sorrows, but we've shared some of them."

"Let our insight lift the veil from your eyes," Feyla added, her voice soft yet firm, like the steady flow of a river carving its path through the stone.

"We have seen the fractures in the world, the tears in the fabric of magic. Let us mend them together."

"Can it be?" Aviara's voice trembled, the black orb's light dimming as her doubt crept in.

"Belief in the possibility, Aviara," Lysandra urged, her dual heritage shining through her plea. "In the possibility of redemption, of restoration. Believe in us."

"Us..." Aviara repeated, and this time, the orb stilled completely. The shadows that had danced wildly across her features slowed, hesitating as if unsure of their hold.

"Believe," Harrow said once more, his voice rising with the crescendo of hope that filled the clearing, mingling with the voices of Lysandra and her companions.

"Believe," they echoed, a united front against the darkness, their words a beacon for a deity teetering on the edge of oblivion.

And in that moment, the bond between mortals and deity, forged in struggle and understanding, glowed with the faintest hint of morning's first light.

The ground quaked beneath their feet as Aviara, the deity they once revered, with no warning, summoned a tempest of shadows that bled into the sky.

Lysandra's heart hammered against her ribcage, a wild drumbeat in the wake of destruction.

She could feel the raw energy pulsing from the earth, a reminder of the cosmic fracture that had marred their world.

"Aviara!" Aerin shouted over the howling wind, his sword gleaming with an ethereal light. "You are the heart of Erenor, not this desolation!"

"The fracture has shadowed your heart,"

Lysandra added, stepping forward, her own power—a blend of human and ethereal—thriving under her skin.

"We know your pain. We've felt it through the vines and the rivers that mourn your absence."

"Loneliness has festered within you," Aerin called out, his voice steady despite the chaos swirling around them.

He clutched his staff, its crystal top pulsing with the fading orb in Aviara's grasp.

"Yet here we stand, together," Eolande chimed in, the air

shimmering around her as she channeled her enchantments.

"Not just as children of Erenor, but as witnesses to your legacy."

"Once you were cherished," Lysandra continued, her words slicing through the tempest with the precision of a blade.

"The other deities have vanished, but we remember. We see the good magic you shared, nurturing every creature, every plant. That essence still resides within you."

Aviara's eyes, dark like the abyss, flickered with the ghost of old storms, the vestige of memories long forsaken. The shadows wavered, their relentless advance pausing as if her resolve had faltered.

"Remember who you were," Lysandra urged, taking another step towards the deity. "Remember what you gave us."

Their plea hung in the turbulent air, a fragile hope amidst the battle that raged on.

Without warning, the earth split open, revealing a chasm of glowing runes and symbols—a trial of the gods etched into the very land they fought upon.

"Stay united," Lysandra instructed, her gaze never leaving Aviara as they navigated the treacherous path ahead.

Each symbol they passed resonated with a piece of history, a fragment of the cosmic fracture's toll on Aviara's spirit.

"Courage, my friends," Harrow's voice boomed, his scales reflecting the myriad of lights below.

He spread his wings, casting a protective aura over the group as they moved in unison, a dance of determination against

Aviara's growing despair.

"Resolve will be our shield," Aerin whispered, his enchantments weaving a web of resilience around them.

"Understanding shall be our guide," he intoned, his staff alight with a beacon of clarity to pierce the encroaching fog of doubt.

As they progressed, each step became a testament to their unwavering spirit, a declaration of their intent to heal not only the deity before them but the fractured land that cried out for salvation.

"Look at us, Aviara," Lysandra beckoned, her relic glowing with an inner fire.

"We face these trials for you, for Erenor. Let us bridge the gap that divides us. Let us restore what was lost together."

With each word, each affirmation of their journey, the deity's barriers crumbled, revealing the glimmer of the goddess they once knew, fighting to emerge from the darkness that had consumed her.

"Let go of the bitterness," Aerin pressed on, his blade cutting through the last shadows that threatened to engulf them.

"Embrace the bond that ties you to this world, to us."

"Your true power lies in creation, not destruction," Lysandra said, reaching out with her heritage and heart. "Let us help you find it again."

In the crucible of conflict and revelation, they forged ahead, undaunted by the trials that sought to test them. Their voices were a chorus of redemption—a symphony of hope for a deity lost to shadow.

Lysandra's breath came in ragged gasps, her muscles screaming as she parried a blow from a shadow hound that lunged towards her.

But it wasn't just her strength or the light of her relic that kept the darkness at bay—it was the fierce loyalty of her companions, their own powers alight with defiant brilliance.

"Shadow, to me!" Lysandra called, and the wolf, fur bristling with electric energy, bounded to her side, its fangs sinking into the ethereal hide of another beast that dared approach.

"Keep focused," Feyla shouted above the din, her voice a clear bell in the cacophony of battle. She danced between enemies, her form a blur of motion, each strike punctuated by the shimmering afterimage of her enchanted daggers.

Master Elarion's staff thrummed with vitality, weaving protective wards around them. His incantations were a steady stream that melded with the chaos, reinforcing their resolve. "We stand united," he cried, his eyes reflecting the conviction of his words.

And there was Aerin, his blade an arc of silver as he cleaved through the darkness, determination etched into his features. "For Erenor!" he bellowed, rallying the others with every swing of his sword.

Above them, Harrow's roar tore through the sky, a thunderous declaration of their unyielding will.

He swooped down, talons outstretched, snatching up shadow hounds and casting them into oblivion.

"Aviara!" Lysandra called out, her voice piercing the turmoil as they cleared a path to the deity. "This ends now!"

The forgotten goddess stood before them, aura pulsating wildly, her gaze fixed on the intruders who dared challenge her dominion over the shadows.

"Futile efforts," Aviara hissed, her voice slicing through the air like a shard of ice.

"Your fury blinds you," Lysandra countered, stepping forward, the relic in her hand a beacon of hope amidst the encircling gloom. "But we see the truth behind your pain."

"Truth?" Aviara spat, her laugh devoid of humor. "You know nothing of my truth!"

"Then enlighten us," Aerin challenged, standing steadfastly beside Lysandra. "Let us bear the weight of your truth together."

"Speak of unity while you battle against me? How quaint," Aviara mocked, yet there was a tremor in her stance, a flicker of uncertainty that betrayed her outward contempt.

"Unity is our strength," Feyla interjected, her voice soft but fierce. "It's what makes us more than the sum of our parts."

"Even corrupted gods can be redeemed," Eolande added his words a soothing balm meant to penetrate the deity's, hardened heart.

"Redemption?" The word seemed to catch in Aviara's throat, and for a moment, the maelstrom of dark energy faltered.

"Remember who you were," Lysandra said, taking another step, her relic's glow intensifying. "We remember you,

Aviara—the protector, the nurturer."

Aviara's expression wavered, torn between the malice that had consumed her and the memories of her past glory.

The battle raged on, a tempest of shadow and light, but at its eye stood two forces—one of ruin, one of restoration—locked in an ultimate confrontation that would determine the fate of Erenor.

The relic in Lysandra's grasp pulsed with a fierce light, casting stark shadows across the clearing where Aviara stood, her form shrouded in the swirling darkness of her own creation.

With each step forward, Lysandra felt the weight of her dual heritage—a lineage steeped in both shadow and light—thrilling through her veins, lending her strength. Her eyes, reflecting the storm within, locked onto Aviara's.

"Aviara, this doesn't have to be your end," Lysandra said, her voice cutting through the howling dark energy winds. "You were once Erenor's shepherd. You can be again."

"Words are feeble against the tide of eons," Aviara retorted, yet the orb in her hands wavered as if it, too, were uncertain.

"Believe in us as we believe in you!" Aerin called out, his hands aglow with healing magic, poised to mend what fractures he could.

"Your heart knows the truth of who you are," Feyla shouted over the din, her mechanical devices whirring, ready to spring into action immediately.

"Let the past guide you back to the light," Eolande urged, his bowstring taut with an arrow meant not to harm but to remind.

Harrow loomed behind them, his scales shimmering with a spectral light that seemed to pierce the surrounding gloom.

He let out a roar that shook the leaves from the trees, a sound that carried the wisdom of ages and the sorrow of witnessing a revered deity fall so far from grace.

"Feel our presence, Aviara," Harrow bellowed. "We stand with you, not against you!"

"Enough talk!" Aviara screamed, her power lashing out in tendrils of shadow toward the group.

Lysandra raised the relic high, and a blinding flash of luminescence momentarily pushed back the darkness. She channeled the essence of her being into the artifact, her spirit reaching for Aviara's core through the maelstrom of corruption.

"Remember the green of the forests, the Song of the Rivers, the dance of the fireflies," Lysandra whispered her words a litany against despair. "Remember your children who walk these lands."

Aviara faltered, her grip on the orb slackening as Lysandra's invocation struck deep into her consciousness.

"My... children?" she murmured, a tear streaking through the grime on her cheek.

"Come back to them," Lysandra pleaded, the relic now a beacon amidst the encroaching shadows.

"Fight with us, Aviara," Aerin said, stepping closer to lend his magic to Lysandra's effort. His voice was a steady drumbeat of solidarity.

"Reclaim the good magic you shared with the world," Feyla

added, her expression fierce with conviction.

"Your connection to Erenor is unbroken," Eolande affirmed, his gaze locked on Aviara's tormented visage.

"We fight for you as you fought for us," Harrow growled, his eyes glowing with an ancient fire.

Together, they formed a circle of defiance around Lysandra, their combined wills a fortress against the cosmic fracture's influence.

The air thrummed with the power of their alliance, Lysandra's relic shining ever brighter, a star in the heart of darkness.

Lysandra's fingers trembled as she held the relic aloft, its light a beacon against the encroaching darkness.

Her allies stood steadfast around her, each drawing on their innermost reserves of strength.

But the shadows were relentless, coiling and lashing like serpents starved of prey.

"Aviara, you are not alone!" Lysandra cried out, her voice breaking through the cacophony of battle. "We stand with you—"

"Watch out!" Aerin's warning sliced through the air.

A shadow Hound, larger and more ferocious than the others, burst from the writhing mass, its eyes a pair of smoldering coals set upon Lysandra. Its jaws gaped wide, revealing rows of teeth sharp enough to cleave spirit from flesh.

Time slowed as the beast lunged.

"NO!" Harrow's roar shattered the momentary stillness.

The dragon, scales shimmering with an ancient aura, interposed his massive form between the Hound and Lysandra.

They collided with a force that shook the earth, a maelstrom of dark energy and Draconic might.

"LYSANDRA!" Eolande's voice filled with panic as he released a volley of arrows into the fray, each resonating with enchantments.

"Keep the connection!" Aerin shouted, his hands weaving intricate patterns in the air, bolstering the protective wards that encased them.

But Harrow endured the assault. The impact was brutal, the sound of rending scales and flesh a visceral agony that echoed in Lysandra's bones.

Harrow's wings beat furiously, driving back the Hound with sheer power, but the damage was done.

"Fall back! Fall back to Harrow!" Lysandra commanded, her heart hammering against her ribs as she moved to the dragon's side.

"Stay with us, old friend," Aerin murmured, placing a hand on Harrow's heaving flank. His magic worked to staunch the flow of silver blood that pooled beneath the dragon.

"Damn it, Harrow, you can't leave us now," Aerin said through gritted teeth, her hands aglow with healing energy that sought the dragon's deepest wounds.

"Your wisdom guides us. Your strength upholds us," Eolande intoned, his voice carrying the weight of an unspoken prayer.

Harrow's breaths came in ragged gasps, yet his eyes met Lysandra's with an unwavering resolve. "For... Erenor," he managed, each word a testament to his indomitable will.

"Fight, Harrow. Fight like the fires of the first dawn," Lysandra whispered, pressing her palm against the dragon's scaled chest, feeling the thrum of his mighty heart.

"Remember who you are, Aviara," she called out once more, hoping the deity would hear her over the din of battle. "Remember who we all are—the guardians of this realm."

As the shadow Hounds regrouped for another assault, the group tightened their circle, each member finding strength in the other. Their resolve was a fortress, their courage a blade, and their love for their companion a flame that refused to be extinguished.

"Come on, Aviara," Lysandra breathed, her gaze locked onto the deity's pained expression. "Come back to us. For Harrow, for Erenor—for all of us."

Harrow's scales gleamed, reflecting the fading light as the sun dipped below the horizon, casting long shadows across the clearing.

The dragon's once vibrant eyes were now dulled with pain, yet within them flickered a spark of something ancient and profound.

"Aviara," Harrow rasped, his voice a mere thread of its usual timbre. "There was...a time. A time before the fracture."

Lysandra knelt beside him, her sword forgotten in the grass. Her hands trembled as she held onto Harrow's massive claw.

She leaned closer, catching each precious syllable that fell from the dragon's lips.

"Speak, Harrow," she urged, her voice laced with desperation.

"Before the fracture... there was unity," Harrow continued, each breath a struggle. "And you, Aviara... sister to the stars, daughter of the dawn... you were not alone."

Aviara's expression wavered as the words seemed to pierce through the veil of darkness that had clouded her being. The orb in her hand flickered it's pulsating energy faltering.

"Remember the Elysian Fields, where we roamed free?" Harrow's voice broke, a single tear rolling down his snout.

"You taught the rivers to curve, the flowers to bloom... You danced upon the winds with joy, not sorrow."

"Is this true?" Aviara's voice quivered, her eyes searching the skies as if trying to recapture a memory lost in the ages.

"Every word," Lysandra affirmed, her own heart aching with the resonance of Harrow's revelation. "You were loved, Aviara. You still are."

"Beloved deity," Aerin spoke up, his staff aglow with supportive power. "Your essence is interwoven with Erenor's lifeblood. We need you whole, as you once were."

"Let go of the fracture," Feyla said softly, her hands clasped in silent supplication. "Embrace the truth of your existence."

The air hummed with tension, with the possibility of redemption or ruin. As Aviara hesitated, Harrow's body shuddered, his life force ebbing away.

"Please…" Eolande whispered, his face a mask of grief.

Harrow turned his gaze to Lysandra one final time. "Heal her," he breathed out, his voice barely audible. "Restore… what was lost."

With a nod, Lysandra drew upon the relic she carried—a pendant that pulsed with the combined lineage of her ancestry.

Closing her eyes, she focused her entire being on the task.

"By the blood of my forebears, by the light of the ancients," she chanted, her voice rising above the wind. "I call upon the pure magic, the sacred bond between deities and mortals."

A luminous glow emanated from the pendant, enveloping Lysandra and Aviara in warmth.

It seeped into their skin, dove into their souls, seeking the broken fragments.

"Feel the connection, Aviara," Lysandra whispered, her voice steady despite the turmoil within. "Feel the love that has never faded. Let it heal you."

Tears streamed down Aviara's cheeks as the black orb disintegrated in her grasp, replaced by a blossoming radiance that grew until it lit the entire clearing.

As the cosmic energy swirled around them, the dark clouds dissipated, revealing a sky punctuated by the first evening stars.

"Forgive me," Aviara gasped, her form beginning to shimmer with the returning purity of her divine essence. "For all I have wrought upon Erenor."

The magic reached its crescendo, and with a last surge, it rushed back into the land, the trees, and the very air they breathed. As the fractures mended, sealing the rift that had once threatened to consume their world, balance was restored to the world as well.

"Thank you," Aviara murmured, her voice clear and resonant. "Thank you, Lysandra, Harrow... my children."

As the deity's form stabilized, her robes became pristine again, her face radiant with an inner light.

She gazed down at Harrow, whose body lay still and peaceful amidst the chaos he had helped to quell.

"Rest now, brave guardian," she said, her voice a gentle benediction. "Your legacy will live on in the hearts you've touched."

The group gathered close, their tears mingling with the dew on the grass, their silence a tribute to the dragon who had sacrificed everything for the land he cherished.

The air hummed with magic as Aviara's form solidified. Her once sullied robes transformed before Lysandra's watchful eyes into a cascade of shimmering fabric that weaved the very light of the stars into its folds.

The deity stood tall and unbroken, the shadows of her corruption vanishing like mist at dawn.

"By the sacred bond between dragon and deity," Aviara proclaimed, her voice echoing with renewed power, "I honor thee, Harrow. No one shall forget your valor. As long as the rivers flow and the mountains stand, so shall my vigil over Erenor endure."

With each word, the surrounding land breathed a sigh of relief, the flora stretching towards the sky as if in gratitude.

Aviara moved gracefully, descending to where Harrow lay. The mighty dragon's scales still glinted like obsidian under the celestial light. Her hands, now free of darkness, cradled his head with a mother's tenderness.

"Great protector," she whispered, tears cresting in her eyes, "your heart beats within the core of this realm, unfaltering, even as you march into the night. With this sacrifice, you've bound us all to a future where hope reigns."

Lysandra felt the weight of the moment, her own grief intertwining with the deity's remorse.

She stepped forward, her hand reaching out to brush against the dragon's cooling hide, her words catching in her throat.

"His wisdom guided us. His strength defended us," Lysandra said, her voice barely above a whisper. "Harrow believed in you, in all of us. We will continue his legacy."

"Indeed, child of two worlds," Aviara replied, recognizing the duality within Lysandra that had helped to restore balance. "Your conviction has been the beacon that led us out of darkness."

The deity's gaze lingered on the companions, her expression a tapestry of sorrow and gratitude. "To each of you who have braved the abyss for the sake of Erenor, I owe a debt that can never truly be repaid."

"Then let his memory guide your way," Eolande implored, his voice steady despite the turmoil.

"Let it be so," Aviara agreed, her smile fragile amid the torrent of emotions.

Gently lifting Harrow's body, Aviara rose to her majestic height.

With a nod of farewell to those who had stood by her, she turned to the heavens.

A brilliant aura enveloped both deity and dragon, their forms blurring as if painted with the strokes of an ethereal artist.

"Walk with me, Harrow, to the lands of our kin," Aviara intoned, her eyes alight with the promise of redemption.

A surge of energy coursed through the clearing, the air crackling with the power of ancient magics reborn.

In the space between heartbeats, a blinding flash enveloped them. When the light receded, Aviara and Harrow were gone, carried away to a realm restored, leaving behind a legacy of sacrifice and a world reborn.

Chapter 24

ERENOR'S DAWN

The wind carried the scent of scorched earth, a solemn reminder of the battle that had raged recently.

Lysandra's gaze lingered on the horizon where the golden dragon had soared for the last time, his brilliance now just a memory against the fading light.

"May your wings find peace in the skies of the divine," she whispered, her voice a soft echo amidst the stillness.

Aerin placed a hand on her shoulder, the warmth of his touch a silent solace. "He was magnificent," he said, his eyes reflecting the shared loss.

"More than that," Eolande added, his voice trembling with emotion. "He was a friend." Feyla nodded, her usual mirth subdued, her fingers absentmindedly twisting a strand of her hair.

"His sacrifice won't be in vain," Aerin stated firmly, the resolve in his voice cutting through the heavy air.

Lysandra looked at each of her allies, their faces etched with the grief of parting yet alight with gratitude for the freedom Harrow and Aviara had found together.

The ties binding them seemed to strengthen with the shared sorrow—an unspoken vow to honor the legacy left behind by the golden dragon.

Collectively, they turned away from the ashen battlefield and toward the gates of Tyrannis. The city loomed before them, its walls imposing yet welcoming, starkly contrasting with the desolation they had traversed.

As they stepped through the archway, the clamor of city life enveloped them like a vibrant tide.

"Home at last," Lysandra murmured, her eyes scanning the tapestry of moving bodies and colorful stalls. She could feel the pulse of the city in her veins, the energy it exuded, igniting a spark within her.

"Keep close," Aerin instructed, his hand finding hers and interlacing their fingers. After so much time in the wilds, the crowds can be overwhelming."

"Or we could just enjoy being anonymous for a while," Feyla suggested, her spirits visibly lifted by the sights and sounds around them.

"Anonymous until someone recognizes the savior of Erenor," Eolande teased gently, earning a playful swat from Lysandra.

"Let's just focus on getting to the castle," Lysandra replied, though a small smile graced her lips.

Navigating through the throngs of people felt like swimming against a current, but there was a rhythm to it—a dance of sorts that Lysandra fell into step with.

Her senses were alert, taking in the vendors hawking their wares, children darting between legs, and the murmur of a thousand conversations melding into one continuous hum.

"Remember this place?" Aerin asked, nodding towards a tiny shop tucked between two larger buildings.

Lysandra's smile widened. "How could I forget? You dared me to steal a kiss from you right outside that very door."

"And you did," he chuckled, his voice mingling with the surrounding noise. Bold as ever."

"Only because I knew I'd win," she retorted, the banter easing the weight of mourning in her chest.

They continued, and the castle grew closer with every step. The familiar stones of the city welcomed them back, whispering tales of past exploits and hinting at future triumphs.

Lysandra felt the anticipation building within her, a rising tide ready to crest. The path ahead was uncertain, but for now, the city of Tyrannis was a bastion—a promise of respite and preparation for the battles that lay in wait.

The cobblestones beneath Lysandra's boots resonated with the heartbeat of Tyrannis, a rhythm both familiar and welcome.

With every step towards the core of her city, the pulse quickened, synchronizing with the thrumming in her chest.

She paused, allowing the essence of home to wash over her, the scents of roasted nuts and fresh bread from nearby stalls intertwining with laughter and haggling.

"Feels like ages since we've been here," Lysandra said, her voice steady yet tinged with an undercurrent of emotion.

"Too long," Feyla agreed, her eyes scanning the perimeter with the vigilance of a hawk. But it seems peace has held in our absence."

A gruff bark sounded beside them as Shadow nudged Lysandra's hand with his snout, his dark fur a stark contrast against the vibrant colors that adorned the market square.

She placed a gloved hand on his head, the connection grounding her swirling thoughts.

"Peace is a tender vine," Lysandra mused. "It requires constant tending, or else it withers."

"Then we shall be its gardeners," Aerin said, his gaze never leaving Lysandra's face. The warrior's stance was relaxed, but the set of his jaw spoke of her readiness to leap into action at a moment's notice.

Lysandra met the eyes of each group member, seeing the mirrored determination reflected at her.

They were battle-worn, each scar a testament to their shared history, each quiet nod a silent oath to stand by her side through the darkness awaiting them.

"Your faith in me... it humbles me," Lysandra acknowledged, feeling the weight of their trust as a mantle upon her shoulders.

"Your strength gives us faith, Lysandra," Aerin said, stepping close enough for his presence to become a tangible warmth.

The unspoken promise between them shimmered in the

air—a bond forged in fire and tempered in sorrow.

"Let us not linger in the shadows of yesterday," Lysandra declared, lifting her chin with resolve.

"We carry Harrow's legacy within us, and with it, we will carve a path toward tomorrow's light."

Aerin nodded, his hand finding hers in a clasp that spoke volumes more than words could convey. Shadow let out a low growl as if acknowledging the gravity of their commitment.

"Lead on," whispered Aerin, his voice barely noticeable over the surrounding din.

"Forward," Lysandra affirmed, her grip tightening around the hilt of her sword. She stepped forth, her allies flanking her, the wolf at her heel, and the spirit of Tyrannis rising to embrace its champions.

The gates of Tyrannis had closed behind them, a resounding clang that severed the past from the present. Lysandra's gaze lingered on the towering ramparts, her mind adrift in the tumultuous sea of memories.

Her fingers brushed over the pommel of her sword, each nick and scratch on the leather grip a silent chronicle of battles fought and demons faced.

She had walked through fire and shadow, each step forging her anew, tempering her spirit into something fierce, something indomitable.

"Quite the journey we've had," Aerin's soft voice drifted to her, laced with the steel of shared trials.

She turned to him, their eyes locking in quiet communion.

They communicated without words; his hands, once used for delicate spells, now bore combat calluses—proof of his evolution beside her.

"Every scar..." she started, her hand rising involuntarily to trace a pale line across his cheek, "a lesson learned."

"Every ache," he continued, his own fingers closing gently over her wrist, "a reminder of our strength."

They stood there, two souls entwined by fate's capricious threads, in the heart of a city that pulsed with life and the echoes of ancient magic.

It was here, amidst the cacophony of market cries and the scent of roasting meats mingling with perfumed oils, that Lysandra felt the magnitude of their bond.

Here, the intangible became palpable, where the ethereal met the earthy.

"Remember when you thought I was just an arrogant witch hunter with more bravado than sense?" Aerin teased, a smile tugging at his lips, diffusing the solemnity of their reflection.

"Arrogant? Never," Lysandra quipped back, allowing a grin to chase away the ghosts of yesteryears. "Infuriatingly self-assured, perhaps."

"Ah, but you saw through me." His arms encircled her waist, pulling her closer with a confidence born of countless days and nights spent in each other's orbit. "You always do."

"And you through me," she admitted, resting her head against his chest, listening to the steady rhythm of his heartbeat—a drumbeat to which her soul had attuned itself.

"You never let me falter, even when shadows clawed at my resolve."

"Nor you, me," he whispered, his breath warm against her hair. "Together, Lysandra, we are unbreakable."

In the embrace they shared, time seemed to slow, the world outside their circle fading to a distant murmur.

The spice-laden air wrapped around them, a testament to the vibrancy of life that thrived beyond the reaches of darkness.

In the silence between heartbeats, a tender moment and sacred pause reaffirmed love and loyalty, defying destiny's relentless march.

"Come," she said at last, her voice steady despite the emotion swelling within her. "We have so much to do."

"Yes, we do," Aerin agreed, releasing her reluctantly but with the promise of return in his touch. "But with you, every challenge is a promise of victory."

They drew apart, but the connection remained, an invisible thread woven through the tapestry of their intertwined fates.

Lysandra cast one last glance at Tyrannis's jagged skyline, then squared her shoulders, facing the future with a warrior's resolve and a lover's hope.

The ornate gates of Tyrannis swung open with a resonance that matched the beating heart within Lysandra Aventis's chest.

The cobblestone streets buzzed with life, merchants hawking wares and children weaving through the crowds, their laughter piercing the air like chimes.

She moved among them, her armor's reflection capturing

snippets of the city she loved.

"Miss Lysandra!" A young boy, only ten, approached with wide-eyed reverence. "My pa says you'll rid us of the darkness."

She knelt to his level, her gaze soft but fierce. "Your pa is right. And what brave task do you hold in this battle?"

"Me?" he squeaked. "I... I can run fast! For messages!"

"Then you are our swiftest ally," she declared, placing a solemn hand on his shoulder. "Every noble quest needs a swift messenger."

His chest puffed out with pride, and he dashed off to boast about his new title.

Lysandra rose, catching the approving nod from an old woman wrapped in shawls.

"You give them hope, my lady," she said, her voice as cracked as the pavement beneath their feet.

"Hope is the light that guides us through the darkness," Lysandra replied, echoing the wisdom Harrow had once shared.

As she continued through the city, each interaction weaved another thread of unity and strength into the tapestry of Tyrannis.

The King had entrusted her with this role, and she embraced it not as a duty but as a calling.

When the last of the day's light dipped below the castle ramparts, Lysandra stole away to the tranquil gardens nestled in the eastern wing—a sanctuary amidst stone and duty. The scent of night-blooming jasmine filled the air, a balm to the weary.

She found a secluded bench by a reflecting pool, its surface reflecting the first stars of the evening. Here, she sat, closing her eyes to the whispers of water and wind.

"Guide me, Harrow," she breathed, welcoming the dragon's memory with sorrow and gratitude. His sacrifice had been her salvation; she only hoped to honor it.

Meditation brought her solace, a calmness that steeled her resolve.

With every inhale, she drew in the courage of those who believed in her; with every exhale, she released the tendrils of doubt.

A shadow passed over her—the physical manifestation of her constant companion, melancholy.

It reminded her of the weight she carried, the expectation of a savior. Yet, as Lysandra opened her eyes to the starlit sky, her spirit soared, knowing she did not carry it alone.

In the garden's quiet, she fortified the fortress of her mind, readying for the battles ahead, with the love of Aerin and the loyalty of her allies as her bastion against the encroaching dark.

Lysandra's boots echoed through the castle's hallowed halls as she made her way to Master Elarion's chambers.

The clink of her sword against her thigh was a rhythmic reminder of the recent battles, the weight of which was both a comfort and a burden.

Her fingertips brushed against ancient stones, each whispering tales of old—a legacy she was now a part of.

Pushing open the heavy oak door, she found Master Elarion surrounded by scrolls and tomes, his brow furrowed in concentration beneath the glow of a solitary candle.

The flame flickered as he looked up, casting dancing shadows across his lined face.

"Master," she began, hesitantly threading her voice, "I have walked through fire and shadow since we last spoke. I need your wisdom."

Elarion gestured her forward, his keen eyes softening. "Tell me your thoughts, child."

She recounted her journey, the surge of magic coursing through her veins, the heart-wrenching loss of Harrow, and the dark tendrils of doubt that sought to entwine her soul.

Her voice trembled but did not break; it was the sound of tempered steel.

"Each challenge has honed you, Lysandra," Elarion said, fingers tentatively smoothing a frayed edge of a scroll. "Your heart bleeds for Erenor, and that is your greatest strength. But remember, even the brightest flame casts a shadow."

"Then how do I fight what lurks within? How do I lead others against the darkness I myself harbor?"

"By acknowledging it," he replied, meeting her gaze. "You wield your inner darkness as one does a blade—with intention, control, and an unwavering hand."

Taking a deep breath, she felt the truth of his words settles around her like a cloak. With a nod of gratitude, she left to gather her allies.

The war room buzzed with energy as her comrades assembled around the table, maps, and markers scattered among them.

Their faces showed lines of determination, illuminated by torchlight.

"Friends," Lysandra addressed them, her voice carrying over the murmur of conversation, "the dragon's sacrifice has afforded us this fleeting peace, yet our path remains riddled with peril."

Eyes locked on her, reflecting trust and camaraderie forged in the crucible of conflict.

"Scouts report remnants of black magic festering in Erenor's veins," she continued, pointing toward the shadowed areas on the map.

"We must extinguish these blights before they fester and spread."

"Striking swiftly is key," Aerin interjected his presence at her side both a comfort and a constant source of strength. His own experiences with the darker arts lent credence to his counsel.

"I agree," Lysandra confirmed. "We will organize ourselves into smaller units."

Whispers of agreement circulated among the group, with each ally prepared to fulfill their role. They had witnessed too many things and endured too many losses to give up or hesitate at this moment.

Feyla's voice echoed with clarity as she declared, "Let us embody the stealth of blades concealed in the dark." "For Erenor, for those we've lost, and for the future we yearn to forge."

A sense of certainty filled the space as they interlocked their hands, a wordless vow passing between them. The impending battle appeared daunting, but they confronted it with a fearless, united front, rendering themselves unstoppable.

Dust kicked up around Lysandra's boots as she pivoted, her sword a silver flash in the dimming light of the training yard.

Her breath came out in short bursts, misting in the chilly air, while her muscles sang with the strain of combat. She was a maelstrom of movement, each strike and parry honed through relentless practice.

"Again," she commanded, her voice leaving no room for argument.

Across from her, an ally nodded, lunging forward with renewed vigor. Steel rang against steel, echoing off the stone walls that enclosed them.

They moved together in a dance as old as war, pushing each other to new limits of endurance and skill.

As twilight deepened into night, their session drew to a close. Lysandra's chest heaved, but her eyes sparkled with an invigorating fire.

She acknowledged her sparring partner with a nod, mutual respect flowing silently between them. They had grown stronger together, bonded by the blade.

Later, within the sanctuary of their chambers, Lysandra found solace in Aerin's arms. Their bodies entwined, tracing the contours of scars and whispered secrets. Each touch rekindled embers of desire, their connection blazing into passion as fervent as their commitment to Erenor's salvation.

In the quiet aftermath, nestled beneath a tapestry of shadows, they shared hushed observations. "Feyla and Eolande think they're stealthy," Aerin murmured against her skin, a smile curling his lips.

Lysandra chuckled softly, tracing a finger along the line of his jaw. "The flush of first love hardly goes unnoticed."

Their laughter was a brief respite from the weight of duty, a momentary escape from the darkness threatening their world.

When dawn's first light crept through the window, Lysandra and Aerin were immersed in ancient texts sprawled across a massive oak table.

The parchment crackled under their fingers as they pored over cryptic runes and faded maps, seeking wisdom from the past to safeguard their future.

Master Elarion joined them, his wise eyes scanning the documents with practiced ease. "This passage speaks of a long-forgotten alliance," he said, tapping a gnarled finger on a dense text block.

Aerin leaned in, his brow furrowing as he deciphered the archaic language. "Could this be the key to rallying support?"

"Indeed," Lysandra replied, her mind alight with strategies. "We need every ally we can muster."

Together, they traced routes and marked locations, their plans growing clearer with each hour spent in research. It was a meticulous task, demanding patience and precision, but they were steadfast in their purpose.

"Here," Lysandra pointed to a range of mountains bordering a desolate plain. "If the legends hold true, we may find aid from those who dwell within the hidden valleys."

"Then it is there we shall seek it," Aerin affirmed, his hand finding hers amidst the scrolls. In that silent promise, they forged their resolve anew.

Their shared vision was clear: to cleanse Erenor of its festering wounds and restore balance to a world teetering on the brink.

With each piece of lore unearthed and every strategy devised, Lysandra felt the burgeoning weight of her destiny—and welcomed it with unyielding resolve.

Lysandra's gaze met in the polished mirror, silently acknowledging the journey etched onto her features.

The last vestiges of youth had given way to the sculpted contours of a warrior, each line and scar a chronicle of battles fought, both within and without.

With steady hands, she lifted the cuirass, the metal cool against her skin, its intricate engravings a testament to her lineage. She secured it. The weight was familiar and strangely comforting.

"An hour longer," Aerin's voice was a warm whisper against her neck, his hands encircling her waist. "The world will keep turning."

She chuckled, catching his gaze in the reflection—a mischievous glint danced in his eyes. "And let our enemies gain another hour's advantage?" Lysandra gently brushed his hands away, turning to face him.

"Time enough for that later," she teased, reaching for his chest plate. Her fingers worked deftly over the clasps and straps, ensuring each piece of his armor sat just right.

He stood patiently, though the quirk of his lips betrayed his impatience—not for battle, but for the respite of their embrace.

"Always later," he murmured, placing a soft kiss on top of her head.

"Of course," she affirmed, stepping back to appraise him, her warrior, her mage, her heart. "Now, we fight."

Together, they joined Feyla and Eolande outside, where the morning sunbathed Tyrannis in a golden glow.

Shadow paced at their side, his coat shimmering like liquid obsidian, a sentinel ever watchful.

Master Elarion waited for them, his presence grounding, a beacon of the wisdom that had guided them through the darkest times.

Upon the grand balcony overlooking the city square, Lysandra stepped forward, her allies forming a steadfast guard behind her.

The people of Tyrannis gathered below. A sea of faces turned upwards, searching for hope amidst the shadows threatening their land.

"Today, we stand on the cusp of a new dawn," Lysandra's voice rose, clear and resonant. "Our path has been wrought with sacrifice, our nights haunted by darkness, but our resolve has never wavered."

"Your safety, your freedom, are the very beats of our hearts," Aerin added, his voice carrying strength and solidarity, a mage unafraid to wield the power of words and magic.

"Look not to the skies for dragons' wings or distant gods." Lysandra lifted her sword, the runes catching the light, casting a radiant dance upon the upturned faces. "For we are the guardians of Erenor, flesh and blood, steel and shadow. And together, we shall reclaim the balance that has been lost."

"United, we stand against the tide of black magic that seeks to engulf us," Feyla declared, her hand resting on the hilt of her blade, her inventor's mind already calculating the mechanics of victory.

"From the hidden valleys to the highest peaks, we call upon all allies," Eolande's voice, usually reserved, now rang with conviction. "Join us, and let our arrows fly true."

A chorus of agreement rose from the crowd, a tangible wave of determination and trust in their protectors. Shadow's howl pierced the air, a primal affirmation of the pact between human and beast.

"Rest now in the peace we fight to preserve," Lysandra concluded, her eyes sweeping across her people, a silent vow to shield them from the darkness. "For today, we battle not just for Tyrannis but for the soul of Erenor itself."

The cheers that followed were not just of adulation but shared courage—a city united under the hope that Lysandra and her comrades had brought.

With a last nod to Master Elarion, she stepped back, her allies close, their readiness an unspoken oath to face whatever perils lay ahead.

The din of celebration faded into the distance as Lysandra led

Aerin and her allies through the castle's labyrinthine halls. The stones whispered beneath their boots, carrying them away from the fervor to a secluded atrium in silver moonlight.

"Every step we've taken has led us here," Lysandra said, her gaze drifting over the faces of those she trusted more than anyone in the world. "And every battle fought has forged this bond between us."

Aerin stepped closer, his hand finding hers, an anchor in the uncertainty ahead. "We are your steel, Lysandra. Where you lead, we follow."

"Indeed," Feyla chimed, her eyes alight with the spark of ingenuity that had saved them countless times. Our minds and weapons are honed and at your service."

Eolande nodded, his quiet demeanor contrasting the fierce loyalty shining in his eyes. "Our arrows will fly together, for the threat we face fears unity above all else."

Lysandra squeezed Aerin's hand, the warmth there a balm to the coldness creeping at the edges of her heart.

She felt a surge of purpose, like a flame reignited by the winds of camaraderie.

"Remember the Dragon," she spoke softly, invoking the memory of sacrifice and freedom that lingered in their souls.

"We carry on in honor of what was given and what was gained."

"His fire burns within us," Aerin affirmed, his voice low but resonant.

"Let's make sure it lights the path to victory," Feyla added, her determination unyielding.

"May our actions reflect his legacy," Eolande concluded with a solemn vow.

They stood in silence, each lost in thoughts of battles past and the ones yet to come. And then, as if by some unspoken signal, they came together in the center of the atrium, their circle unbreakable.

Lysandra looked around at the faces illuminated by the celestial glow from above—faces marked by resilience, courage, and love. Her chest swelled with conviction so fierce it banished any lingering shadows of doubt.

"Tomorrow, we may walk into the jaws of chaos," she declared, her voice cutting through the night with crystalline clarity. "But we walk as one. And we shall emerge not just unscathed but triumphant."

The vows they exchanged were silent but binding, each nod and touch sealing their promise to stand as one against the encroaching darkness.

"Then let us rest," Aerin suggested, though his eyes betrayed the same restless energy that coursed through Lysandra. "For tonight, we find solace in our unity."

"Rest, but keep your blades sharp," Lysandra replied, a wry smile dancing on her lips.

"Always," Feyla and Eolande responded in unison, their own smiles mirroring hers.

Lysandra remained in the atrium as they dispersed, her gaze lifting to the stars that peeked through the open ceiling. They twinkled back at her, distant witnesses to the trials of mortals below.

Aerin lingered, watching her with a tenderness that could melt the coldest iron. He approached, wrapping his arms around her waist, his breath warm on her neck.

"Whatever comes," he whispered, "we face it together."

"Forever," Lysandra replied, turning in his embrace to meet his kiss—an affirmation of their shared future.

With hearts fortified by love and spirits buoyed by unwavering resolve, Lysandra knew that no matter how dark the nights grew or how fierce the battles raged, they were ready. Together, they would reclaim the balance of Erenor or die trying.

About the author Kim Bock

KIM BOCK BOOKS

Kim Bock is a successful bilingual Indie author and co-owner of a thriving website design business based in South Africa, which she runs with her husband, Eitel. She has already published a historical romance novel in South Africa and released the final book in her trilogy, "The Chronicles of Erenor," on Amazon—Kim's writing benefits from her varied viewpoints and love of storytelling, which she draws on. While working on a website design with her husband, she dedicates her free time to crafting captivating fiction that draws readers into new realms of imagination. Join Kim Bock on her literary adventure, where her novels reflect her diverse experiences and offer readers a glimpse into her imaginative world.

You can find out more on her website at www.kimbock-books.com

Also by Kim Bock

ERENOR'S DAWN & THE LAST MAGE

This book is also available on Amazon Kindle. It takes you back to the enchanting world of Erenor, where the victory over King Draven and the revival of magic has brought a fragile peace. Lysandra hailed as the savior, grapples with her lineage's dark secrets while a new shadow looms.

A forgotten mythical deity, a remnant of Erenor's ancient

KIM BOCK

past, stirs, threatening to unravel the fabric of magic. Lysandra travels beyond the known boundaries of magic with steadfast allies like Aerin, Feyla, the wise Elarion, and Harrow, the fearless dragon.

This thrilling sequel tests alliances, and passionate love blossoms amidst the chaos. Feyla finds unexpected love with Eolande, an enigmatic elf, while Lysandra and Aerin's bond deepens, and they fall deeply in love amidst the trials.

Lysandra faces her most formidable challenge yet: will her powers be enough to preserve Erenor's delicate balance?

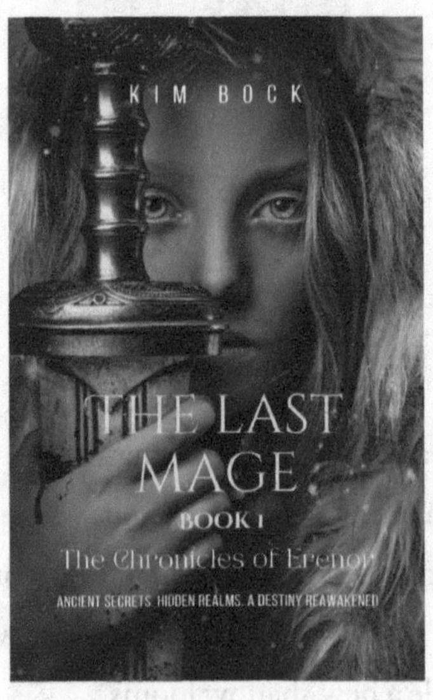

"The Last Mage" is the first book in the Chronicles of

Erenor series, following Lysandra, a hidden mage and skilled swordswoman, on her quest to restore balance to her world. She battles King Draven's oppressive rule and evil forces with the help of her loyal black wolf, Shadow, the hunter Aerin, and the inventor, Feyla. Along the way, Lysandra confronts ancient secrets and combats evil creatures like the Shadow Hounds and the corrupted dragon, The Harrow. In the process, she unexpectedly finds love and embraces her destiny as the last descendant of the First Mage.

After defeating King Draven and restoring Erenor's magic, Lysandra and her allies discover an even greater danger looming—a mysterious evil wielding black magic and the power to summon ancient creatures. In an explosive battle, Lysandra faces the shocking truth about her connection to this demon and the struggle between her light and dark sides. With the help of her companions, she emerges victorious, but the triumph is bittersweet as new threats arise from the celestial fracture.

"The Last Mage" is an enthralling fantasy adventure that intertwines themes of magic, bravery, love, and the eternal battle between light and darkness. This book is ideal for fans of stories featuring mythical creatures, loyal companionship, and the quest for balance in a fractured world. Join Lysandra on her epic journey in The Chronicles of Erenor and discover a realm where the fate of all hangs in the balance.

Special Request by Kim Bock

PLEASE BE SO KIND TO REVIEW THE BOOK

Dear Reader,

Thank you for joining me on this journey through *The Chronicles of Erenor*. Your support means the world to me, and I hope you've enjoyed exploring the realms of Erenor as much as I've enjoyed crafting them.

If you found yourself lost in the adventures of Lysandra, Aerin, and their companions, or if the story moved you in any way, I would be incredibly grateful if you could take a moment to share your thoughts with other readers.

Your review can be as brief or detailed as you like. It will help others discover "The Chronicles of Erenor" and embark on a similar journey.

To leave your review, visit the book's page on Amazon.Or at your preferred online bookstore! Here's the revised text:

Again, thank you for your support and participation in this epic adventure!